GFFs

GHOST FRIENDS FOREVER

charmz

MORE GRAPHIC NOVELS AVAILABLE FROM

Charmz™

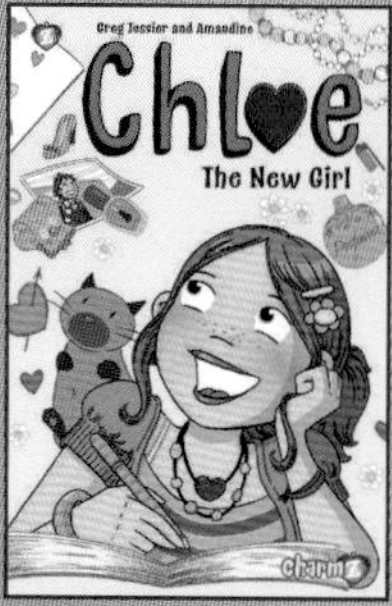
Greg Tessier and Amandine
Chloe
The New Girl
charmz

CHLOE #1
"THE NEW GIRL"

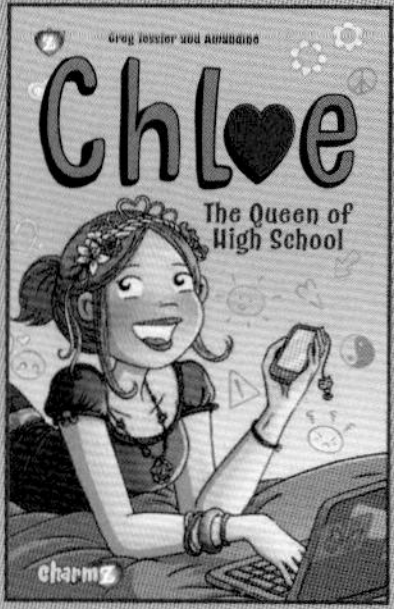
Greg Tessier and Amandine
Chloe
The Queen of High School
charmz

CHLOE #2
"THE QUEEN OF HIGH SCHOOL"

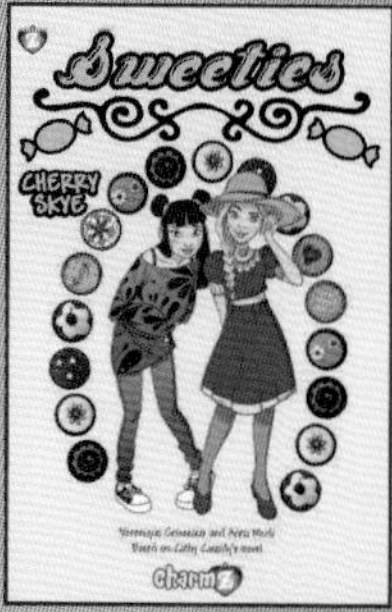
Sweeties
CHERRY SKYE
charmz

SWEETIES #1
"CHERRY SKYE"

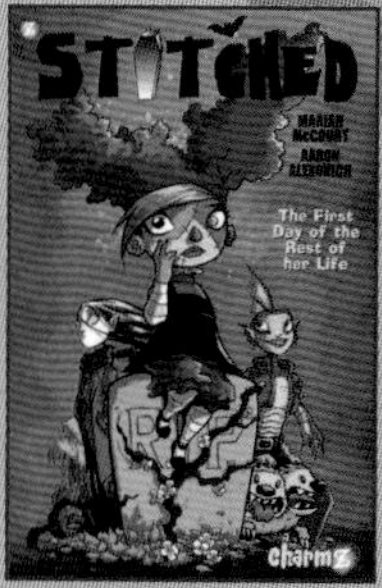
STITCHED
MARIAH McCOURT
AARON ALEXOVICH
The First Day of the Rest of her Life
charmz

STITCHED #1
"THE FIRST DAY OF THE REST OF HER LIFE"

COMING SOON

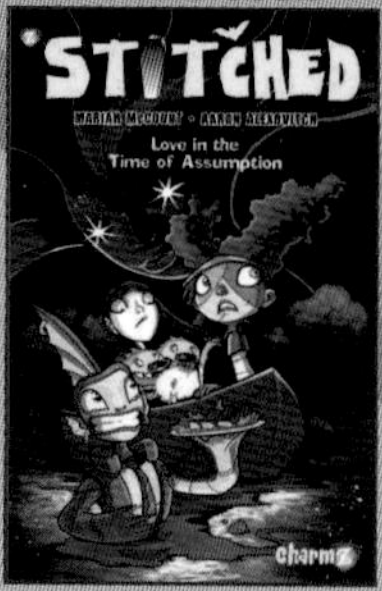
STITCHED
Love in the Time of Assumption
charmz

STITCHED #2
"LOVE IN THE TIME OF ASSUMPTION"

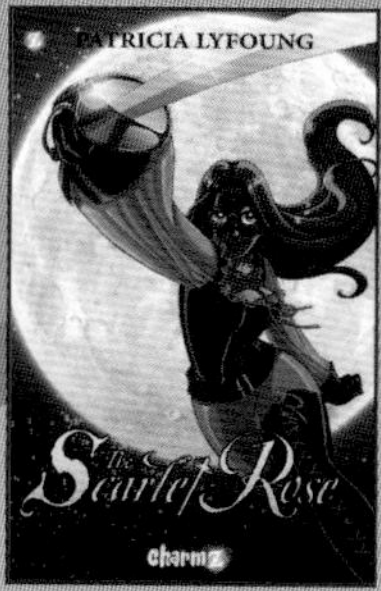
PATRICIA LYFOUNG
The Scarlet Rose
charmz

SCARLET ROSE #1
"I KNEW I'D MEET YOU"

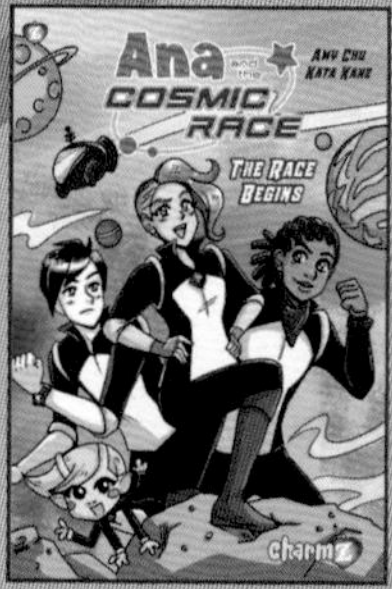
Ana
COSMIC RACE
THE RACE BEGINS
charmz

ANA AND THE COSMIC RACE #1
"THE RACE BEGINS"

Charmz graphic novels are available for $9.99 in paperback, and $14.99 in hardcover. Available from booksellers everywhere. You can also order online from www.papercutz.com. Or call 1-800-886-1223, Monday through Friday, 9–5 EST. MC, Visa, and AmEx accepted. To order by mail, please add $5.00 for postage and handling for first book ordered, $1.00 for each additional book and make check payable to NBM Publishing. Send to: Charmz, 160 Broadway, Suite 700, East Wing, New York, NY 10038.

Charmz graphic novels are also available wherever e-books are sold.

GFFs

GHOST FRIENDS FOREVER

MY HEART LIES IN THE 90s

STORY BY MONICA GALLAGHER
ART BY KATA KANE

charmz

NEW YORK

GFFs
GHOST FRIENDS FOREVER

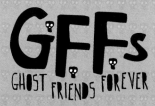

#1 "MY HEART LIES IN THE 90s"

MONICA GALLAGHER – STORY
KATA KANE – ART & COVER
MATT HERMS – COLORS
BRYAN SENKA – LETTERING

CHARMZ BOOKS MAY BE PURCHASED FOR BUSINESS OR PROMOTIONAL USE. FOR INFORMATION ON BULK PURCHASES PLEASE CONTACT MACMILLAN CORPORATE AND PREMIUM SALES DEPARTMENT AT (800) 221-7945 X5442

DAWN GUZZO – PRODUCTION AND DESIGN
MARIAH MCCOURT – EDITOR
JEFF WHITMAN – ASSISTANT MANAGING EDITOR
JIM SALICRUP
EDITOR-IN-CHIEF

PB ISBN: 978-1-62991-802-0
HC ISBN: 978-1-62991-803-7

PRINTED IN CHINA, NOVEMBER 2017

DISTRIBUTED BY MACMILLAN
FIRST PRINTING

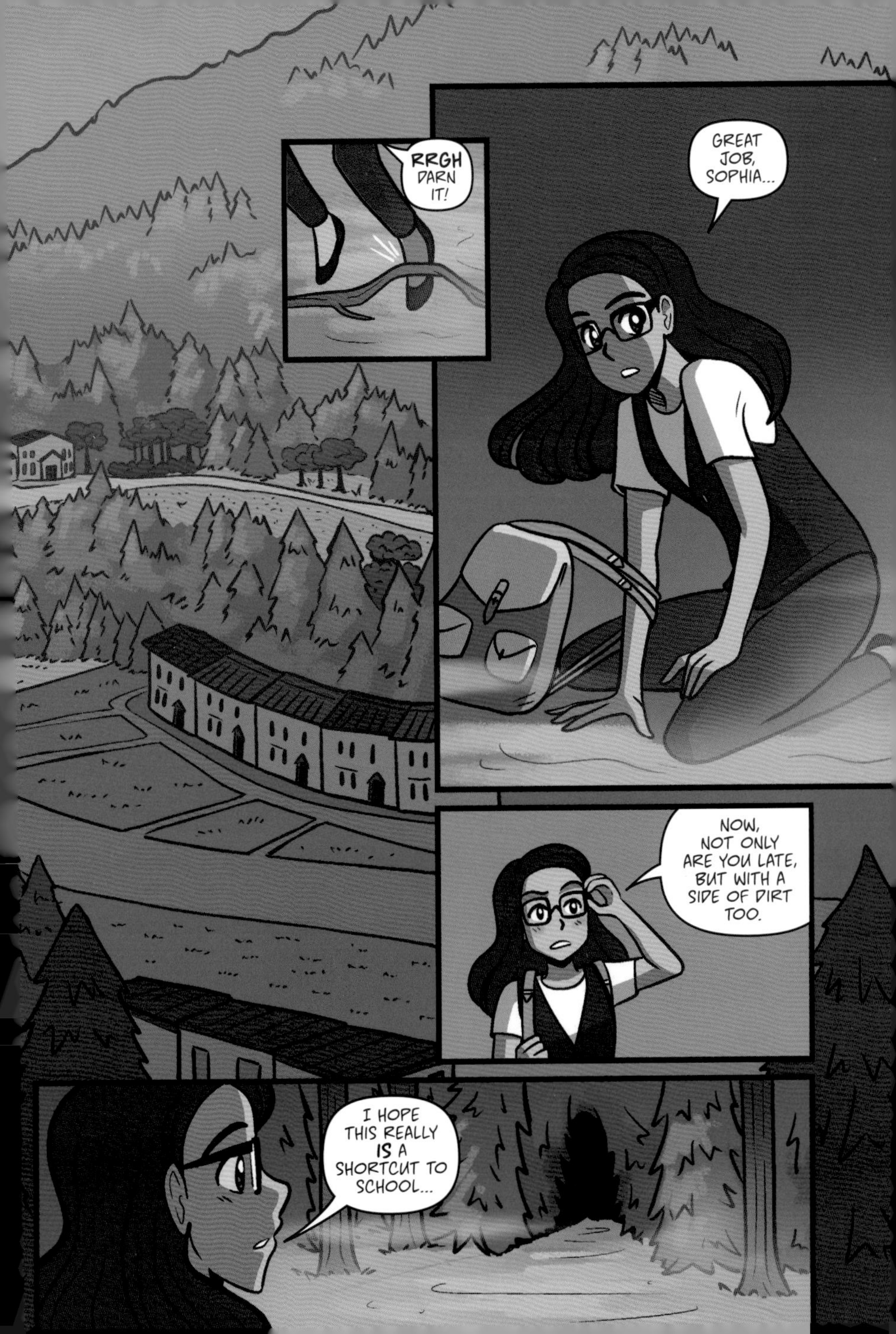
RRGH DARN IT!
GREAT JOB, SOPHIA...
NOW, NOT ONLY ARE YOU LATE, BUT WITH A SIDE OF DIRT TOO.
I HOPE THIS REALLY IS A SHORTCUT TO SCHOOL...

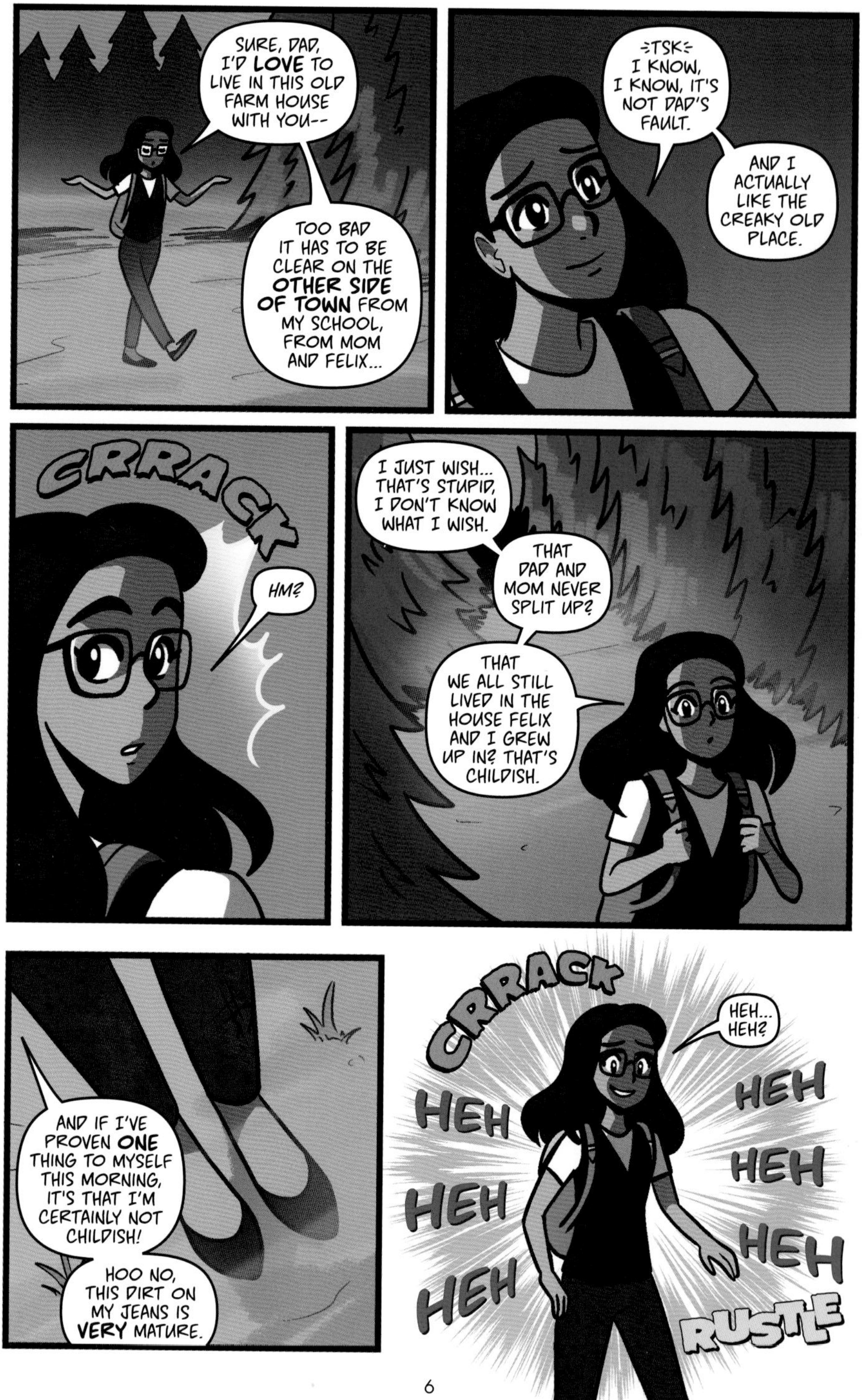
SURE, DAD, I'D LOVE TO LIVE IN THIS OLD FARM HOUSE WITH YOU--
TOO BAD IT HAS TO BE CLEAR ON THE OTHER SIDE OF TOWN FROM MY SCHOOL, FROM MOM AND FELIX...
TSK I KNOW, I KNOW, IT'S NOT DAD'S FAULT.
AND I ACTUALLY LIKE THE CREAKY OLD PLACE.
CRRACK
HM?
I JUST WISH... THAT'S STUPID, I DON'T KNOW WHAT I WISH.
THAT DAD AND MOM NEVER SPLIT UP?
THAT WE ALL STILL LIVED IN THE HOUSE FELIX AND I GREW UP IN? THAT'S CHILDISH.
AND IF I'VE PROVEN ONE THING TO MYSELF THIS MORNING, IT'S THAT I'M CERTAINLY NOT CHILDISH!
HOO NO, THIS DIRT ON MY JEANS IS VERY MATURE.
CRRACK
HEH... HEH?
HEH
HEH
HEH
HEH
HEH
HEH
RUSTLE

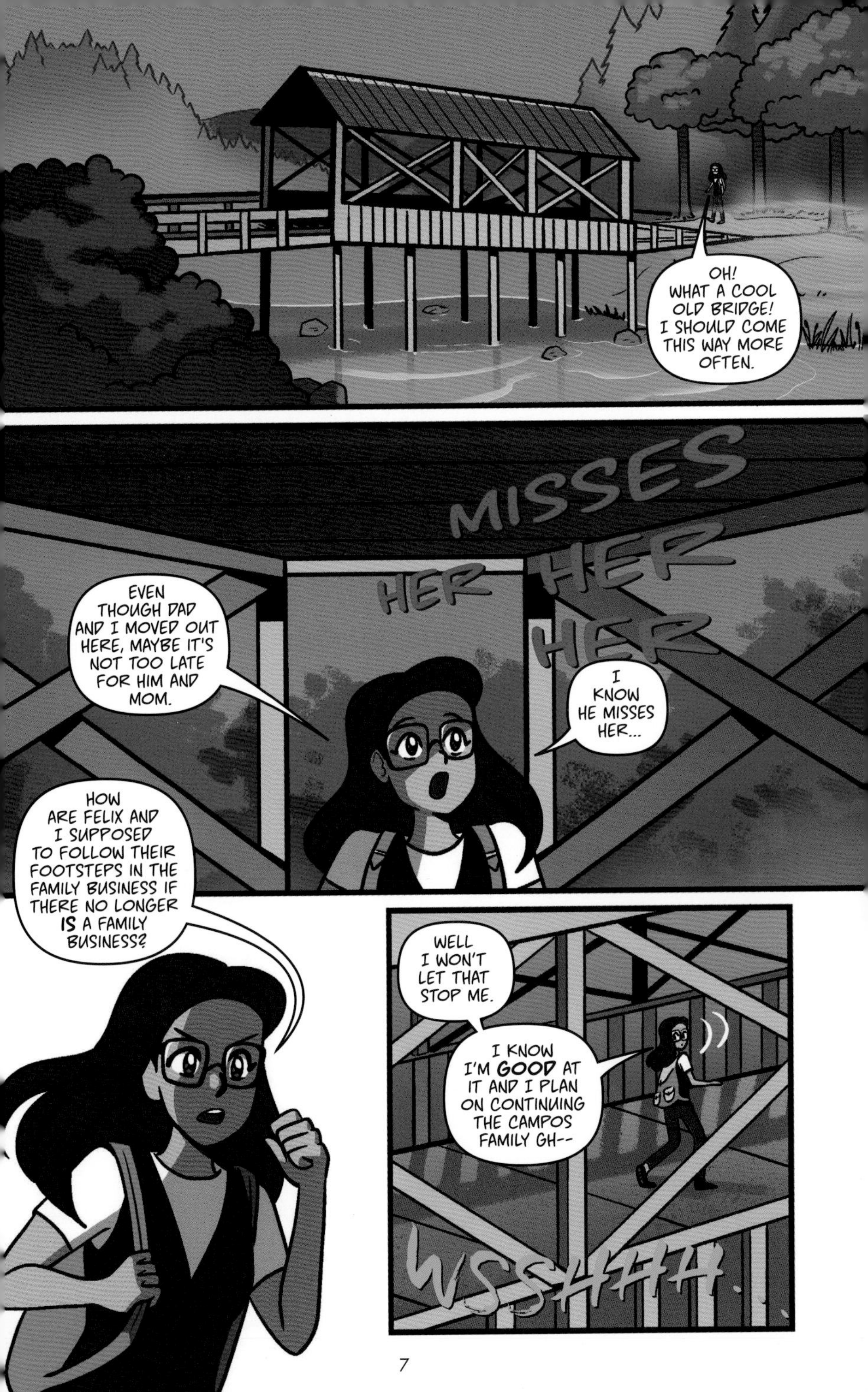
OH! WHAT A COOL OLD BRIDGE! I SHOULD COME THIS WAY MORE OFTEN.
MISSES
HER HER HER
EVEN THOUGH DAD AND I MOVED OUT HERE, MAYBE IT'S NOT TOO LATE FOR HIM AND MOM.
I KNOW HE MISSES HER...
HOW ARE FELIX AND I SUPPOSED TO FOLLOW THEIR FOOTSTEPS IN THE FAMILY BUSINESS IF THERE NO LONGER **IS** A FAMILY BUSINESS?
WELL I WON'T LET THAT STOP ME.
I KNOW I'M **GOOD** AT IT AND I PLAN ON CONTINUING THE CAMPOS FAMILY GH--
WSSHHH

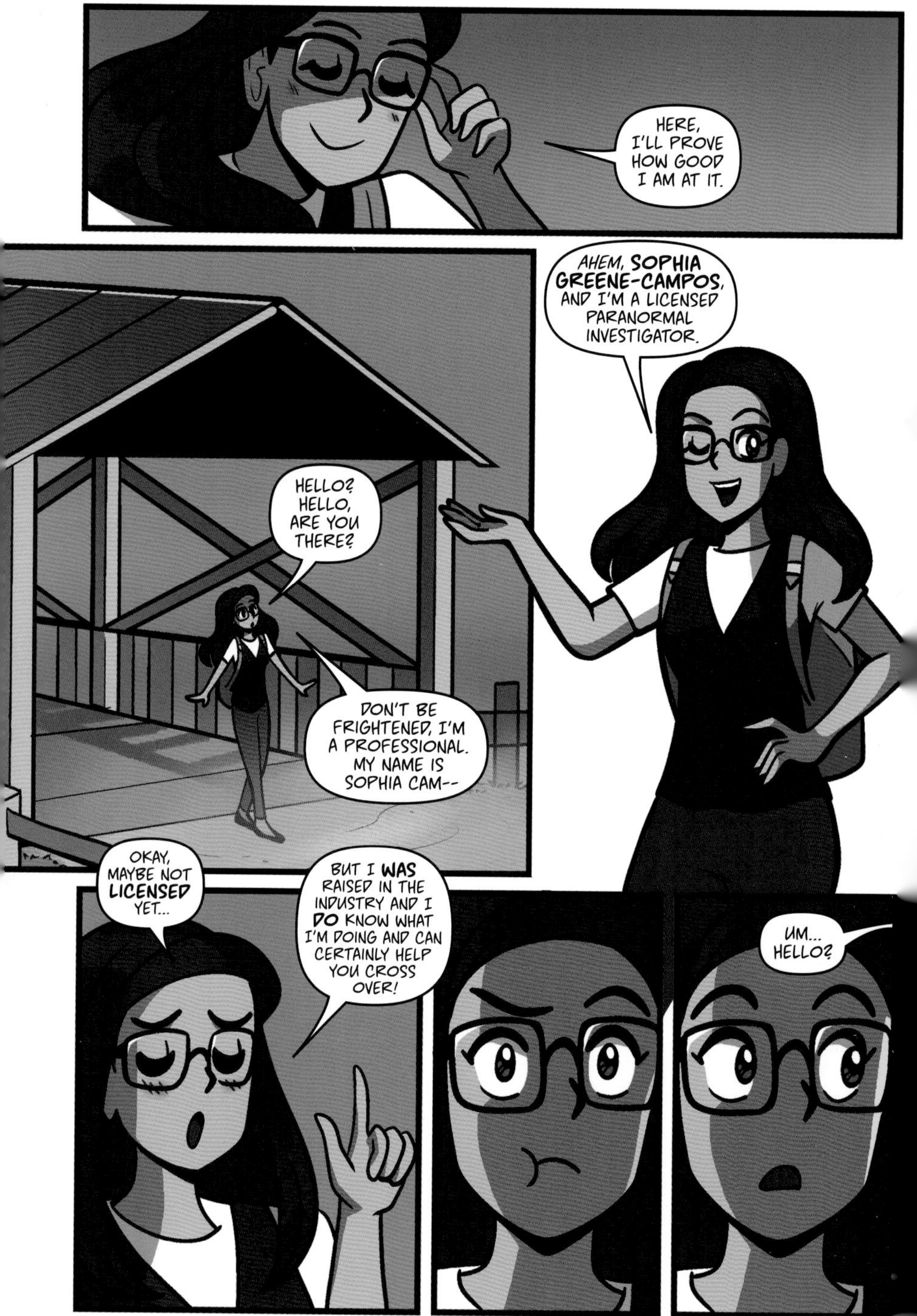
HERE, I'LL PROVE HOW GOOD I AM AT IT.
HELLO? HELLO, ARE YOU THERE?
DON'T BE FRIGHTENED, I'M A PROFESSIONAL. MY NAME IS SOPHIA CAM--
AHEM, SOPHIA GREENE-CAMPOS, AND I'M A LICENSED PARANORMAL INVESTIGATOR.
OKAY, MAYBE NOT LICENSED YET...
BUT I WAS RAISED IN THE INDUSTRY AND I DO KNOW WHAT I'M DOING AND CAN CERTAINLY HELP YOU CROSS OVER!
UM... HELLO?

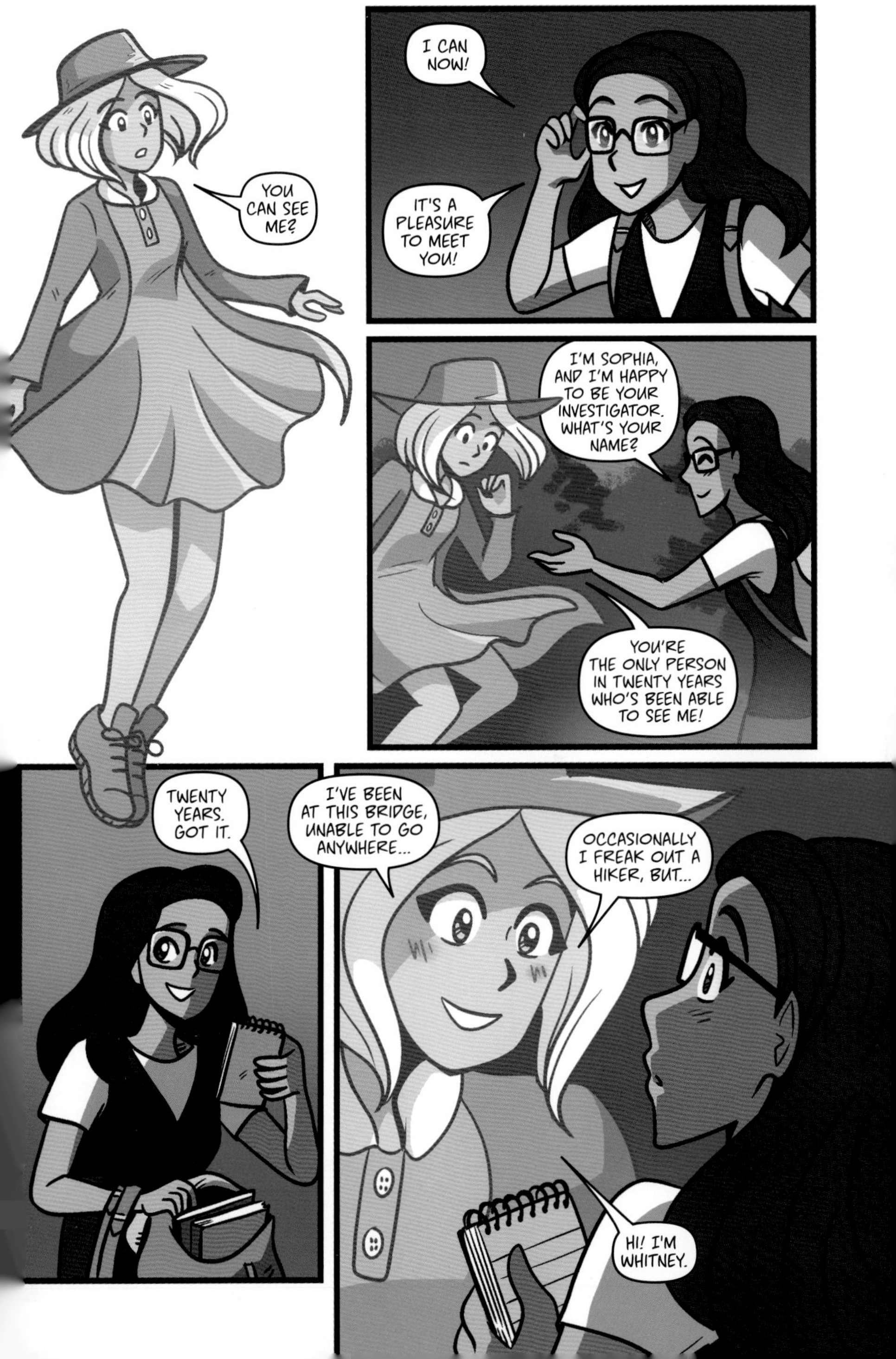
YOU CAN SEE ME?
I CAN NOW!
IT'S A PLEASURE TO MEET YOU!
I'M SOPHIA, AND I'M HAPPY TO BE YOUR INVESTIGATOR. WHAT'S YOUR NAME?
YOU'RE THE ONLY PERSON IN TWENTY YEARS WHO'S BEEN ABLE TO SEE ME!
TWENTY YEARS. GOT IT.
I'VE BEEN AT THIS BRIDGE, UNABLE TO GO ANYWHERE...
OCCASIONALLY I FREAK OUT A HIKER, BUT...
HI! I'M WHITNEY.

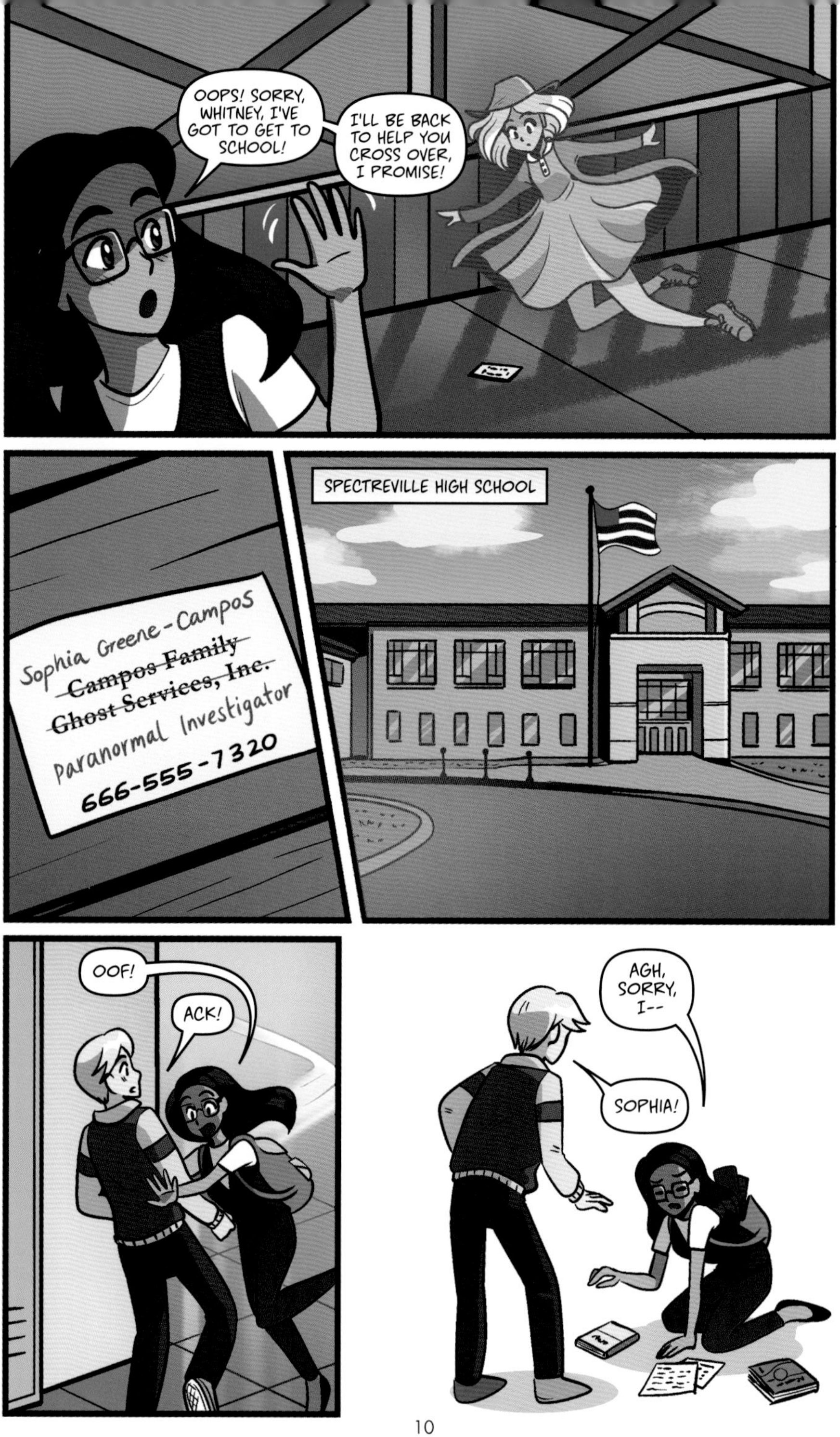
OOPS! SORRY, WHITNEY, I'VE GOT TO GET TO SCHOOL!
I'LL BE BACK TO HELP YOU CROSS OVER, I PROMISE!
Sophia Greene-Campos
Campos Family Ghost Services, Inc.
paranormal Investigator
666-555-7320
SPECTREVILLE HIGH SCHOOL
OOF!
ACK!
AGH, SORRY, I--
SOPHIA!

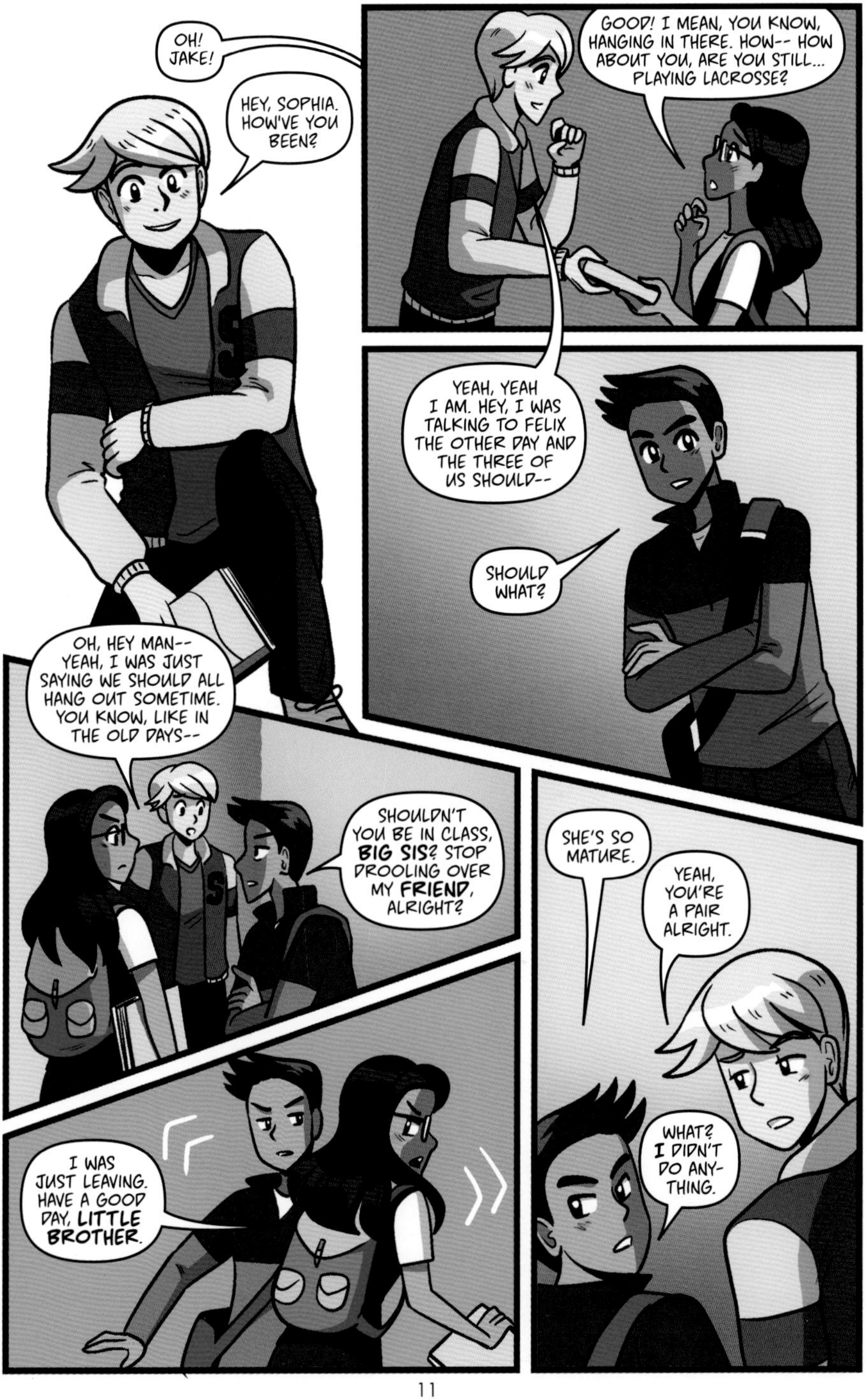

OH! JAKE!
HEY, SOPHIA. HOW'VE YOU BEEN?
GOOD! I MEAN, YOU KNOW, HANGING IN THERE. HOW-- HOW ABOUT YOU, ARE YOU STILL... PLAYING LACROSSE?
YEAH, YEAH I AM. HEY, I WAS TALKING TO FELIX THE OTHER DAY AND THE THREE OF US SHOULD--
SHOULD WHAT?
OH, HEY MAN-- YEAH, I WAS JUST SAYING WE SHOULD ALL HANG OUT SOMETIME. YOU KNOW, LIKE IN THE OLD DAYS--
SHOULDN'T YOU BE IN CLASS, **BIG SIS**? STOP DROOLING OVER MY **FRIEND**, ALRIGHT?
I WAS JUST LEAVING. HAVE A GOOD DAY, **LITTLE BROTHER**.
SHE'S SO MATURE.
YEAH, YOU'RE A PAIR ALRIGHT.
WHAT? **I** DIDN'T DO ANY-THING.

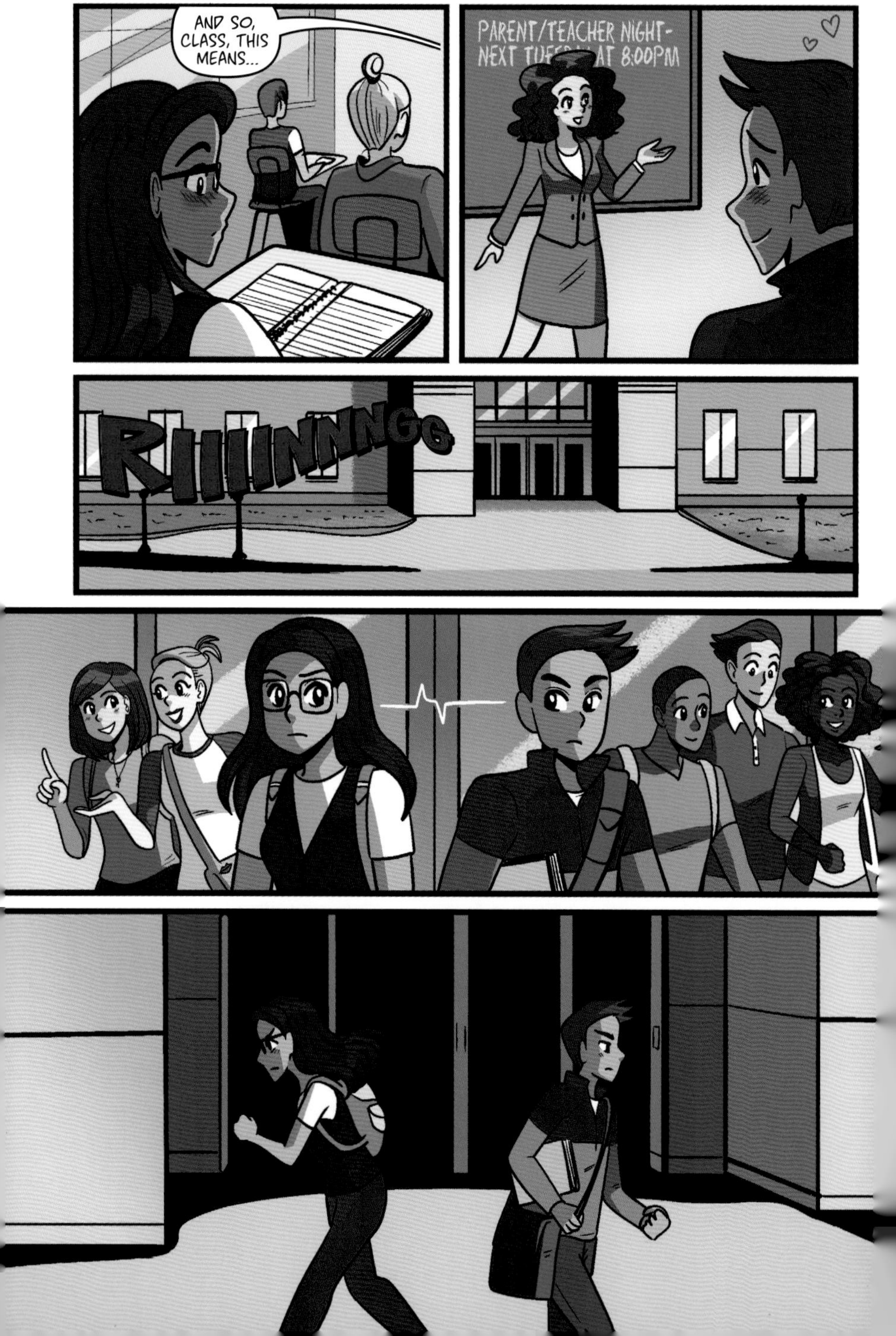
AND SO, CLASS, THIS MEANS...
PARENT/TEACHER NIGHT-
RIIIINNNGG

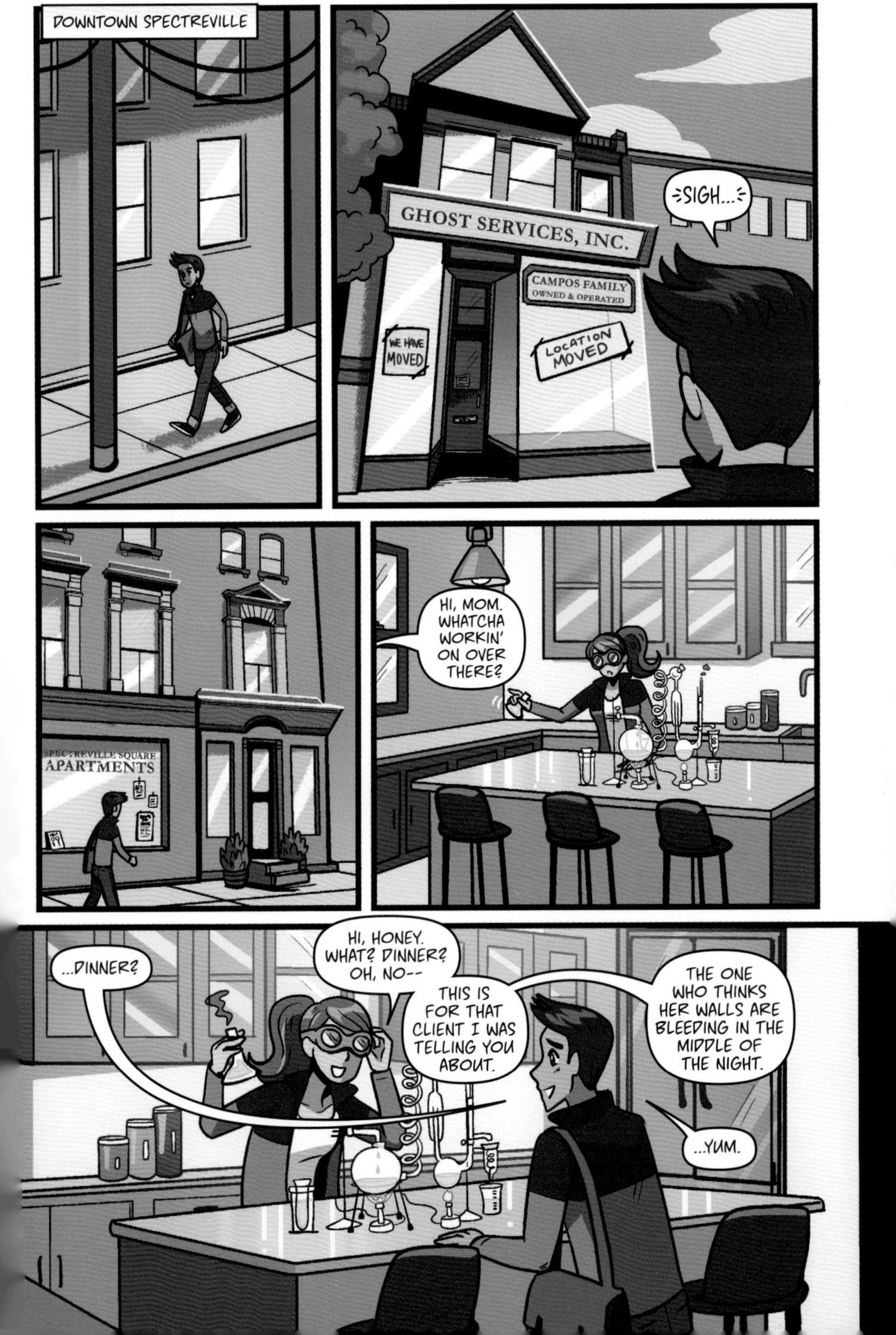
DOWNTOWN SPECTREVILLE
GHOST SERVICES, INC.
CAMPOS FAMILY OWNED & OPERATED
WE HAVE MOVED
LOCATION MOVED
SIGH...
SPECTREVILLE SQUARE APARTMENTS
HI, MOM. WHATCHA WORKIN' ON OVER THERE?
...DINNER?
HI, HONEY. WHAT? DINNER? OH, NO--
THIS IS FOR THAT CLIENT I WAS TELLING YOU ABOUT.
THE ONE WHO THINKS HER WALLS ARE BLEEDING IN THE MIDDLE OF THE NIGHT.
...YUM.

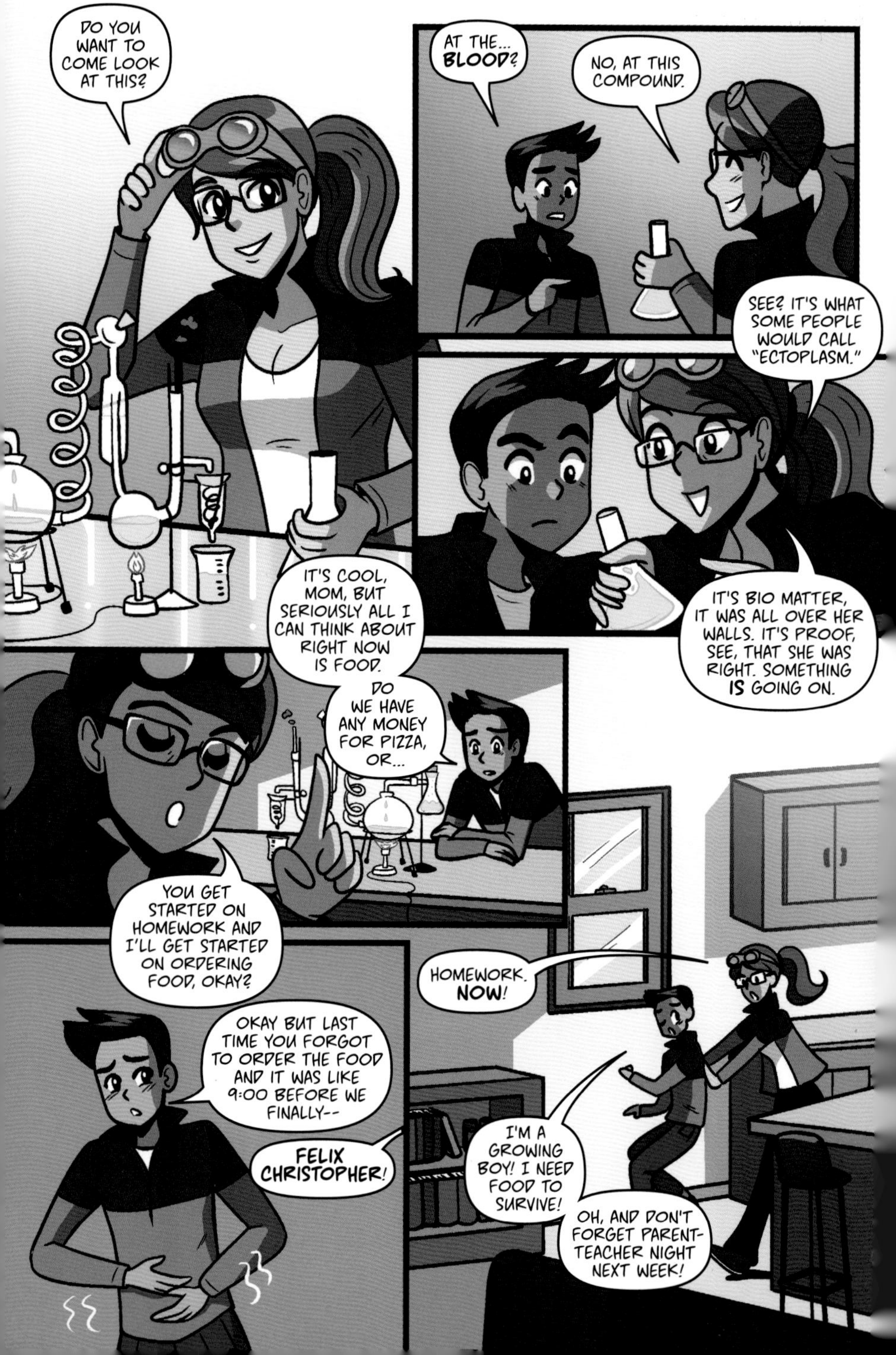
DO YOU WANT TO COME LOOK AT THIS?
AT THE... BLOOD?
NO, AT THIS COMPOUND.
SEE? IT'S WHAT SOME PEOPLE WOULD CALL "ECTOPLASM."
IT'S BIO MATTER, IT WAS ALL OVER HER WALLS. IT'S PROOF, SEE, THAT SHE WAS RIGHT. SOMETHING IS GOING ON.
IT'S COOL, MOM, BUT SERIOUSLY ALL I CAN THINK ABOUT RIGHT NOW IS FOOD.
DO WE HAVE ANY MONEY FOR PIZZA, OR...
YOU GET STARTED ON HOMEWORK AND I'LL GET STARTED ON ORDERING FOOD, OKAY?
OKAY BUT LAST TIME YOU FORGOT TO ORDER THE FOOD AND IT WAS LIKE 9:00 BEFORE WE FINALLY--
FELIX CHRISTOPHER!
HOMEWORK. NOW!
I'M A GROWING BOY! I NEED FOOD TO SURVIVE!
OH, AND DON'T FORGET PARENT-TEACHER NIGHT NEXT WEEK!

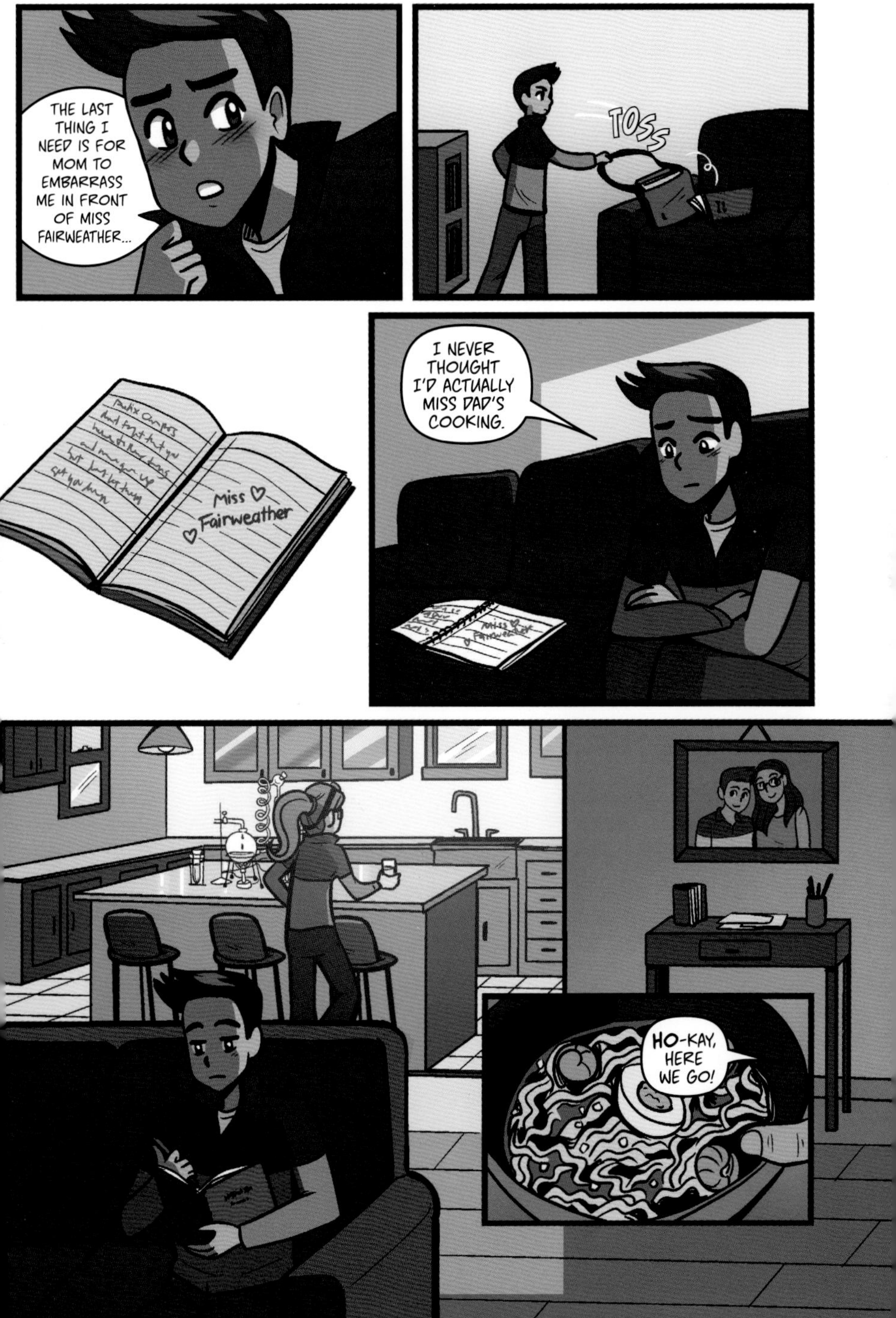
THE LAST THING I NEED IS FOR MOM TO EMBARRASS ME IN FRONT OF MISS FAIRWEATHER...
TOSS
Miss Fairweather
I NEVER THOUGHT I'D ACTUALLY MISS DAD'S COOKING.
HO-KAY, HERE WE GO!

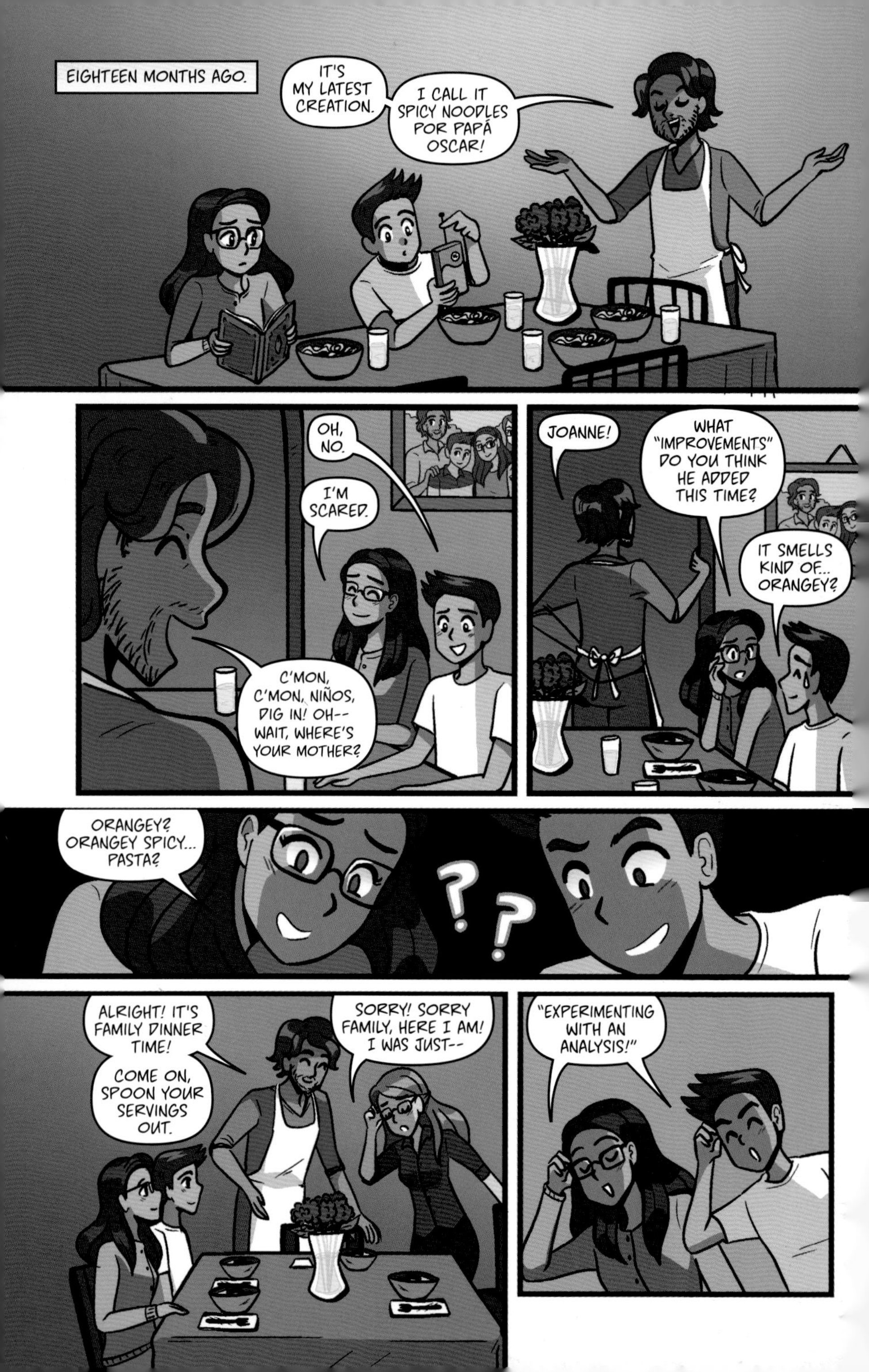
EIGHTEEN MONTHS AGO.
IT'S MY LATEST CREATION.
I CALL IT SPICY NOODLES POR PAPÁ OSCAR!
OH, NO.
I'M SCARED.
C'MON, C'MON, NIÑOS, DIG IN! OH-- WAIT, WHERE'S YOUR MOTHER?
JOANNE!
WHAT "IMPROVEMENTS" DO YOU THINK HE ADDED THIS TIME?
IT SMELLS KIND OF... ORANGEY?
ORANGEY? ORANGEY SPICY... PASTA?
??
ALRIGHT! IT'S FAMILY DINNER TIME!
COME ON, SPOON YOUR SERVINGS OUT.
SORRY! SORRY FAMILY, HERE I AM! I WAS JUST--
"EXPERIMENTING WITH AN ANALYSIS!"

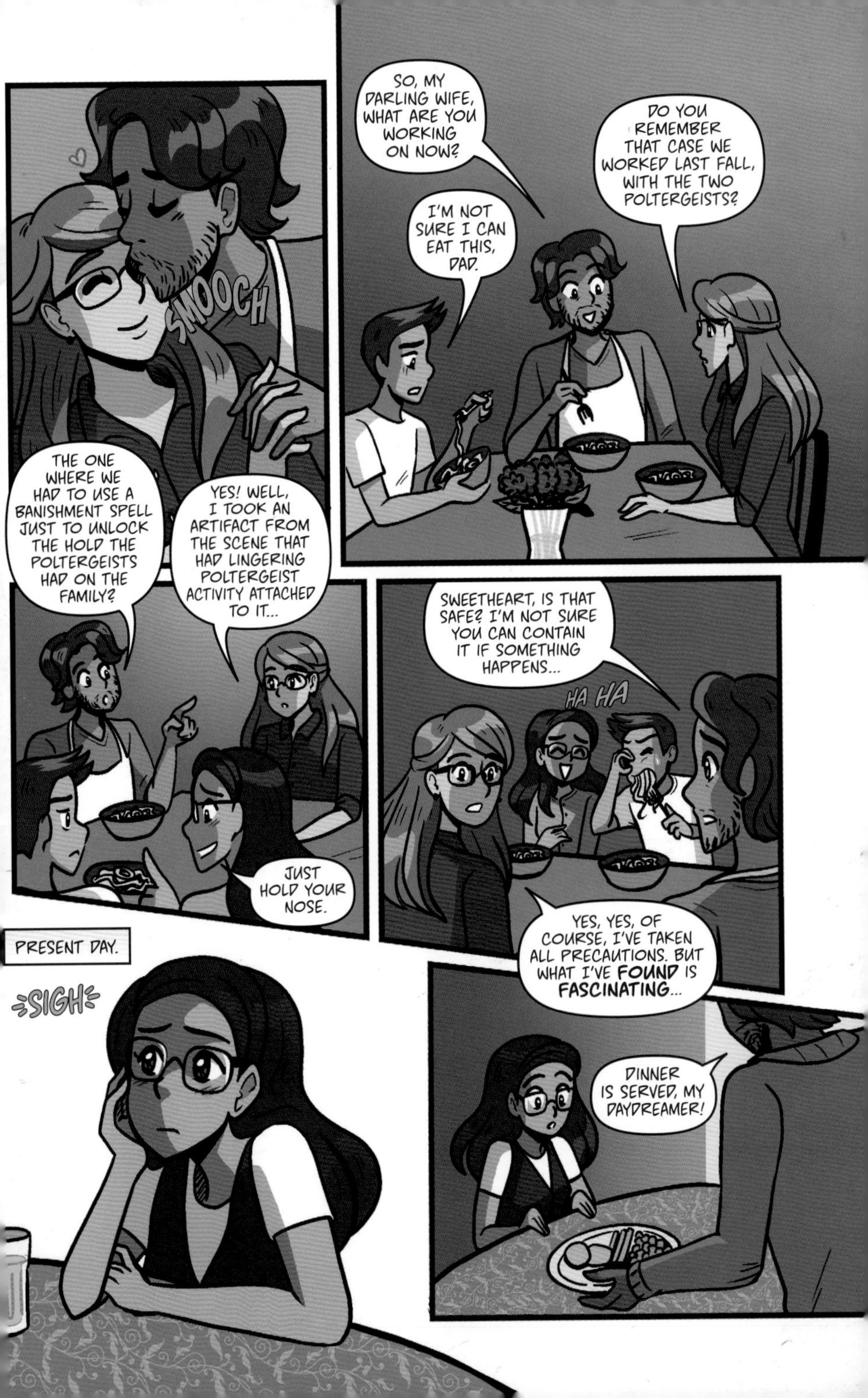
SMOOCH
SO, MY DARLING WIFE, WHAT ARE YOU WORKING ON NOW?
DO YOU REMEMBER THAT CASE WE WORKED LAST FALL, WITH THE TWO POLTERGEISTS?
I'M NOT SURE I CAN EAT THIS, DAD.
THE ONE WHERE WE HAD TO USE A BANISHMENT SPELL JUST TO UNLOCK THE HOLD THE POLTERGEISTS HAD ON THE FAMILY?
YES! WELL, I TOOK AN ARTIFACT FROM THE SCENE THAT HAD LINGERING POLTERGEIST ACTIVITY ATTACHED TO IT...
JUST HOLD YOUR NOSE.
SWEETHEART, IS THAT SAFE? I'M NOT SURE YOU CAN CONTAIN IT IF SOMETHING HAPPENS...
HA HA
YES, YES, OF COURSE, I'VE TAKEN ALL PRECAUTIONS. BUT WHAT I'VE **FOUND** IS **FASCINATING**...
PRESENT DAY.
SIGH
DINNER IS SERVED, MY DAYDREAMER!

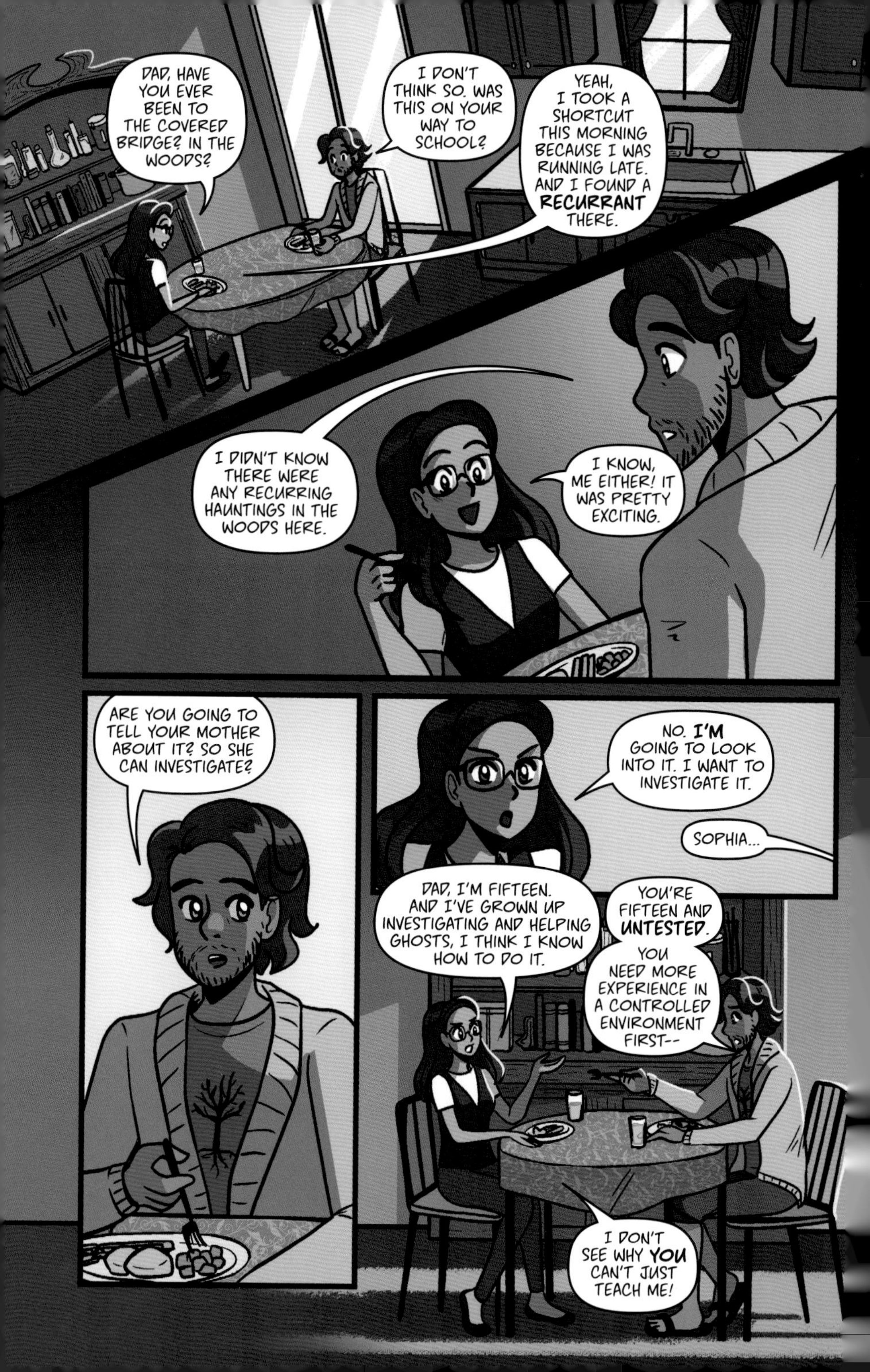
DAD, HAVE YOU EVER BEEN TO THE COVERED BRIDGE? IN THE WOODS?
I DON'T THINK SO. WAS THIS ON YOUR WAY TO SCHOOL?
YEAH, I TOOK A SHORTCUT THIS MORNING BECAUSE I WAS RUNNING LATE. AND I FOUND A **RECURRANT** THERE.
I DIDN'T KNOW THERE WERE ANY RECURRING HAUNTINGS IN THE WOODS HERE.
I KNOW, ME EITHER! IT WAS PRETTY EXCITING.
ARE YOU GOING TO TELL YOUR MOTHER ABOUT IT? SO SHE CAN INVESTIGATE?
NO. **I'M** GOING TO LOOK INTO IT. I WANT TO INVESTIGATE IT.
SOPHIA...
DAD, I'M FIFTEEN. AND I'VE GROWN UP INVESTIGATING AND HELPING GHOSTS, I THINK I KNOW HOW TO DO IT.
YOU'RE FIFTEEN AND **UNTESTED**.
YOU NEED MORE EXPERIENCE IN A CONTROLLED ENVIRONMENT FIRST--
I DON'T SEE WHY **YOU** CAN'T JUST TEACH ME!

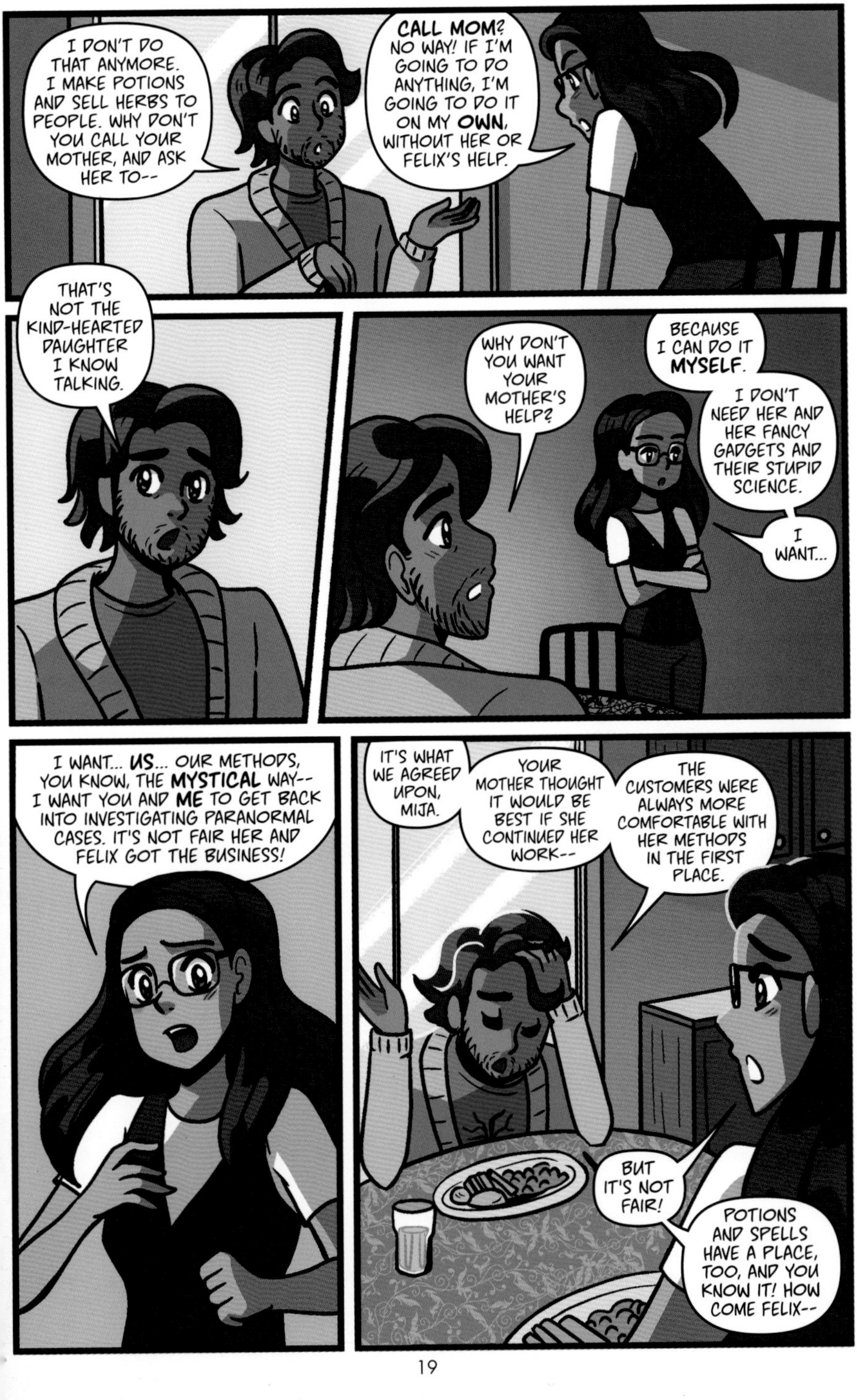
I DON'T DO THAT ANYMORE. I MAKE POTIONS AND SELL HERBS TO PEOPLE. WHY DON'T YOU CALL YOUR MOTHER, AND ASK HER TO--
CALL MOM? NO WAY! IF I'M GOING TO DO ANYTHING, I'M GOING TO DO IT ON MY OWN, WITHOUT HER OR FELIX'S HELP.
THAT'S NOT THE KIND-HEARTED DAUGHTER I KNOW TALKING.
WHY DON'T YOU WANT YOUR MOTHER'S HELP?
BECAUSE I CAN DO IT MYSELF.
I DON'T NEED HER AND HER FANCY GADGETS AND THEIR STUPID SCIENCE.
I WANT...
I WANT... US... OUR METHODS, YOU KNOW, THE MYSTICAL WAY-- I WANT YOU AND ME TO GET BACK INTO INVESTIGATING PARANORMAL CASES. IT'S NOT FAIR HER AND FELIX GOT THE BUSINESS!
IT'S WHAT WE AGREED UPON, MIJA.
YOUR MOTHER THOUGHT IT WOULD BE BEST IF SHE CONTINUED HER WORK--
THE CUSTOMERS WERE ALWAYS MORE COMFORTABLE WITH HER METHODS IN THE FIRST PLACE.
BUT IT'S NOT FAIR!
POTIONS AND SPELLS HAVE A PLACE, TOO, AND YOU KNOW IT! HOW COME FELIX--

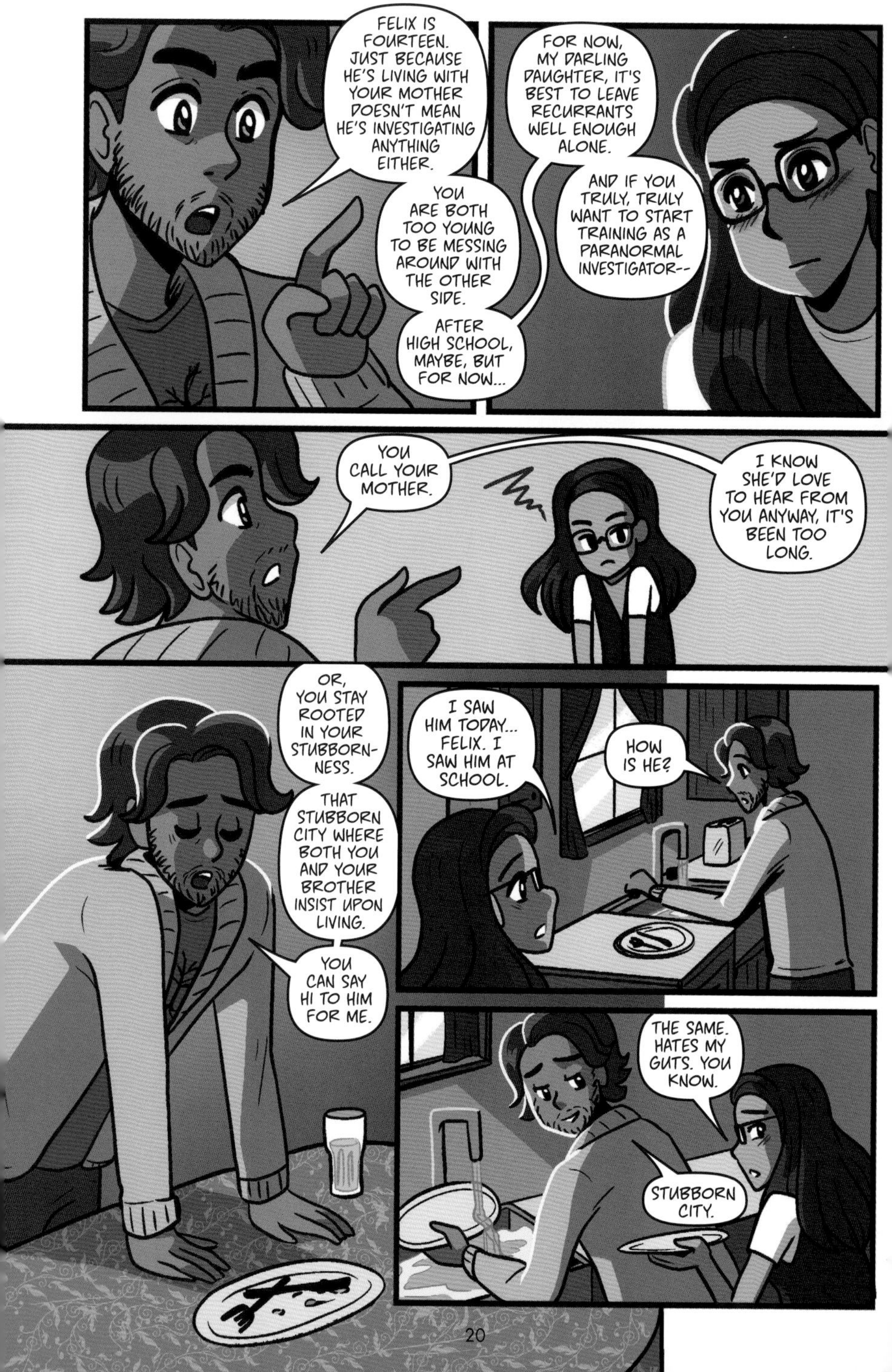
FELIX IS FOURTEEN. JUST BECAUSE HE'S LIVING WITH YOUR MOTHER DOESN'T MEAN HE'S INVESTIGATING ANYTHING EITHER.
YOU ARE BOTH TOO YOUNG TO BE MESSING AROUND WITH THE OTHER SIDE.
AFTER HIGH SCHOOL, MAYBE, BUT FOR NOW...
FOR NOW, MY DARLING DAUGHTER, IT'S BEST TO LEAVE RECURRANTS WELL ENOUGH ALONE.
AND IF YOU TRULY, TRULY WANT TO START TRAINING AS A PARANORMAL INVESTIGATOR--
YOU CALL YOUR MOTHER.
I KNOW SHE'D LOVE TO HEAR FROM YOU ANYWAY, IT'S BEEN TOO LONG.
OR, YOU STAY ROOTED IN YOUR STUBBORN-NESS.
THAT STUBBORN CITY WHERE BOTH YOU AND YOUR BROTHER INSIST UPON LIVING.
YOU CAN SAY HI TO HIM FOR ME.
I SAW HIM TODAY... FELIX. I SAW HIM AT SCHOOL.
HOW IS HE?
THE SAME. HATES MY GUTS. YOU KNOW.
STUBBORN CITY.

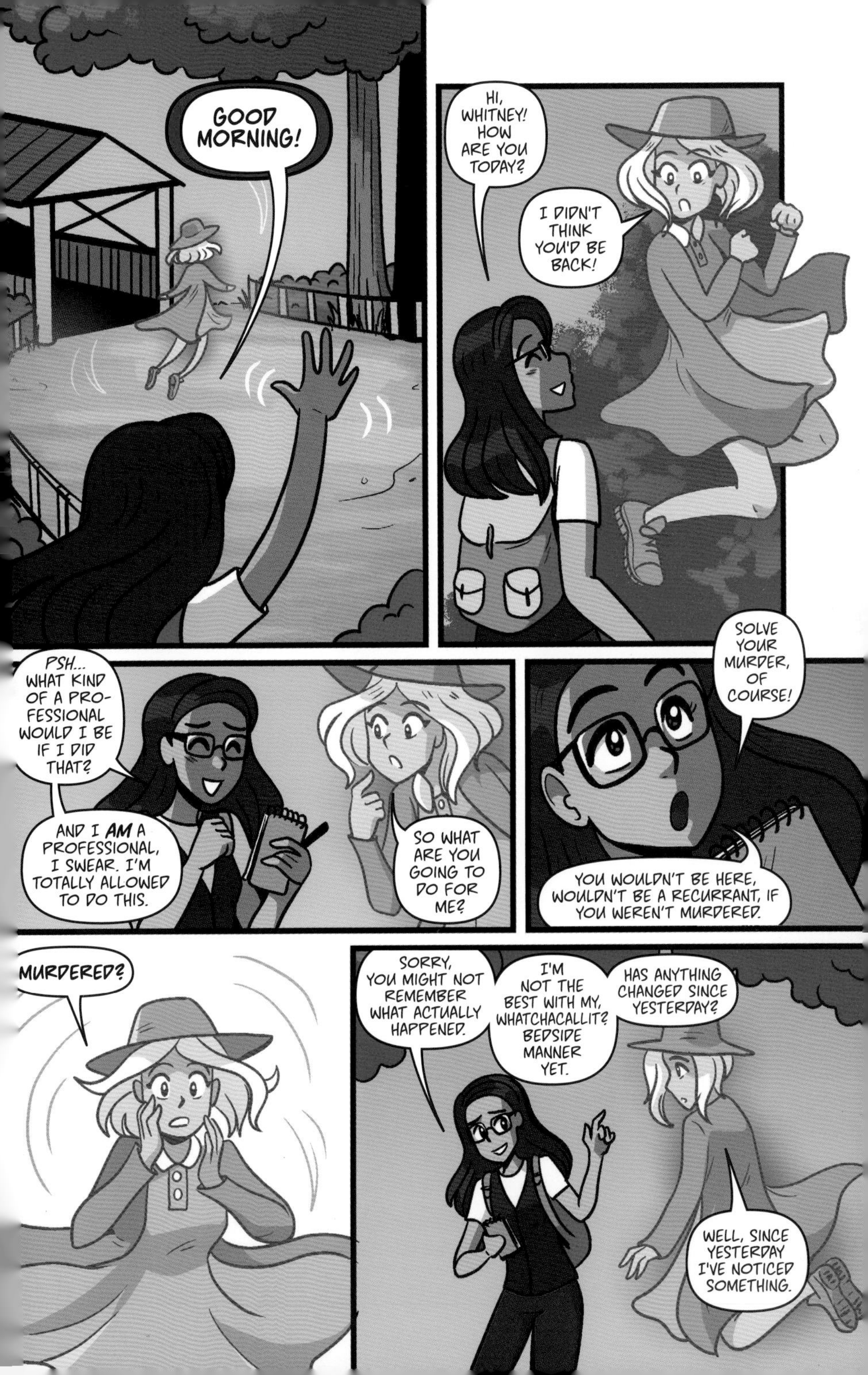
GOOD MORNING!
HI, WHITNEY! HOW ARE YOU TODAY?
I DIDN'T THINK YOU'D BE BACK!
PSH... WHAT KIND OF A PRO-FESSIONAL WOULD I BE IF I DID THAT?
AND I AM A PROFESSIONAL, I SWEAR. I'M TOTALLY ALLOWED TO DO THIS.
SO WHAT ARE YOU GOING TO DO FOR ME?
SOLVE YOUR MURDER, OF COURSE!
YOU WOULDN'T BE HERE, WOULDN'T BE A RECURRANT, IF YOU WEREN'T MURDERED.
MURDERED?
SORRY, YOU MIGHT NOT REMEMBER WHAT ACTUALLY HAPPENED.
I'M NOT THE BEST WITH MY, WHATCHACALLIT? BEDSIDE MANNER YET.
HAS ANYTHING CHANGED SINCE YESTERDAY?
WELL, SINCE YESTERDAY I'VE NOTICED SOMETHING.

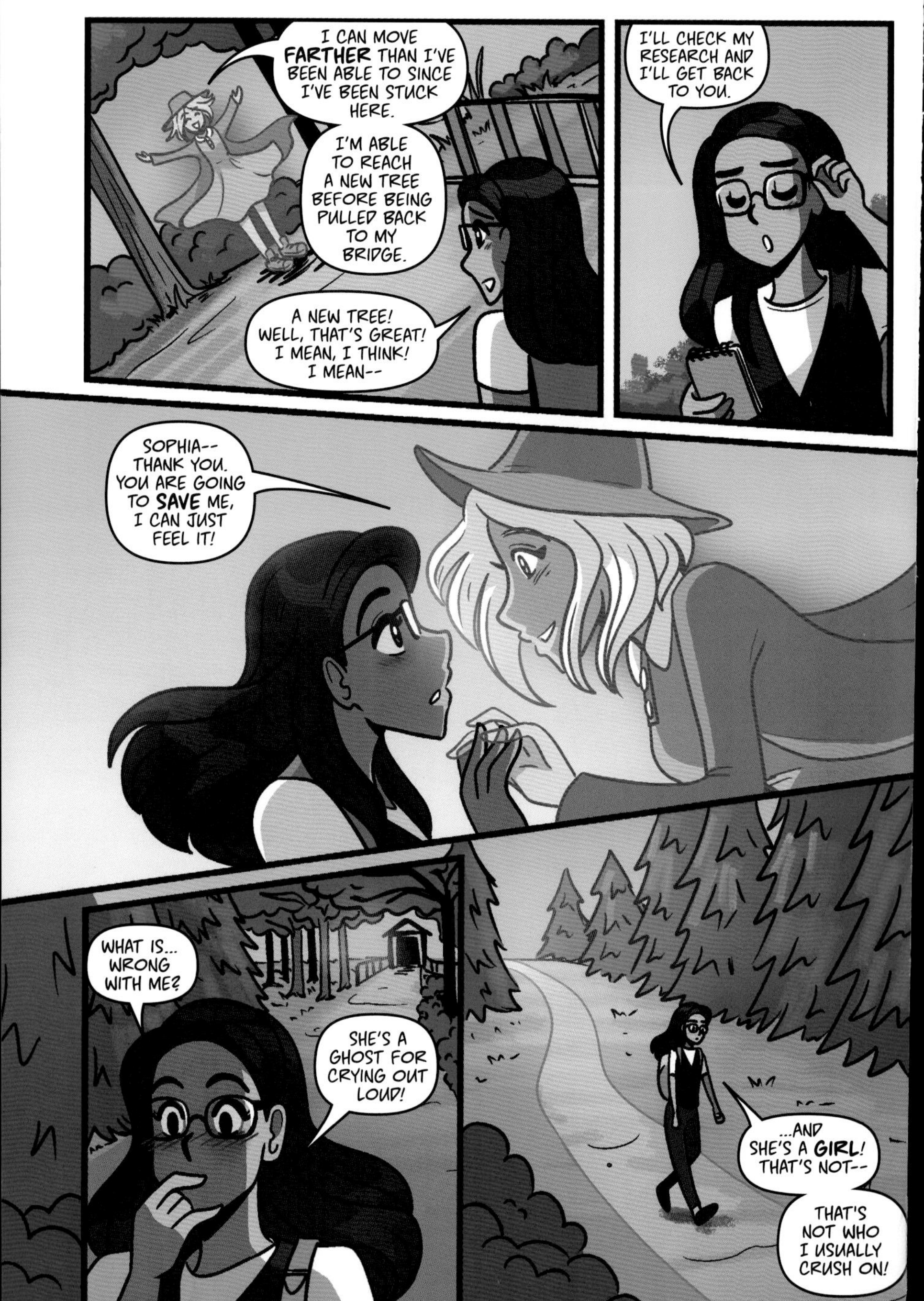
I CAN MOVE FARTHER THAN I'VE BEEN ABLE TO SINCE I'VE BEEN STUCK HERE.
I'M ABLE TO REACH A NEW TREE BEFORE BEING PULLED BACK TO MY BRIDGE.
A NEW TREE! WELL, THAT'S GREAT! I MEAN, I THINK! I MEAN--
I'LL CHECK MY RESEARCH AND I'LL GET BACK TO YOU.
SOPHIA-- THANK YOU. YOU ARE GOING TO SAVE ME, I CAN JUST FEEL IT!
WHAT IS... WRONG WITH ME?
SHE'S A GHOST FOR CRYING OUT LOUD!
...AND SHE'S A GIRL! THAT'S NOT--
THAT'S NOT WHO I USUALLY CRUSH ON!

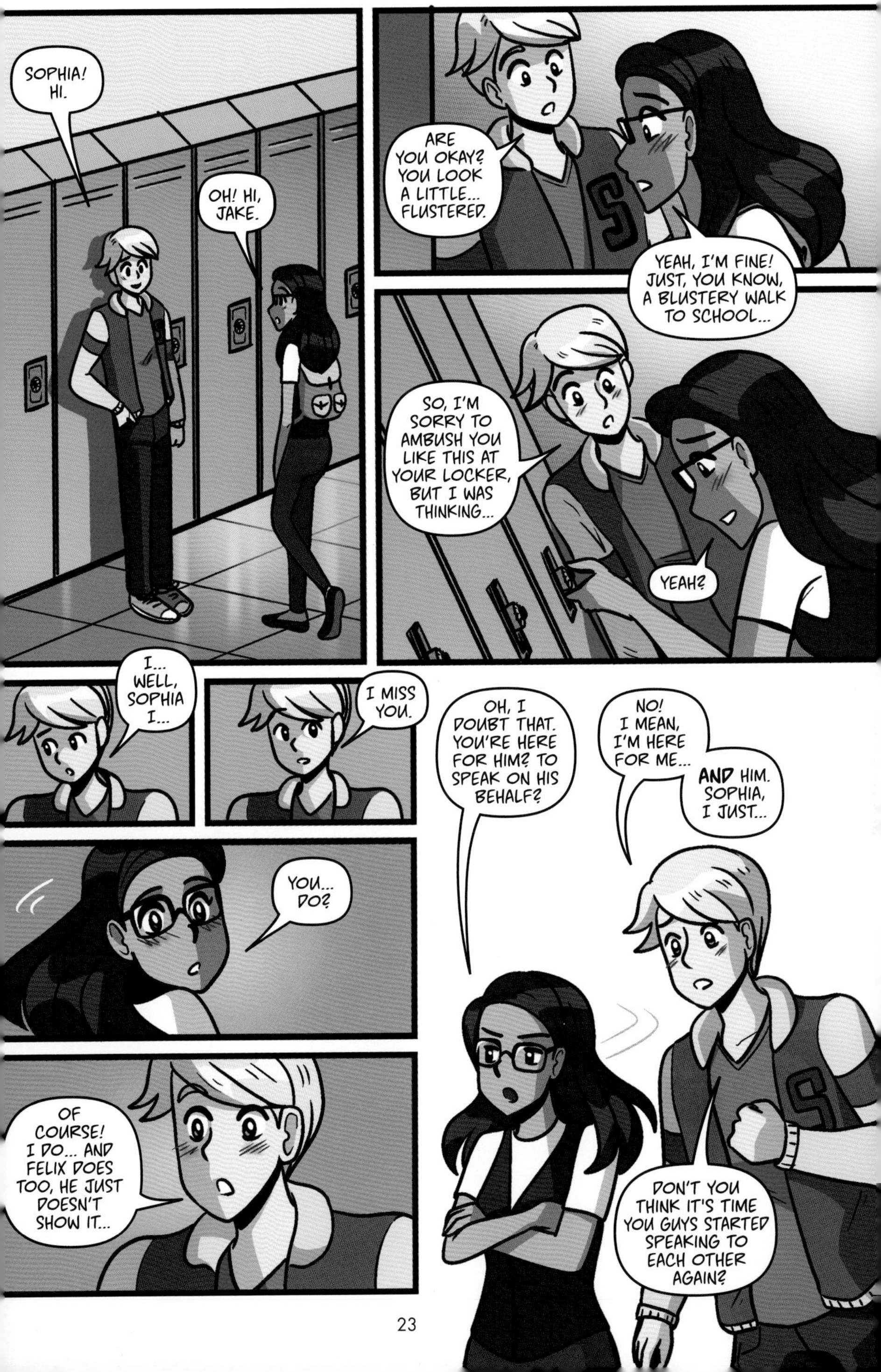

SOPHIA! HI.
OH! HI, JAKE.
ARE YOU OKAY? YOU LOOK A LITTLE... FLUSTERED.
YEAH, I'M FINE! JUST, YOU KNOW, A BLUSTERY WALK TO SCHOOL...
SO, I'M SORRY TO AMBUSH YOU LIKE THIS AT YOUR LOCKER, BUT I WAS THINKING...
YEAH?
I... WELL, SOPHIA I...
I MISS YOU.
YOU... DO?
OF COURSE! I DO... AND FELIX DOES TOO, HE JUST DOESN'T SHOW IT...
OH, I DOUBT THAT. YOU'RE HERE FOR HIM? TO SPEAK ON HIS BEHALF?
NO! I MEAN, I'M HERE FOR ME...
AND HIM. SOPHIA, I JUST...
DON'T YOU THINK IT'S TIME YOU GUYS STARTED SPEAKING TO EACH OTHER AGAIN?

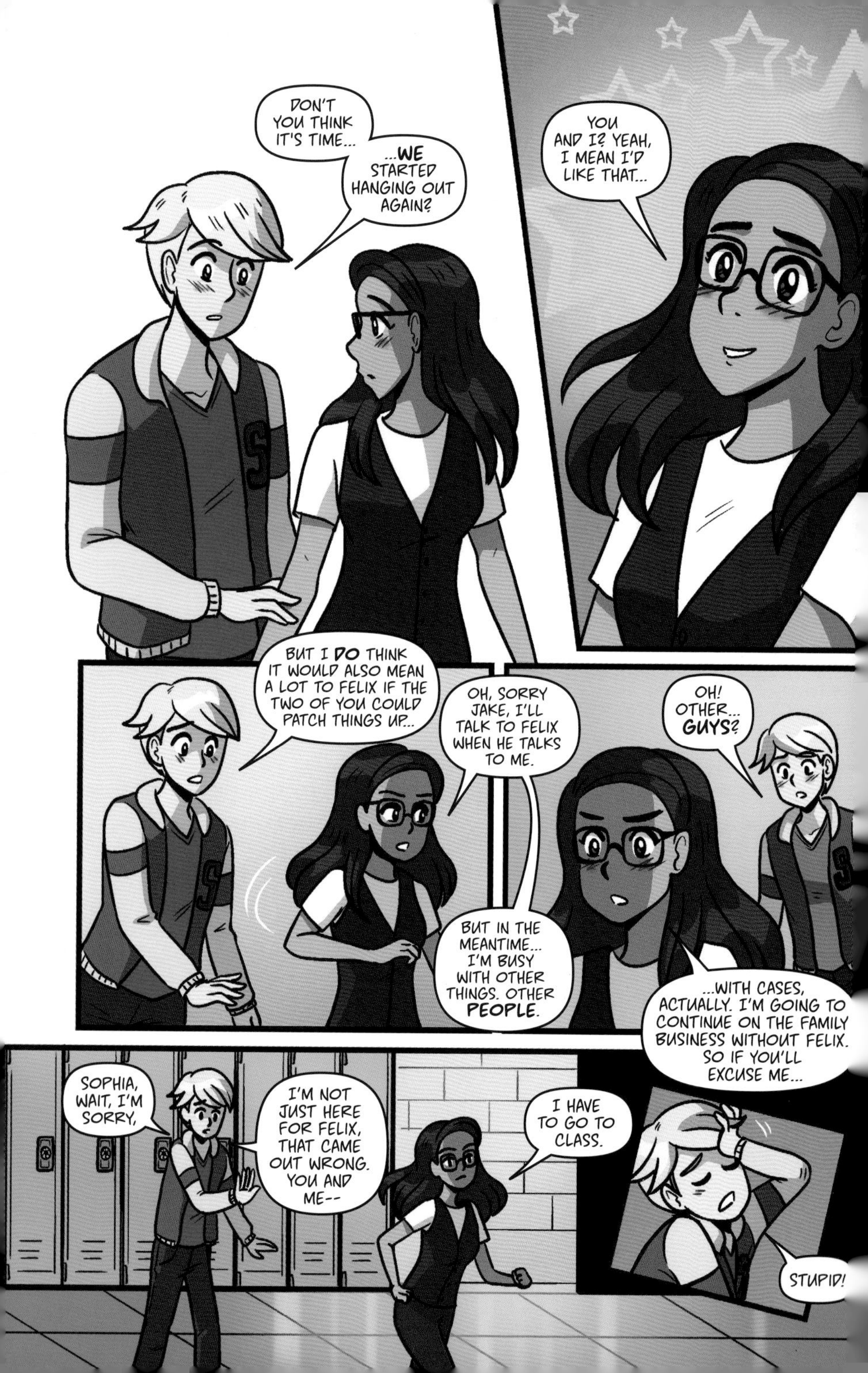
DON'T YOU THINK IT'S TIME...
...WE STARTED HANGING OUT AGAIN?
YOU AND I? YEAH, I MEAN I'D LIKE THAT...
BUT I DO THINK IT WOULD ALSO MEAN A LOT TO FELIX IF THE TWO OF YOU COULD PATCH THINGS UP...
OH, SORRY JAKE, I'LL TALK TO FELIX WHEN HE TALKS TO ME.
BUT IN THE MEANTIME... I'M BUSY WITH OTHER THINGS. OTHER PEOPLE.
OH! OTHER... GUYS?
...WITH CASES, ACTUALLY. I'M GOING TO CONTINUE ON THE FAMILY BUSINESS WITHOUT FELIX. SO IF YOU'LL EXCUSE ME...
SOPHIA, WAIT, I'M SORRY,
I'M NOT JUST HERE FOR FELIX, THAT CAME OUT WRONG. YOU AND ME--
I HAVE TO GO TO CLASS.
STUPID!

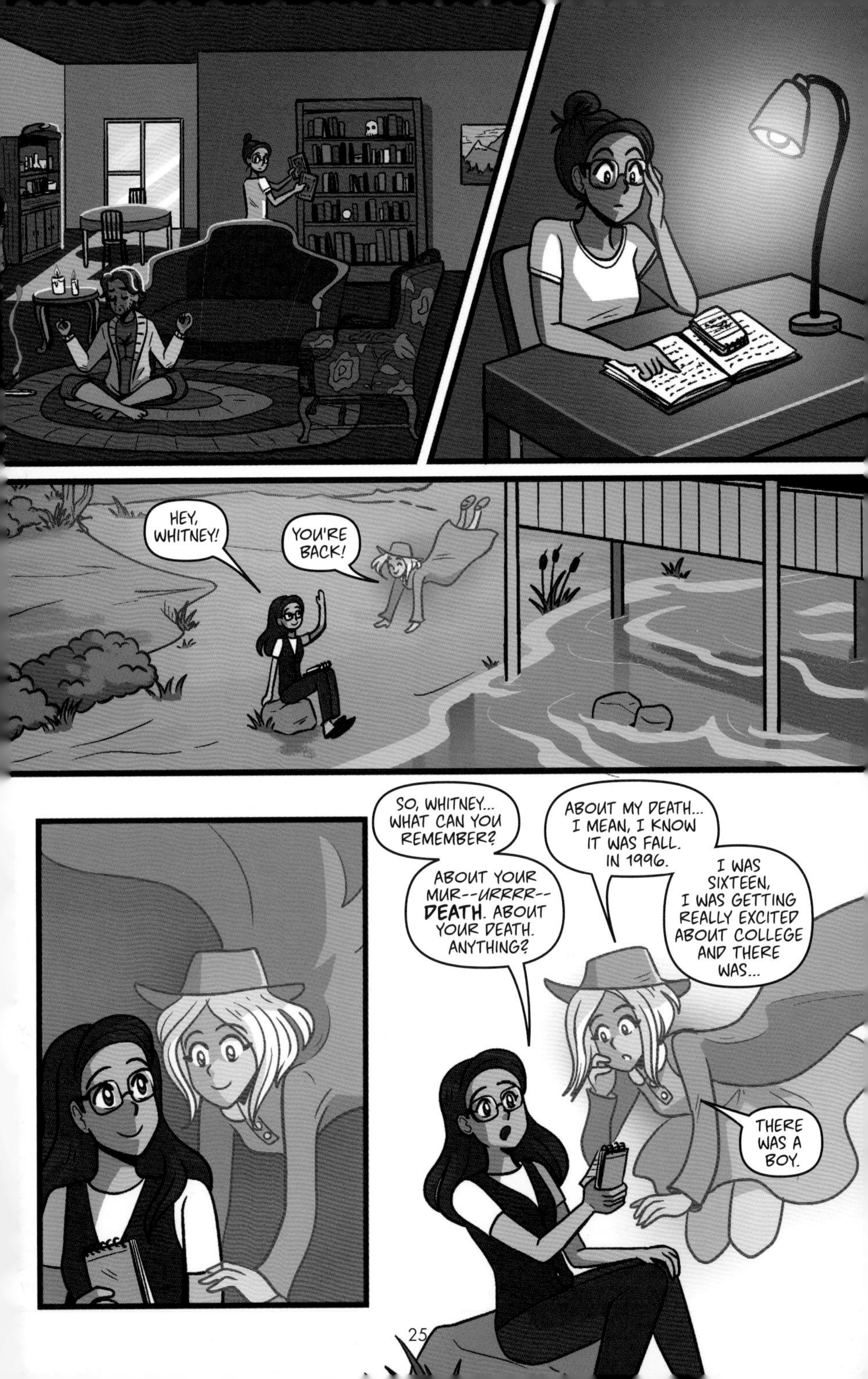
HEY, WHITNEY!
YOU'RE BACK!
SO, WHITNEY... WHAT CAN YOU REMEMBER?
ABOUT YOUR MUR--URRRR--**DEATH**. ABOUT YOUR DEATH. ANYTHING?
ABOUT MY DEATH... I MEAN, I KNOW IT WAS FALL. IN 1996.
I WAS SIXTEEN, I WAS GETTING REALLY EXCITED ABOUT COLLEGE AND THERE WAS...
THERE WAS A BOY.

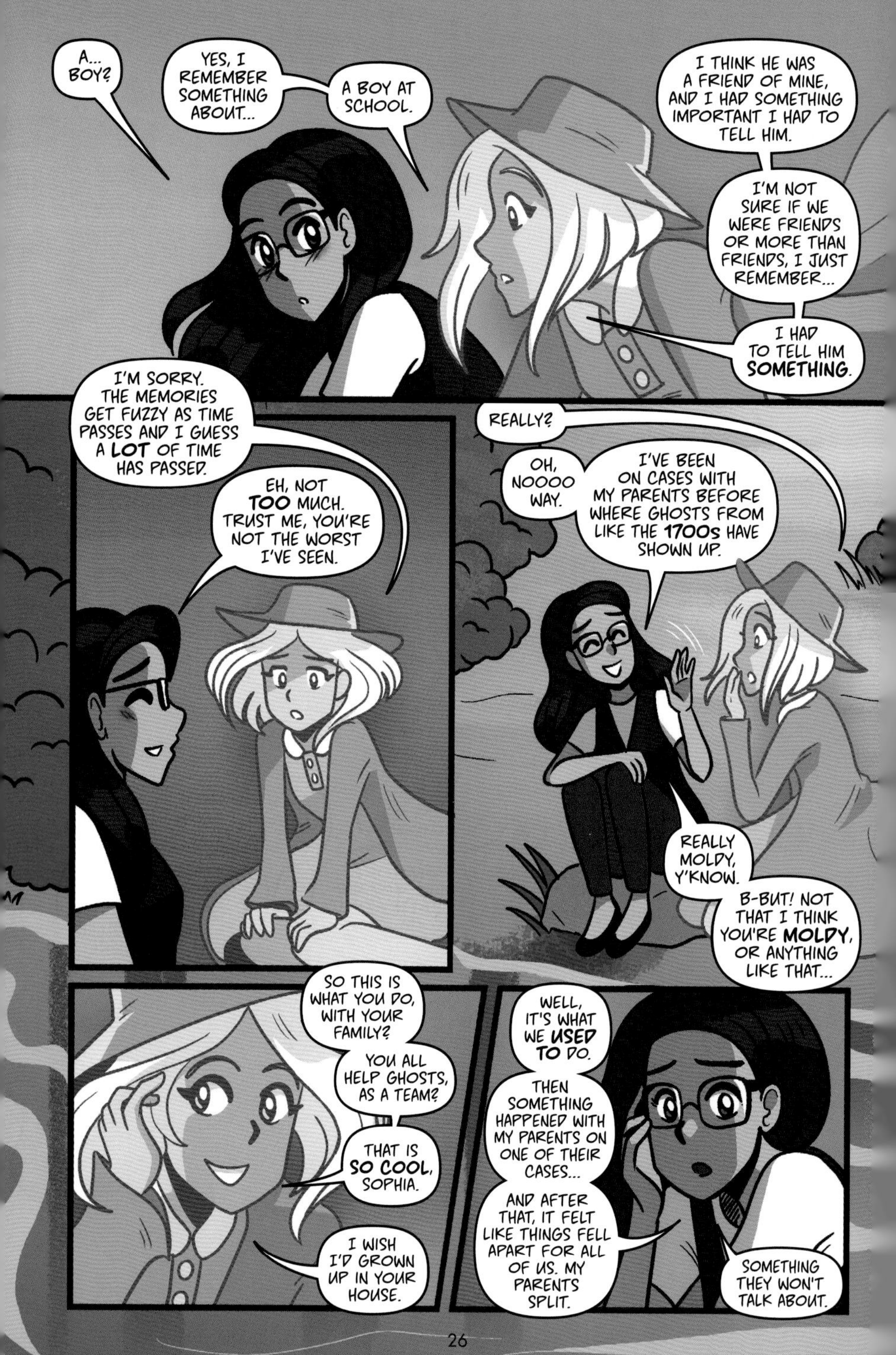
A... BOY?
YES, I REMEMBER SOMETHING ABOUT...
A BOY AT SCHOOL.
I THINK HE WAS A FRIEND OF MINE, AND I HAD SOMETHING IMPORTANT I HAD TO TELL HIM.
I'M NOT SURE IF WE WERE FRIENDS OR MORE THAN FRIENDS, I JUST REMEMBER...
I HAD TO TELL HIM **SOMETHING**.
I'M SORRY. THE MEMORIES GET FUZZY AS TIME PASSES AND I GUESS A **LOT** OF TIME HAS PASSED.
EH, NOT **TOO** MUCH. TRUST ME, YOU'RE NOT THE WORST I'VE SEEN.
REALLY?
OH, NOOOO WAY.
I'VE BEEN ON CASES WITH MY PARENTS BEFORE WHERE GHOSTS FROM LIKE THE **1700s** HAVE SHOWN UP.
REALLY MOLDY, Y'KNOW.
B-BUT! NOT THAT I THINK YOU'RE **MOLDY**, OR ANYTHING LIKE THAT...
SO THIS IS WHAT YOU DO, WITH YOUR FAMILY?
YOU ALL HELP GHOSTS, AS A TEAM?
THAT IS **SO COOL**, SOPHIA.
I WISH I'D GROWN UP IN YOUR HOUSE.
WELL, IT'S WHAT WE **USED TO** DO.
THEN SOMETHING HAPPENED WITH MY PARENTS ON ONE OF THEIR CASES...
AND AFTER THAT, IT FELT LIKE THINGS FELL APART FOR ALL OF US. MY PARENTS SPLIT.
SOMETHING THEY WON'T TALK ABOUT.

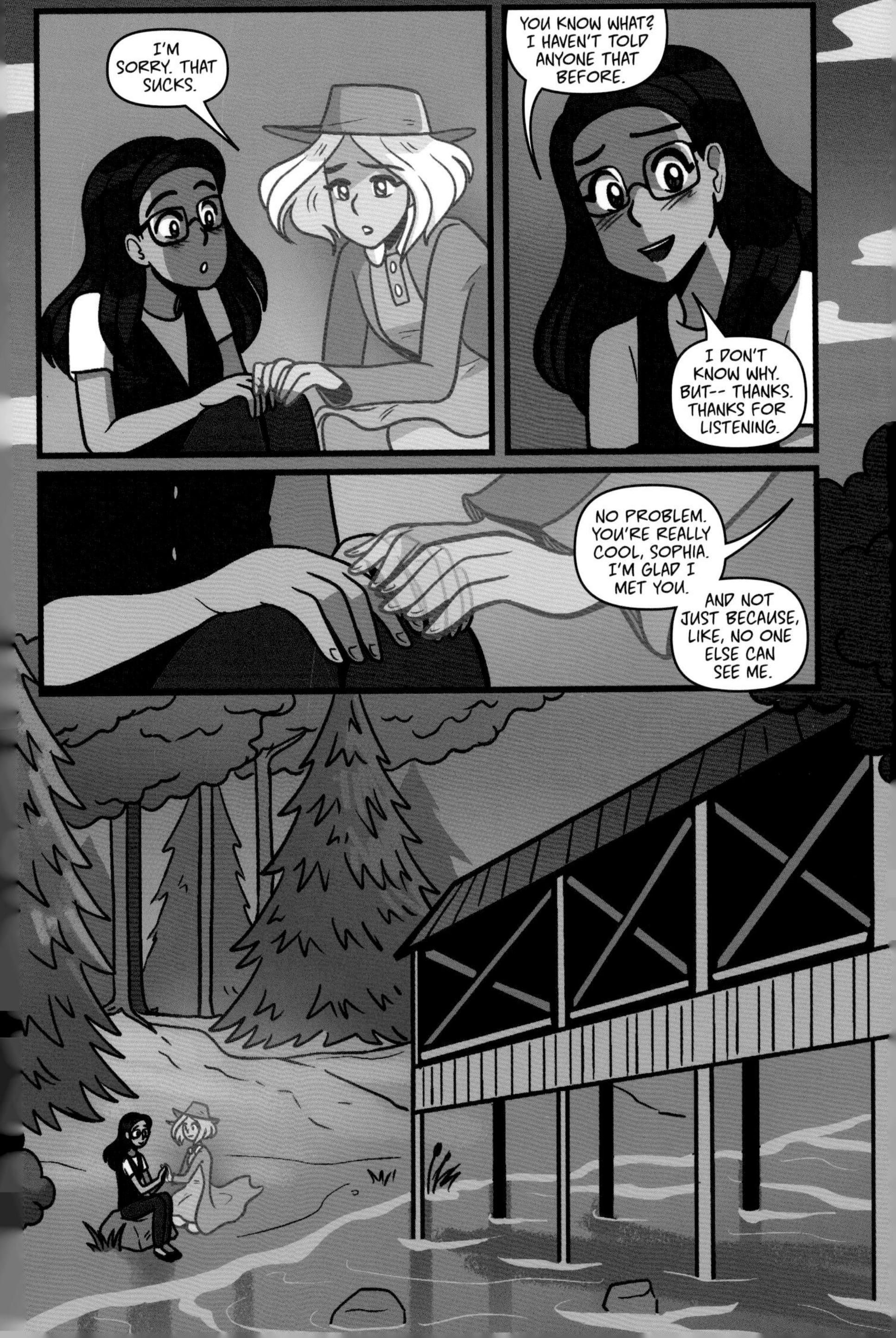
I'M SORRY. THAT SUCKS.
YOU KNOW WHAT? I HAVEN'T TOLD ANYONE THAT BEFORE.
I DON'T KNOW WHY. BUT-- THANKS. THANKS FOR LISTENING.
NO PROBLEM. YOU'RE REALLY COOL, SOPHIA. I'M GLAD I MET YOU.
AND NOT JUST BECAUSE, LIKE, NO ONE ELSE CAN SEE ME.

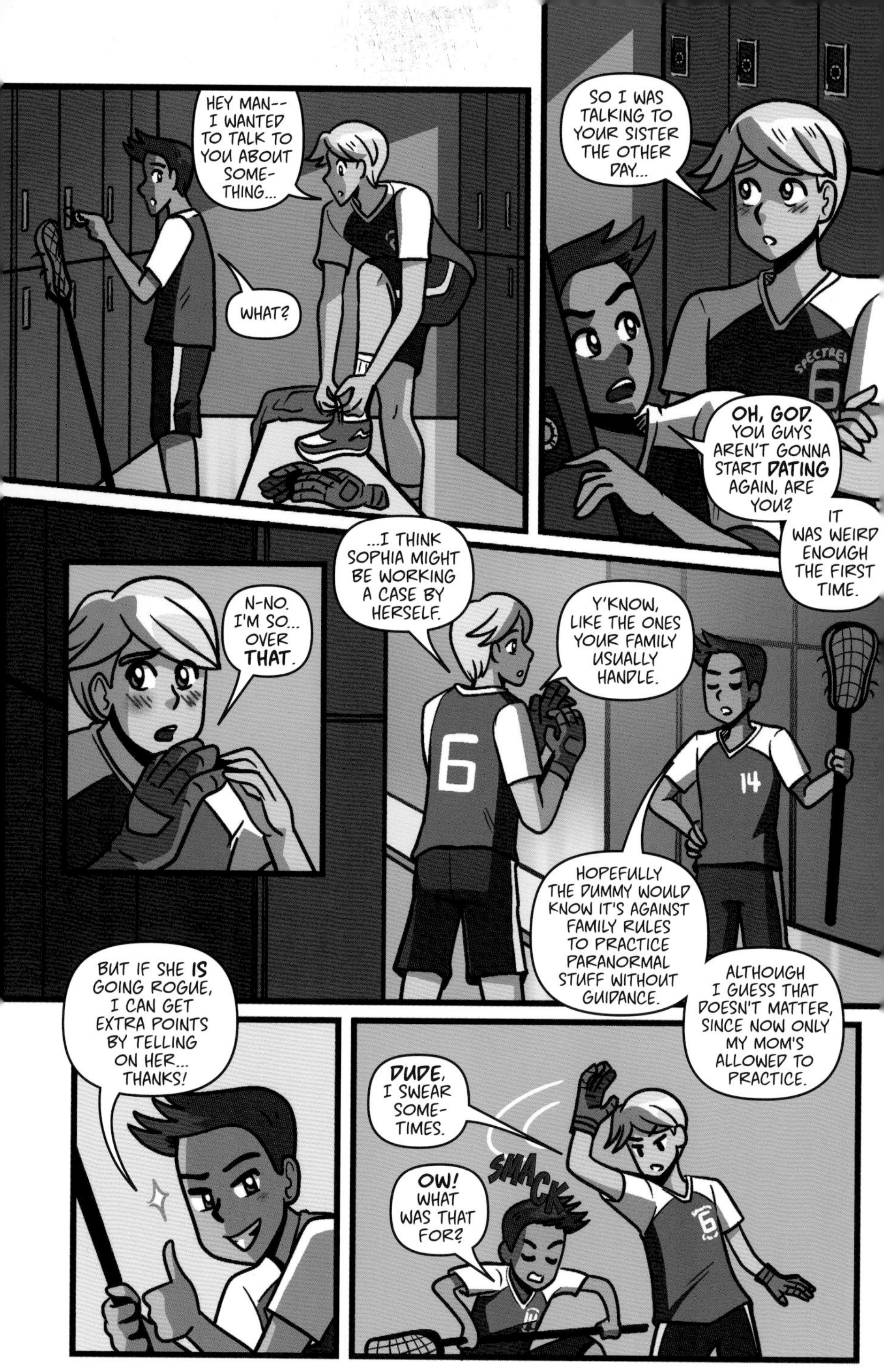
HEY MAN-- I WANTED TO TALK TO YOU ABOUT SOME-THING...
WHAT?
SO I WAS TALKING TO YOUR SISTER THE OTHER DAY...
OH, GOD. YOU GUYS AREN'T GONNA START DATING AGAIN, ARE YOU?
IT WAS WEIRD ENOUGH THE FIRST TIME.
N-NO. I'M SO... OVER THAT.
...I THINK SOPHIA MIGHT BE WORKING A CASE BY HERSELF.
Y'KNOW, LIKE THE ONES YOUR FAMILY USUALLY HANDLE.
HOPEFULLY THE DUMMY WOULD KNOW IT'S AGAINST FAMILY RULES TO PRACTICE PARANORMAL STUFF WITHOUT GUIDANCE.
ALTHOUGH I GUESS THAT DOESN'T MATTER, SINCE NOW ONLY MY MOM'S ALLOWED TO PRACTICE.
BUT IF SHE IS GOING ROGUE, I CAN GET EXTRA POINTS BY TELLING ON HER... THANKS!
DUDE, I SWEAR SOME-TIMES.
SMACK
OW! WHAT WAS THAT FOR?

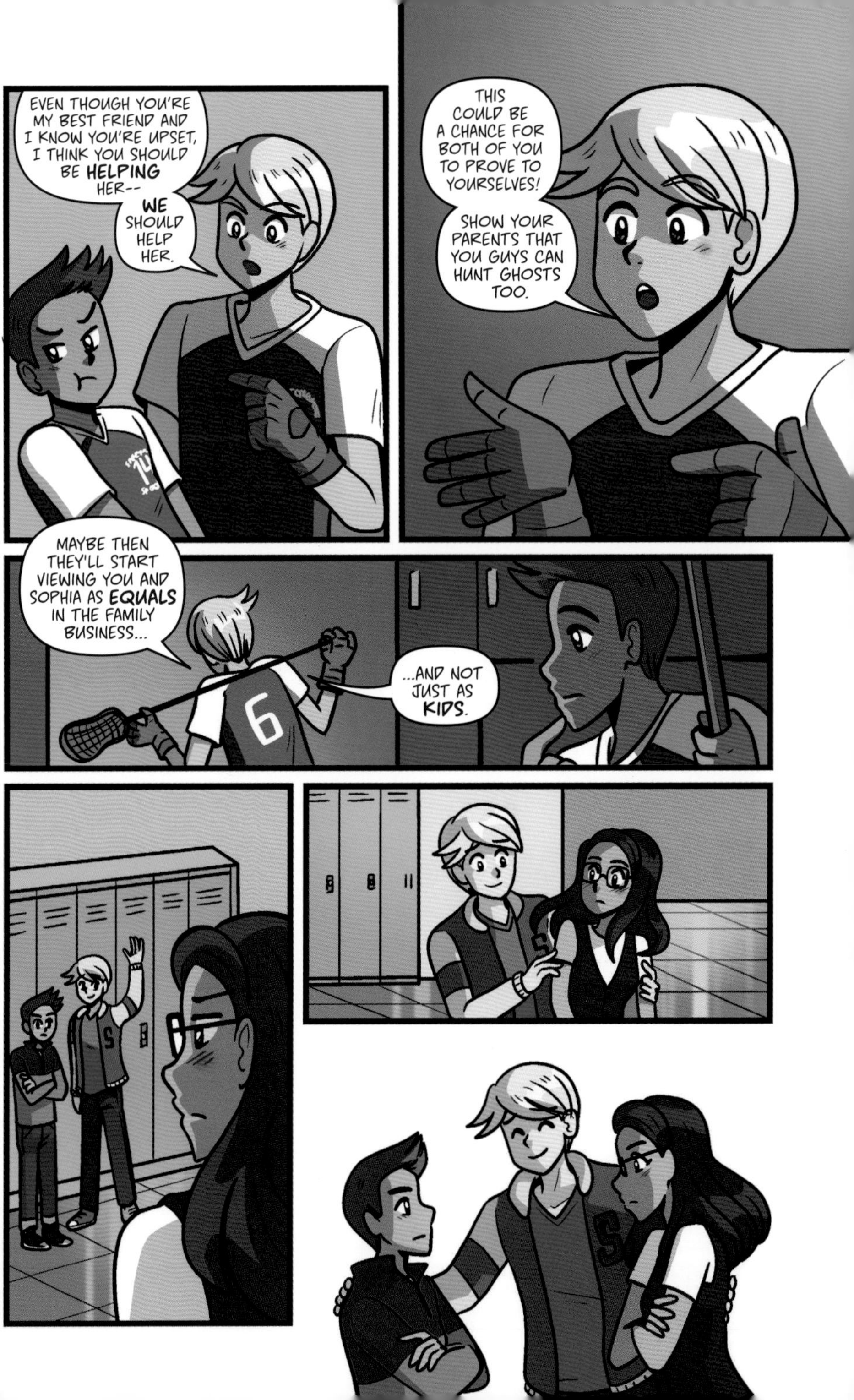
EVEN THOUGH YOU'RE MY BEST FRIEND AND I KNOW YOU'RE UPSET, I THINK YOU SHOULD BE **HELPING** HER--
WE SHOULD HELP HER.
THIS COULD BE A CHANCE FOR BOTH OF YOU TO PROVE TO YOURSELVES!
SHOW YOUR PARENTS THAT YOU GUYS CAN HUNT GHOSTS TOO.
MAYBE THEN THEY'LL START VIEWING YOU AND SOPHIA AS **EQUALS** IN THE FAMILY BUSINESS...
...AND NOT JUST AS **KIDS**.

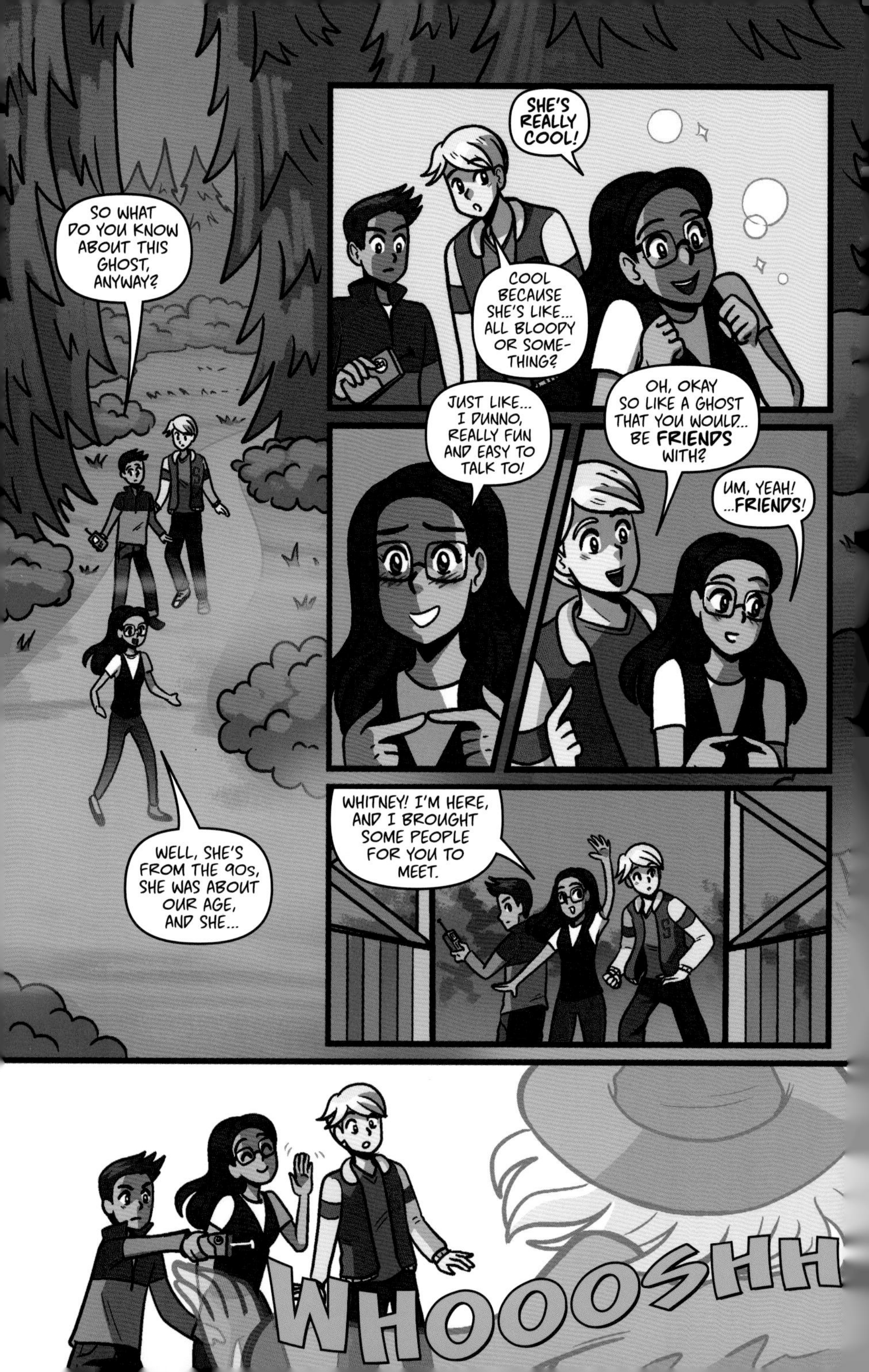
SO WHAT DO YOU KNOW ABOUT THIS GHOST, ANYWAY?
WELL, SHE'S FROM THE 90s, SHE WAS ABOUT OUR AGE, AND SHE...
SHE'S REALLY COOL!
COOL BECAUSE SHE'S LIKE... ALL BLOODY OR SOME-THING?
JUST LIKE... I DUNNO, REALLY FUN AND EASY TO TALK TO!
OH, OKAY SO LIKE A GHOST THAT YOU WOULD... BE FRIENDS WITH?
UM, YEAH! ...FRIENDS!
WHITNEY! I'M HERE, AND I BROUGHT SOME PEOPLE FOR YOU TO MEET.
WHOOOOSHH

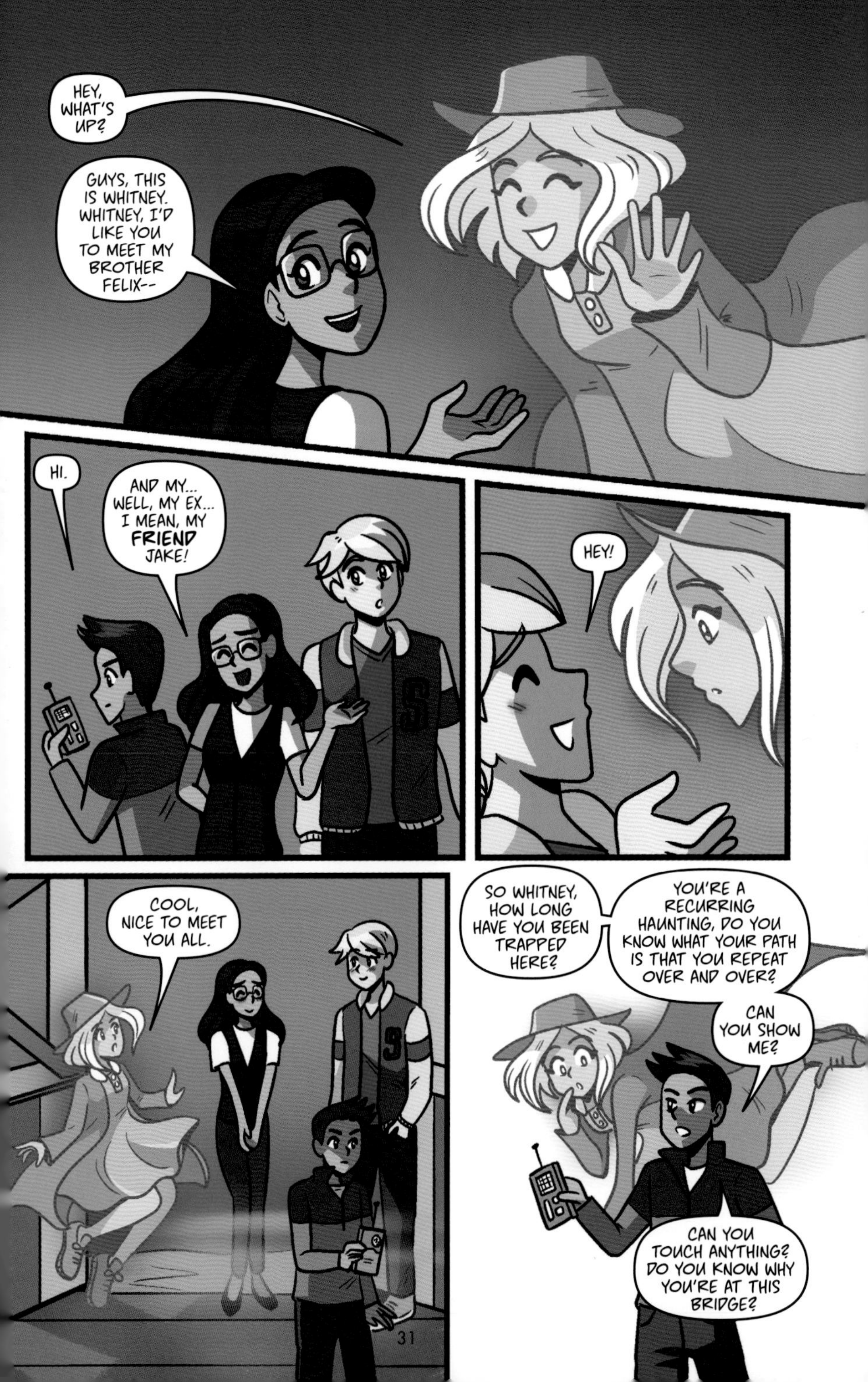
HEY, WHAT'S UP?
GUYS, THIS IS WHITNEY. WHITNEY, I'D LIKE YOU TO MEET MY BROTHER FELIX--
HI.
AND MY... WELL, MY EX... I MEAN, MY **FRIEND** JAKE!
HEY!
COOL, NICE TO MEET YOU ALL.
SO WHITNEY, HOW LONG HAVE YOU BEEN TRAPPED HERE?
YOU'RE A RECURRING HAUNTING, DO YOU KNOW WHAT YOUR PATH IS THAT YOU REPEAT OVER AND OVER?
CAN YOU SHOW ME?
CAN YOU TOUCH ANYTHING? DO YOU KNOW WHY YOU'RE AT THIS BRIDGE?

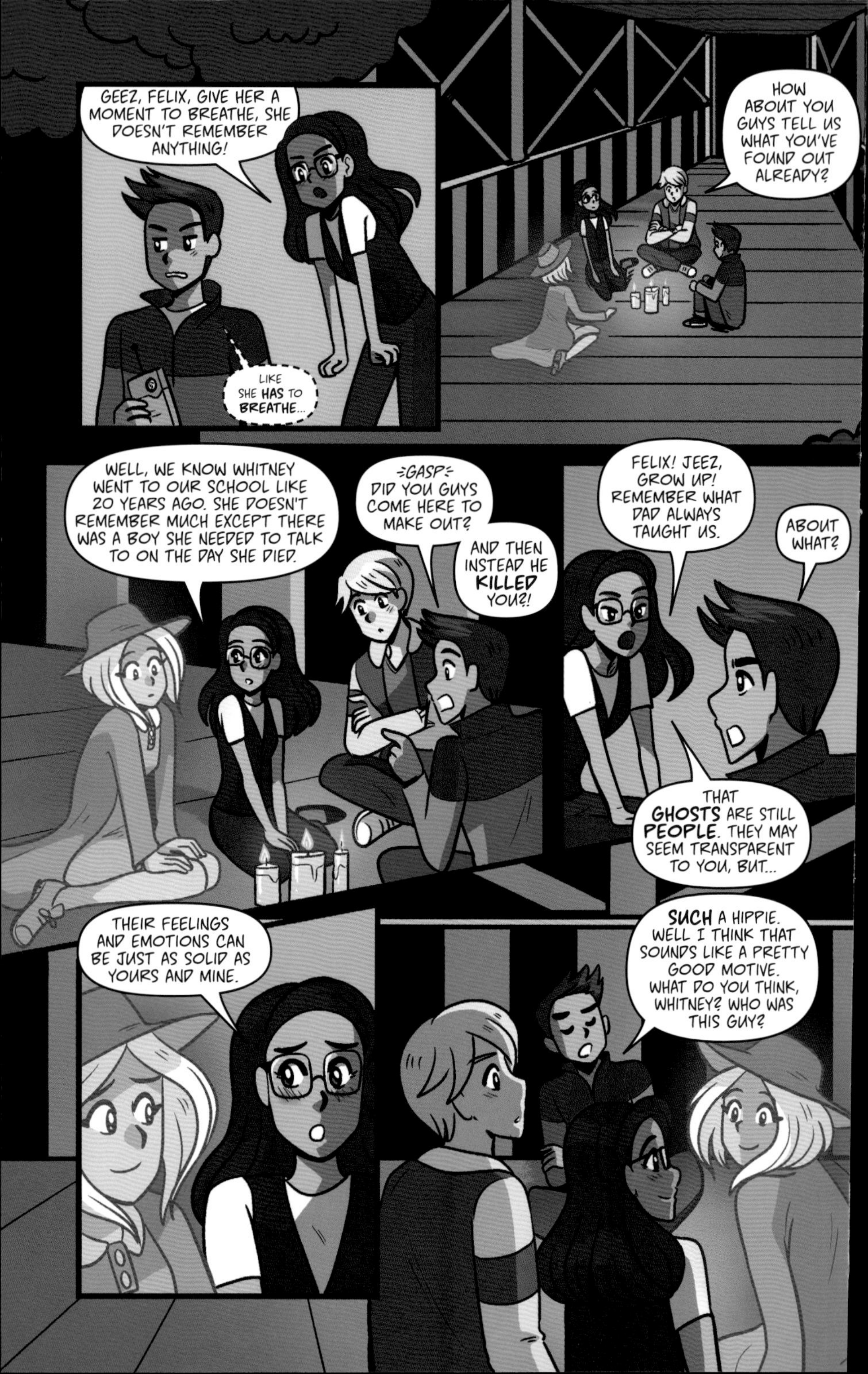

GEEZ, FELIX, GIVE HER A MOMENT TO BREATHE, SHE DOESN'T REMEMBER ANYTHING!
LIKE SHE HAS TO BREATHE...
HOW ABOUT YOU GUYS TELL US WHAT YOU'VE FOUND OUT ALREADY?
WELL, WE KNOW WHITNEY WENT TO OUR SCHOOL LIKE 20 YEARS AGO. SHE DOESN'T REMEMBER MUCH EXCEPT THERE WAS A BOY SHE NEEDED TO TALK TO ON THE DAY SHE DIED.
GASP
DID YOU GUYS COME HERE TO MAKE OUT?
AND THEN INSTEAD HE KILLED YOU?!
FELIX! JEEZ, GROW UP! REMEMBER WHAT DAD ALWAYS TAUGHT US.
ABOUT WHAT?
THAT GHOSTS ARE STILL PEOPLE. THEY MAY SEEM TRANSPARENT TO YOU, BUT...
THEIR FEELINGS AND EMOTIONS CAN BE JUST AS SOLID AS YOURS AND MINE.
SUCH A HIPPIE. WELL I THINK THAT SOUNDS LIKE A PRETTY GOOD MOTIVE. WHAT DO YOU THINK, WHITNEY? WHO WAS THIS GUY?

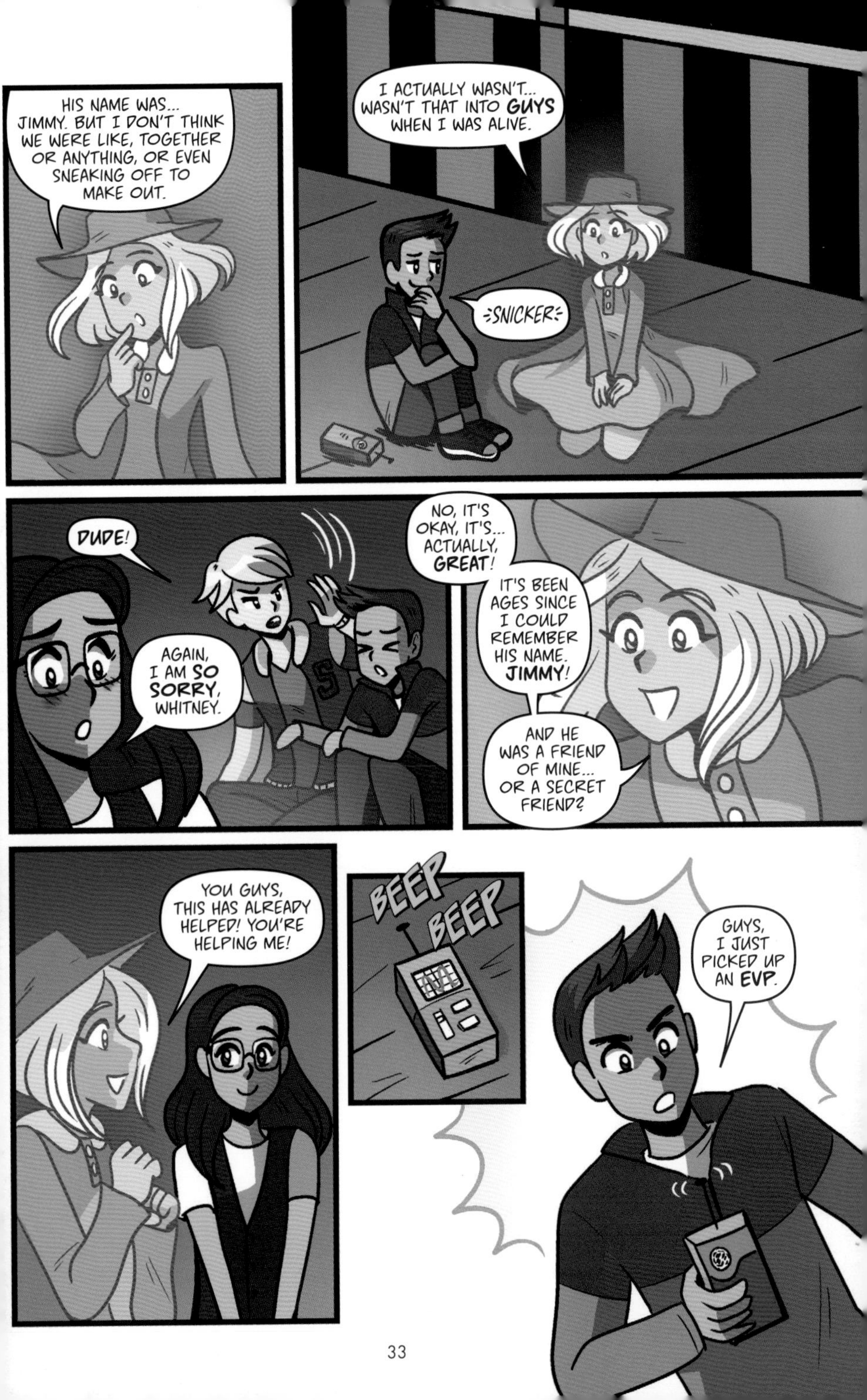
HIS NAME WAS... JIMMY. BUT I DON'T THINK WE WERE LIKE, TOGETHER OR ANYTHING, OR EVEN SNEAKING OFF TO MAKE OUT.
I ACTUALLY WASN'T... WASN'T THAT INTO **GUYS** WHEN I WAS ALIVE.
SNICKER
DUDE!
AGAIN, I AM **SO SORRY**, WHITNEY.
NO, IT'S OKAY, IT'S... ACTUALLY, **GREAT**!
IT'S BEEN AGES SINCE I COULD REMEMBER HIS NAME. **JIMMY**!
AND HE WAS A FRIEND OF MINE... OR A SECRET FRIEND?
YOU GUYS, THIS HAS ALREADY HELPED! YOU'RE HELPING ME!
BEEP
BEEP
GUYS, I JUST PICKED UP AN **EVP**.

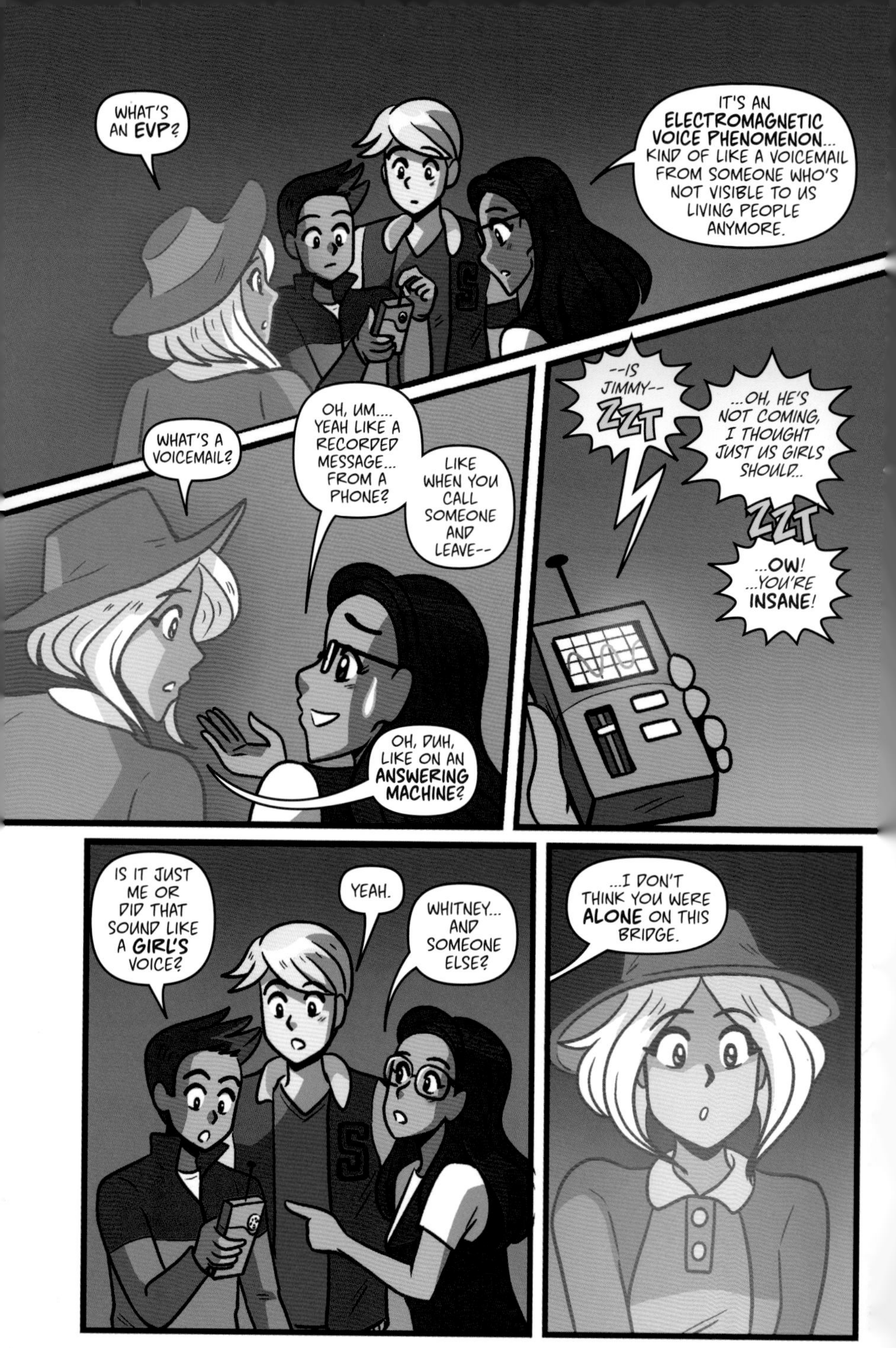
WHAT'S AN EVP?
IT'S AN ELECTROMAGNETIC VOICE PHENOMENON... KIND OF LIKE A VOICEMAIL FROM SOMEONE WHO'S NOT VISIBLE TO US LIVING PEOPLE ANYMORE.
WHAT'S A VOICEMAIL?
OH, UM.... YEAH LIKE A RECORDED MESSAGE... FROM A PHONE?
LIKE WHEN YOU CALL SOMEONE AND LEAVE--
OH, DUH, LIKE ON AN ANSWERING MACHINE?
--IS JIMMY--
ZZT
...OH, HE'S NOT COMING, I THOUGHT JUST US GIRLS SHOULD...
ZZT
...OW! ...YOU'RE INSANE!
IS IT JUST ME OR DID THAT SOUND LIKE A GIRL'S VOICE?
YEAH.
WHITNEY... AND SOMEONE ELSE?
...I DON'T THINK YOU WERE ALONE ON THIS BRIDGE.

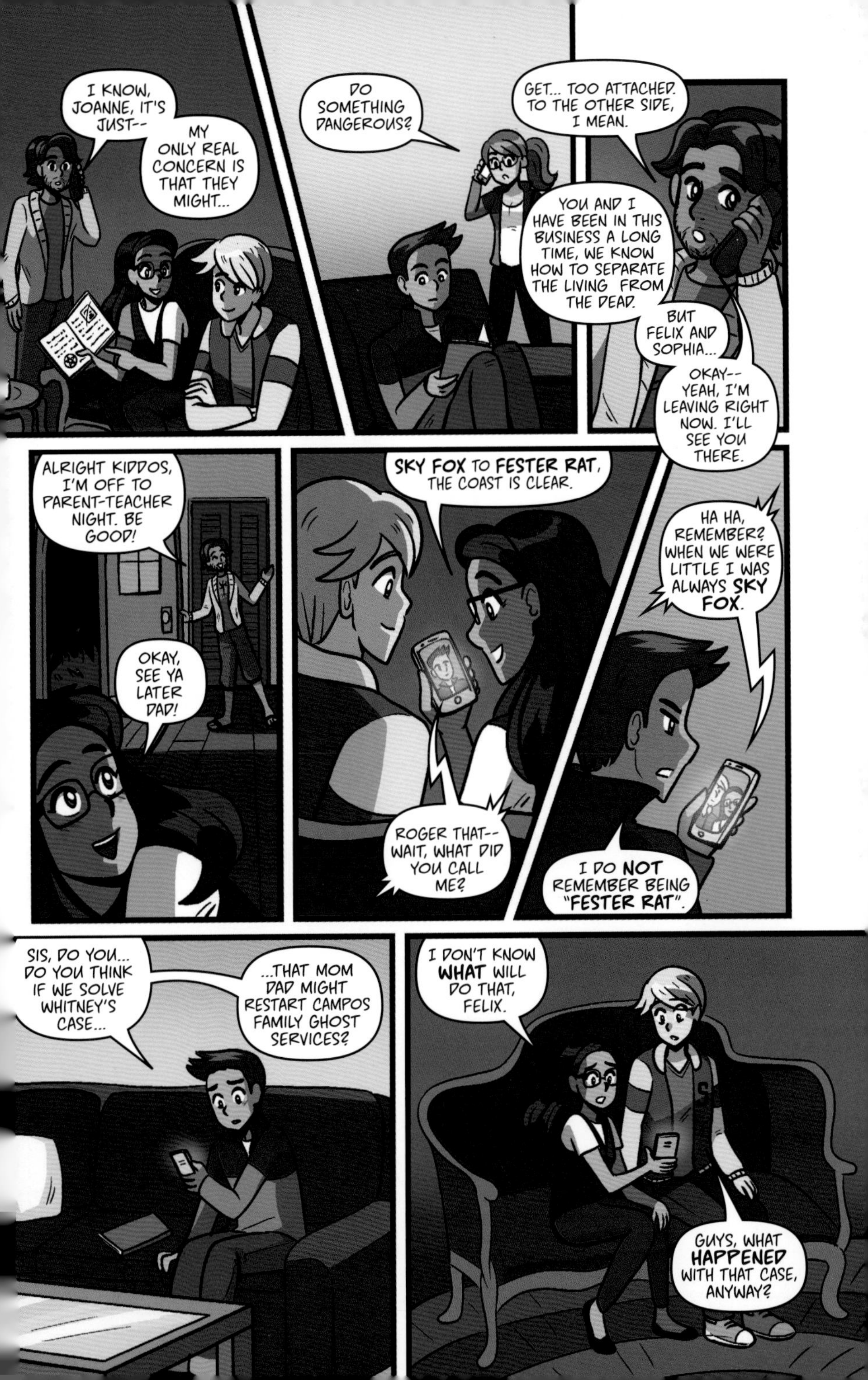
I KNOW, JOANNE, IT'S JUST--
MY ONLY REAL CONCERN IS THAT THEY MIGHT...
DO SOMETHING DANGEROUS?
GET... TOO ATTACHED. TO THE OTHER SIDE, I MEAN.
YOU AND I HAVE BEEN IN THIS BUSINESS A LONG TIME, WE KNOW HOW TO SEPARATE THE LIVING FROM THE DEAD.
BUT FELIX AND SOPHIA...
OKAY-- YEAH, I'M LEAVING RIGHT NOW. I'LL SEE YOU THERE.
ALRIGHT KIDDOS, I'M OFF TO PARENT-TEACHER NIGHT. BE GOOD!
OKAY, SEE YA LATER DAD!
SKY FOX TO **FESTER RAT**, THE COAST IS CLEAR.
ROGER THAT-- WAIT, WHAT DID YOU CALL ME?
HA HA, REMEMBER? WHEN WE WERE LITTLE I WAS ALWAYS **SKY FOX**.
I DO **NOT** REMEMBER BEING "**FESTER RAT**".
SIS, DO YOU... DO YOU THINK IF WE SOLVE WHITNEY'S CASE...
...THAT MOM DAD MIGHT RESTART CAMPOS FAMILY GHOST SERVICES?
I DON'T KNOW **WHAT** WILL DO THAT, FELIX.
GUYS, WHAT **HAPPENED** WITH THAT CASE, ANYWAY?

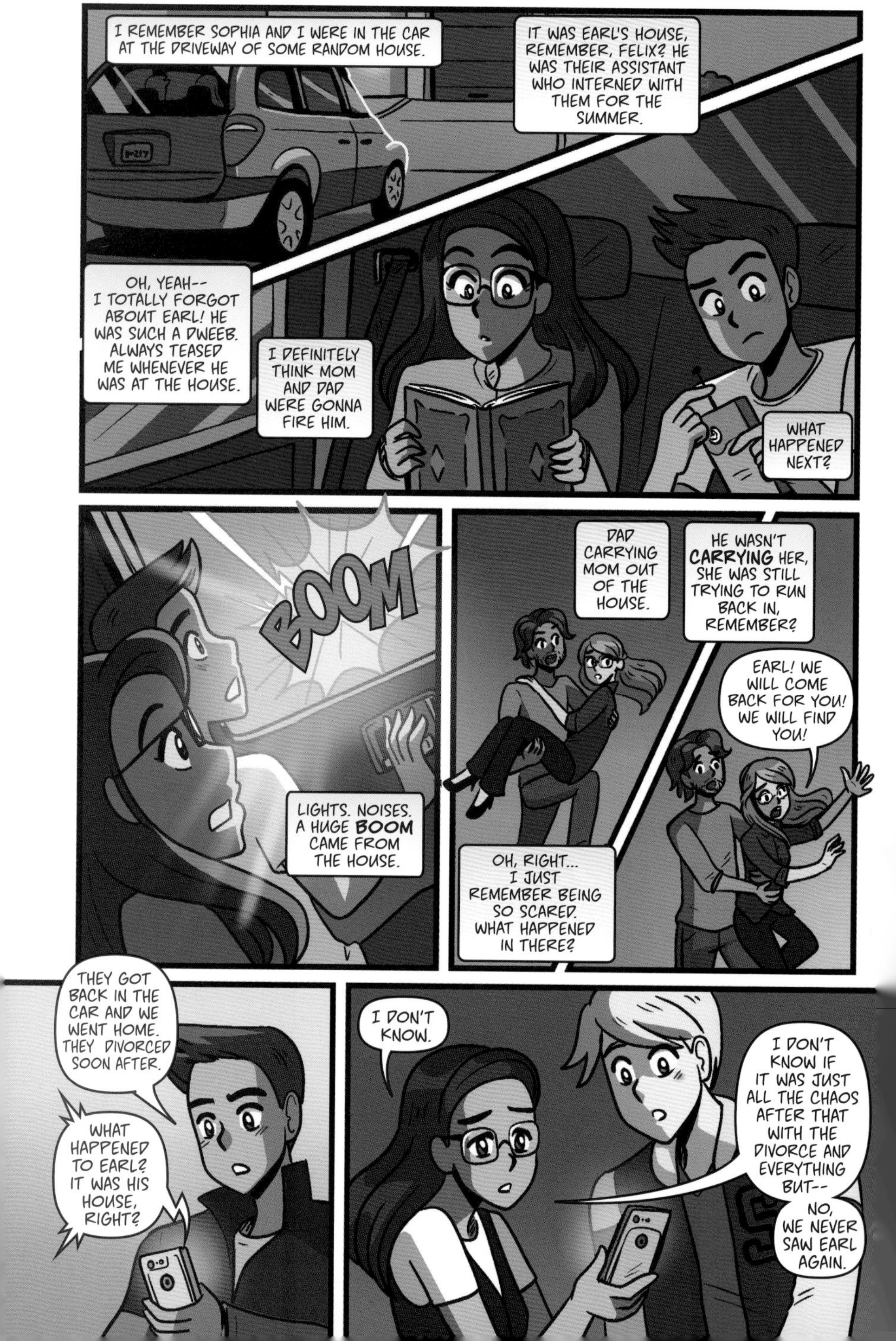
I REMEMBER SOPHIA AND I WERE IN THE CAR AT THE DRIVEWAY OF SOME RANDOM HOUSE.
IT WAS EARL'S HOUSE, REMEMBER, FELIX? HE WAS THEIR ASSISTANT WHO INTERNED WITH THEM FOR THE SUMMER.
OH, YEAH-- I TOTALLY FORGOT ABOUT EARL! HE WAS SUCH A DWEEB. ALWAYS TEASED ME WHENEVER HE WAS AT THE HOUSE.
I DEFINITELY THINK MOM AND DAD WERE GONNA FIRE HIM.
WHAT HAPPENED NEXT?
BOOM
LIGHTS. NOISES. A HUGE **BOOM** CAME FROM THE HOUSE.
DAD CARRYING MOM OUT OF THE HOUSE.
HE WASN'T **CARRYING** HER, SHE WAS STILL TRYING TO RUN BACK IN, REMEMBER?
EARL! WE WILL COME BACK FOR YOU! WE WILL FIND YOU!
OH, RIGHT... I JUST REMEMBER BEING SO SCARED. WHAT HAPPENED IN THERE?
THEY GOT BACK IN THE CAR AND WE WENT HOME. THEY DIVORCED SOON AFTER.
WHAT HAPPENED TO EARL? IT WAS HIS HOUSE, RIGHT?
I DON'T KNOW.
I DON'T KNOW IF IT WAS JUST ALL THE CHAOS AFTER THAT WITH THE DIVORCE AND EVERYTHING BUT--
NO, WE NEVER SAW EARL AGAIN.

PARENT TEACHER NIGHT

MISS FAIRWEATHER, WE'VE HEARD SO MUCH ABOUT YOU FROM OUR FELIX. I THINK YOU'RE HIS FAVORITE TEACHER.

FELIX HAS KEPT UP WITH ALL HIS HOMEWORK, I'VE MADE SURE OF THAT.

AW, THAT'S SO NICE. FELIX IS ONE OF MY FAVORITES, TOO! OVERALL HE'S DOING FANTASTIC IN MY CLASS. IT'S JUST SOMETIMES HE EXPERIENCES... BOUTS OF DAYDREAMING, OR TURNS IN PAPERS TO ME LIKE THIS--

A creative essay is any short... written with specific attention to its aesthetic qualities and presentation that is written from point-of-view of the author. Creative essays are a form of creative nonfiction, a genre used to describe any type of imaginative authoring that... find creativity in... My essay is going... and there are... world...

WE USED TO. NOW I RUN A BOUTIQUE PARANORMAL INVESTIGATION CLINIC, AND OSCAR RUNS AN HERB AND POTION SHOP.

SURELY YOU'RE AWARE THAT WE'VE BEEN DIVORCED--

YOU ALL RUN THAT FAMILY GHOST BUSINESS, DON'T YOU? FORGIVE ME, I'M BLANKING ON THE NAME--

AN HERB AND POTION SHOP? THAT SOUNDS LOVELY. I'LL HAVE TO PAY YOU A VISIT THERE SOME TIME.

OF COURSE. MY HOURS ARE 10-6, MONDAY THROUGH FRIDAY.

LATER...

DO WE NEED TO HAVE A TALK?

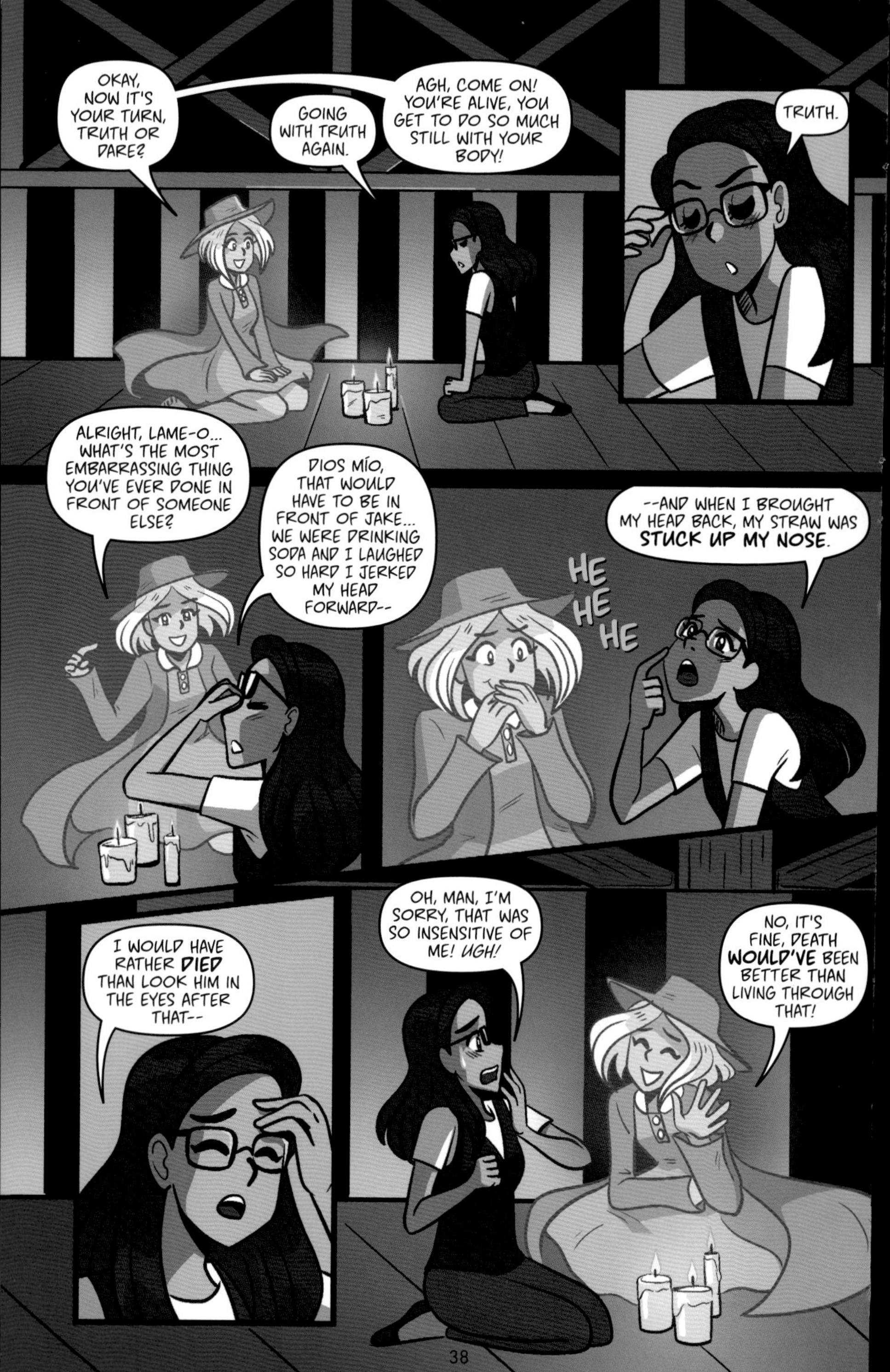
OKAY, NOW IT'S YOUR TURN, TRUTH OR DARE?
GOING WITH TRUTH AGAIN.
AGH, COME ON! YOU'RE ALIVE, YOU GET TO DO SO MUCH STILL WITH YOUR BODY!
TRUTH.
ALRIGHT, LAME-O... WHAT'S THE MOST EMBARRASSING THING YOU'VE EVER DONE IN FRONT OF SOMEONE ELSE?
DIOS MÍO, THAT WOULD HAVE TO BE IN FRONT OF JAKE... WE WERE DRINKING SODA AND I LAUGHED SO HARD I JERKED MY HEAD FORWARD--
--AND WHEN I BROUGHT MY HEAD BACK, MY STRAW WAS **STUCK UP MY NOSE**.
HE HE HE
I WOULD HAVE RATHER **DIED** THAN LOOK HIM IN THE EYES AFTER THAT--
OH, MAN, I'M SORRY, THAT WAS SO INSENSITIVE OF ME! *UGH!*
NO, IT'S FINE, DEATH **WOULD'VE** BEEN BETTER THAN LIVING THROUGH THAT!

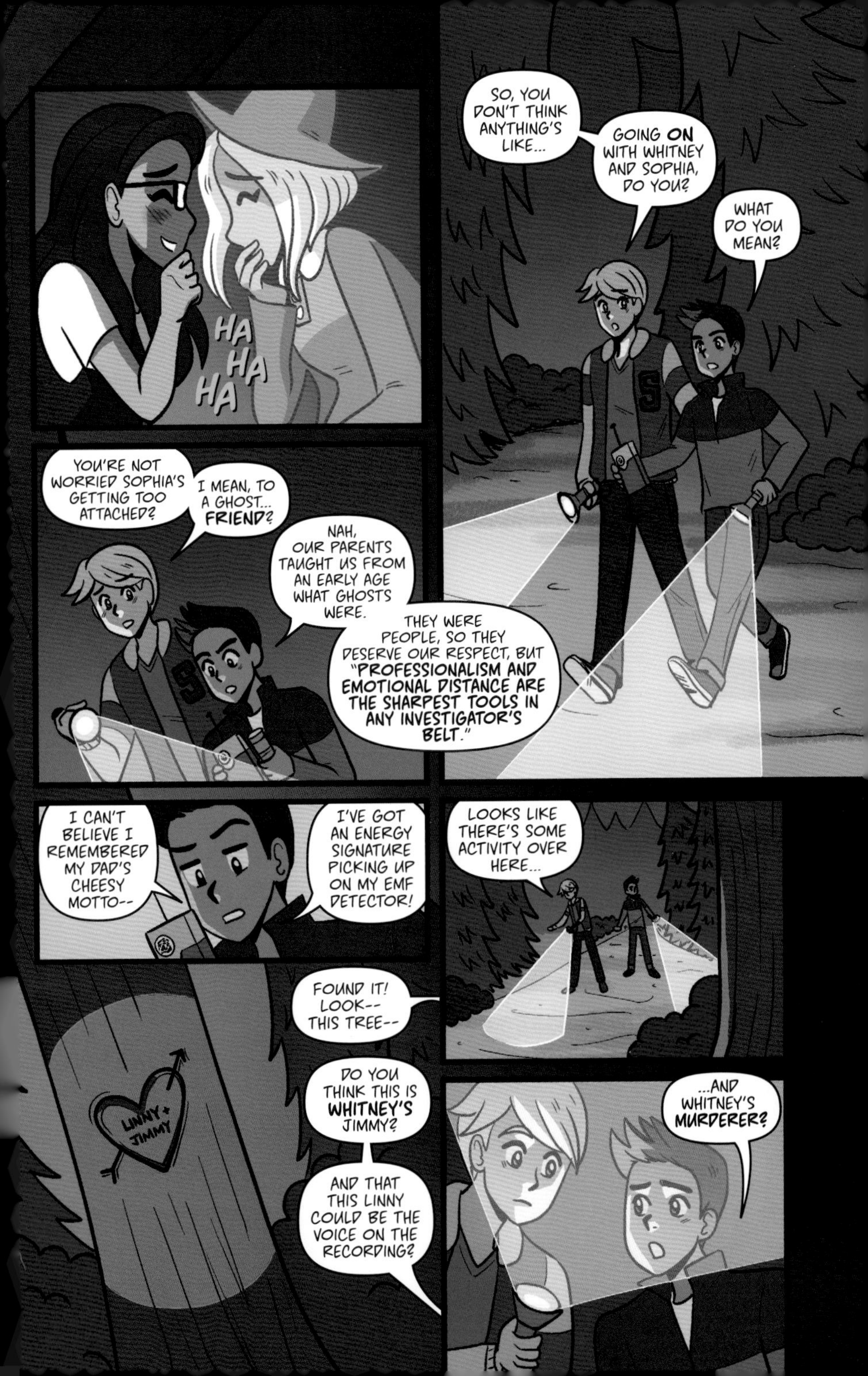
HA HA HA
SO, YOU DON'T THINK ANYTHING'S LIKE...
GOING **ON** WITH WHITNEY AND SOPHIA, DO YOU?
WHAT DO YOU MEAN?
YOU'RE NOT WORRIED SOPHIA'S GETTING TOO ATTACHED?
I MEAN, TO A GHOST... **FRIEND?**
NAH, OUR PARENTS TAUGHT US FROM AN EARLY AGE WHAT GHOSTS WERE.
THEY WERE PEOPLE, SO THEY DESERVE OUR RESPECT, BUT **"PROFESSIONALISM AND EMOTIONAL DISTANCE ARE THE SHARPEST TOOLS IN ANY INVESTIGATOR'S BELT."**
I CAN'T BELIEVE I REMEMBERED MY DAD'S CHEESY MOTTO--
I'VE GOT AN ENERGY SIGNATURE PICKING UP ON MY EMF DETECTOR!
LOOKS LIKE THERE'S SOME ACTIVITY OVER HERE...
FOUND IT! LOOK-- THIS TREE--
LINNY + JIMMY
DO YOU THINK THIS IS **WHITNEY'S** JIMMY?
AND THAT THIS LINNY COULD BE THE VOICE ON THE RECORDING?
...AND WHITNEY'S **MURDERER?**

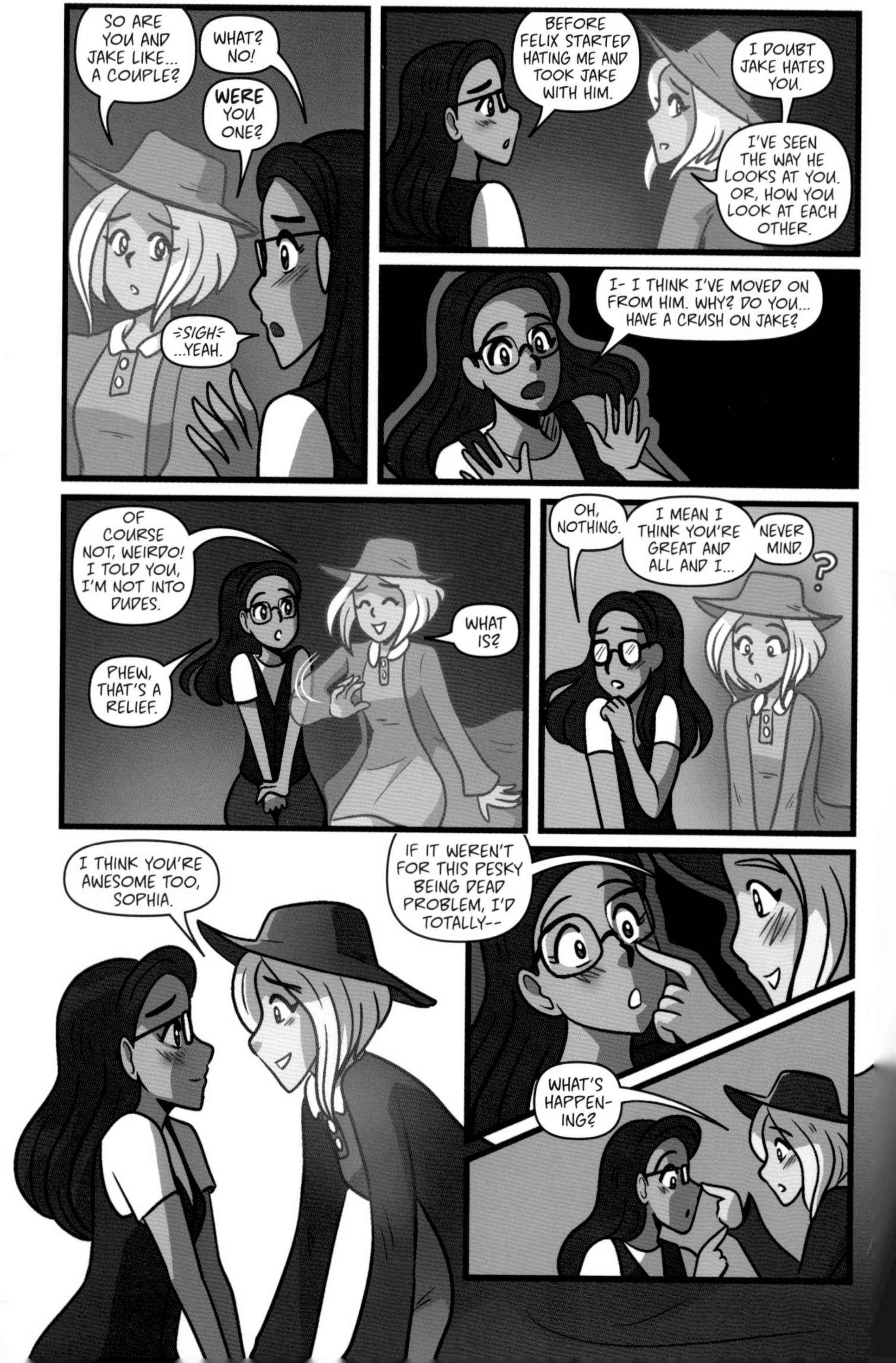
SO ARE YOU AND JAKE LIKE... A COUPLE?
WHAT? NO!
WERE YOU ONE?
=SIGH= ...YEAH.
BEFORE FELIX STARTED HATING ME AND TOOK JAKE WITH HIM.
I DOUBT JAKE HATES YOU.
I'VE SEEN THE WAY HE LOOKS AT YOU. OR, HOW YOU LOOK AT EACH OTHER.
I- I THINK I'VE MOVED ON FROM HIM. WHY? DO YOU... HAVE A CRUSH ON JAKE?
OF COURSE NOT, WEIRDO! I TOLD YOU, I'M NOT INTO DUDES.
PHEW, THAT'S A RELIEF.
WHAT IS?
OH, NOTHING.
I MEAN I THINK YOU'RE GREAT AND ALL AND I...
NEVER MIND.
?
I THINK YOU'RE AWESOME TOO, SOPHIA.
IF IT WEREN'T FOR THIS PESKY BEING DEAD PROBLEM, I'D TOTALLY--
WHAT'S HAPPEN-ING?

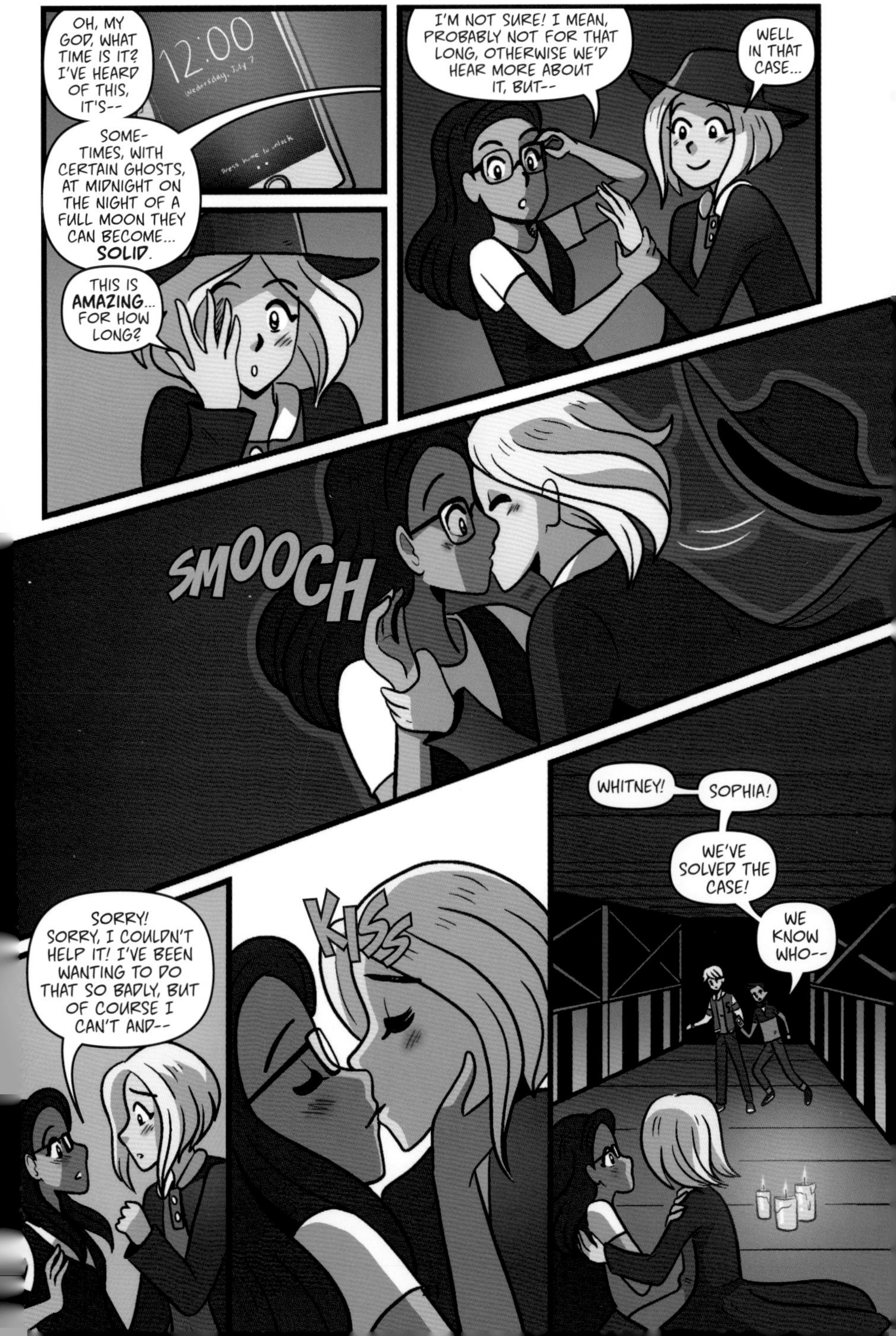
OH, MY GOD, WHAT TIME IS IT? I'VE HEARD OF THIS, IT'S--
12:00
Wednesday, July 7
Press home to unlock
SOMETIMES, WITH CERTAIN GHOSTS, AT MIDNIGHT ON THE NIGHT OF A FULL MOON THEY CAN BECOME... SOLID.
THIS IS AMAZING... FOR HOW LONG?
I'M NOT SURE! I MEAN, PROBABLY NOT FOR THAT LONG, OTHERWISE WE'D HEAR MORE ABOUT IT, BUT--
WELL IN THAT CASE...
SMOOCH
SORRY! SORRY, I COULDN'T HELP IT! I'VE BEEN WANTING TO DO THAT SO BADLY, BUT OF COURSE I CAN'T AND--
KISS
WHITNEY!
SOPHIA!
WE'VE SOLVED THE CASE!
WE KNOW WHO--

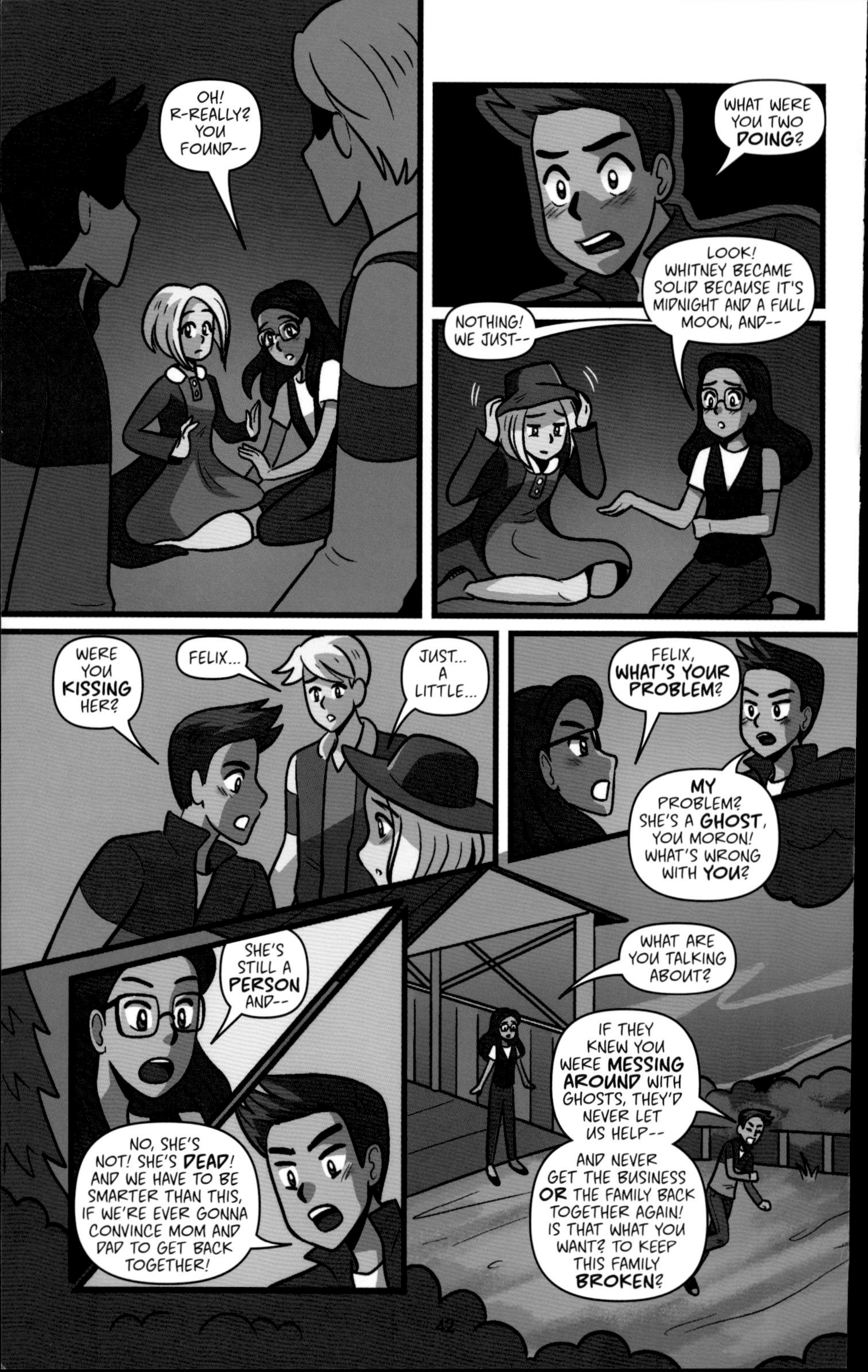
OH! R-REALLY? YOU FOUND--
WHAT WERE YOU TWO DOING?
NOTHING! WE JUST--
LOOK! WHITNEY BECAME SOLID BECAUSE IT'S MIDNIGHT AND A FULL MOON, AND--
WERE YOU KISSING HER?
FELIX...
JUST... A LITTLE...
FELIX, WHAT'S YOUR PROBLEM?
MY PROBLEM? SHE'S A GHOST, YOU MORON! WHAT'S WRONG WITH YOU?
SHE'S STILL A PERSON AND--
NO, SHE'S NOT! SHE'S DEAD! AND WE HAVE TO BE SMARTER THAN THIS, IF WE'RE EVER GONNA CONVINCE MOM AND DAD TO GET BACK TOGETHER!
WHAT ARE YOU TALKING ABOUT?
IF THEY KNEW YOU WERE MESSING AROUND WITH GHOSTS, THEY'D NEVER LET US HELP--
AND NEVER GET THE BUSINESS OR THE FAMILY BACK TOGETHER AGAIN! IS THAT WHAT YOU WANT? TO KEEP THIS FAMILY BROKEN?

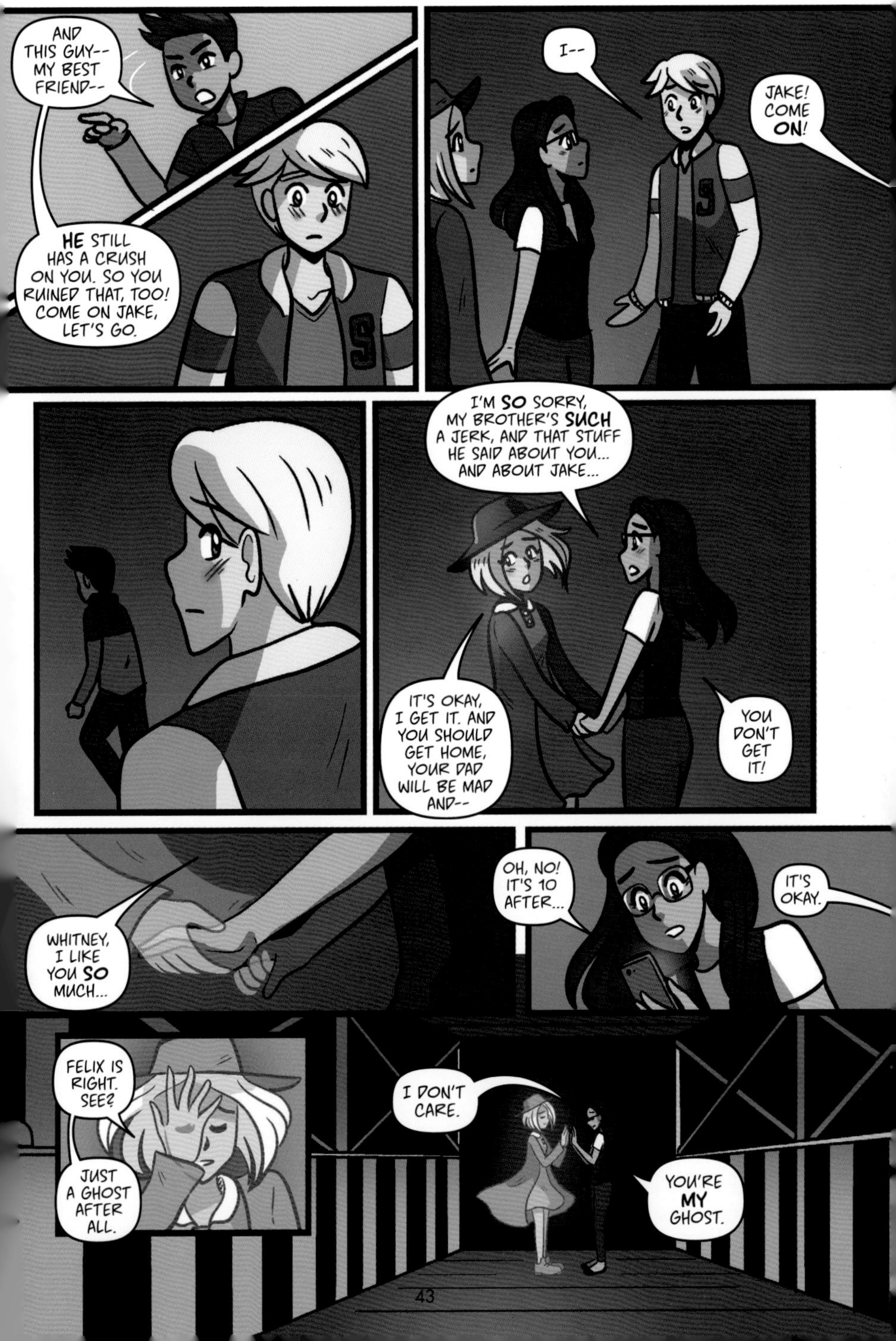
AND THIS GUY-- MY BEST FRIEND--
HE STILL HAS A CRUSH ON YOU. SO YOU RUINED THAT, TOO! COME ON JAKE, LET'S GO.
I--
JAKE! COME ON!
I'M SO SORRY, MY BROTHER'S SUCH A JERK, AND THAT STUFF HE SAID ABOUT YOU... AND ABOUT JAKE...
IT'S OKAY, I GET IT. AND YOU SHOULD GET HOME, YOUR DAD WILL BE MAD AND--
YOU DON'T GET IT!
WHITNEY, I LIKE YOU SO MUCH...
OH, NO! IT'S 10 AFTER...
IT'S OKAY.
FELIX IS RIGHT. SEE?
JUST A GHOST AFTER ALL.
I DON'T CARE.
YOU'RE MY GHOST.

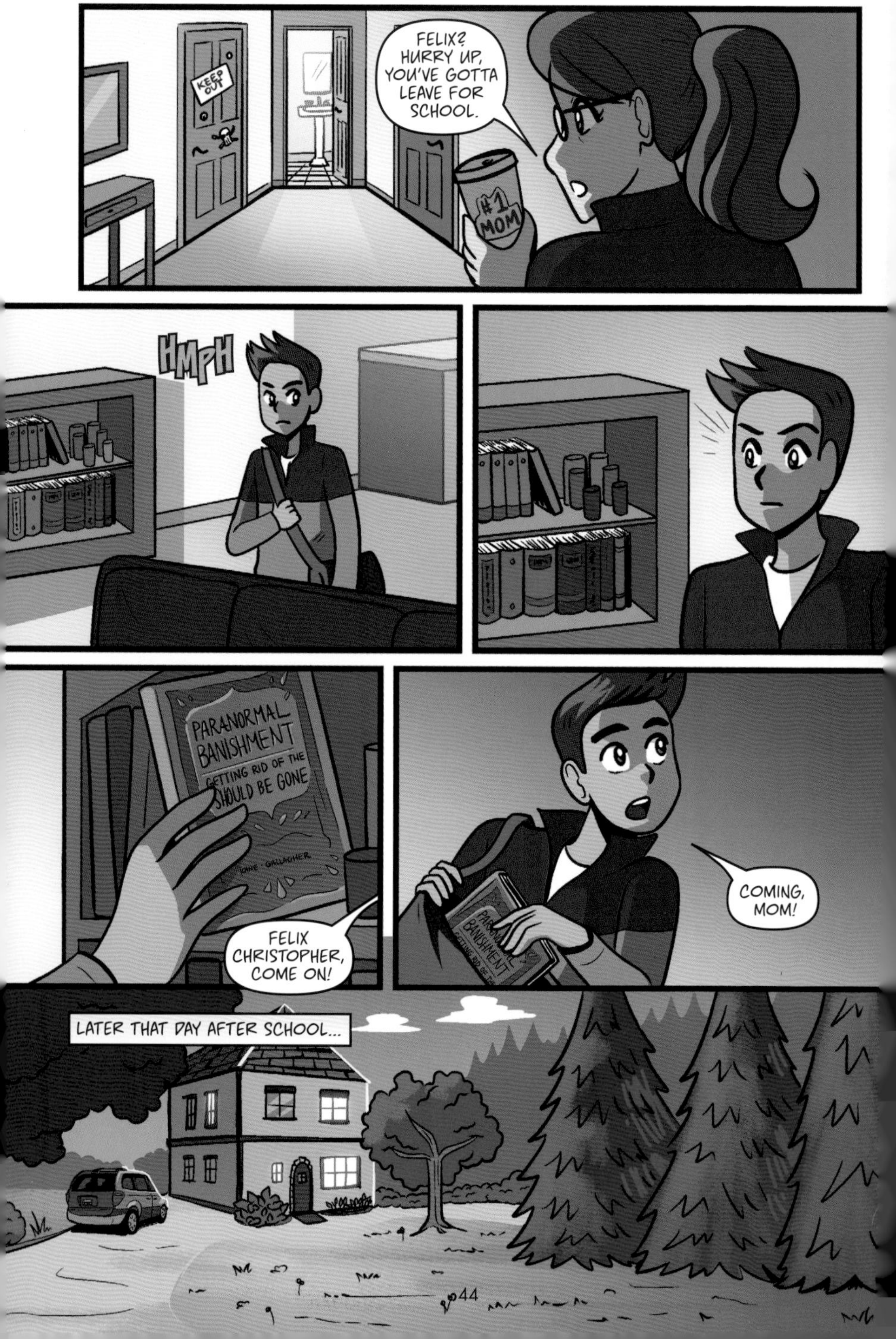
KEEP OUT
FELIX? HURRY UP, YOU'VE GOTTA LEAVE FOR SCHOOL.
#1 MOM
HMPH
PARANORMAL BANISHMENT
GETTING RID OF THE SHOULD BE GONE
FELIX CHRISTOPHER, COME ON!
COMING, MOM!
LATER THAT DAY AFTER SCHOOL...

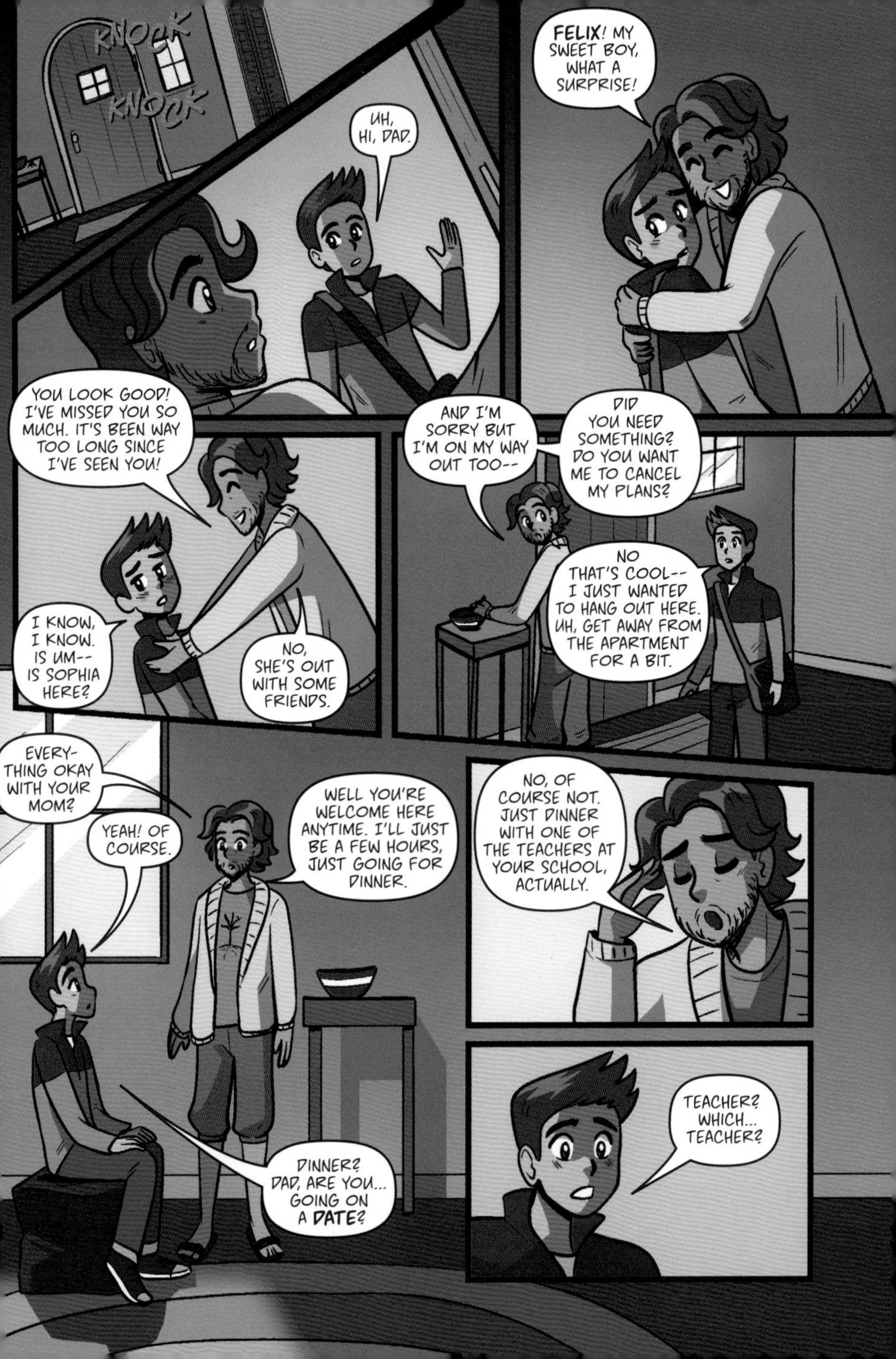
KNOCK
KNOCK
UH, HI, DAD.
FELIX! MY SWEET BOY, WHAT A SURPRISE!
YOU LOOK GOOD! I'VE MISSED YOU SO MUCH. IT'S BEEN WAY TOO LONG SINCE I'VE SEEN YOU!
I KNOW, I KNOW. IS UM-- IS SOPHIA HERE?
NO, SHE'S OUT WITH SOME FRIENDS.
DID YOU NEED SOMETHING? DO YOU WANT ME TO CANCEL MY PLANS?
AND I'M SORRY BUT I'M ON MY WAY OUT TOO--
NO THAT'S COOL-- I JUST WANTED TO HANG OUT HERE. UH, GET AWAY FROM THE APARTMENT FOR A BIT.
EVERY-THING OKAY WITH YOUR MOM?
YEAH! OF COURSE.
WELL YOU'RE WELCOME HERE ANYTIME. I'LL JUST BE A FEW HOURS, JUST GOING FOR DINNER.
DINNER? DAD, ARE YOU... GOING ON A DATE?
NO, OF COURSE NOT. JUST DINNER WITH ONE OF THE TEACHERS AT YOUR SCHOOL, ACTUALLY.
TEACHER? WHICH... TEACHER?

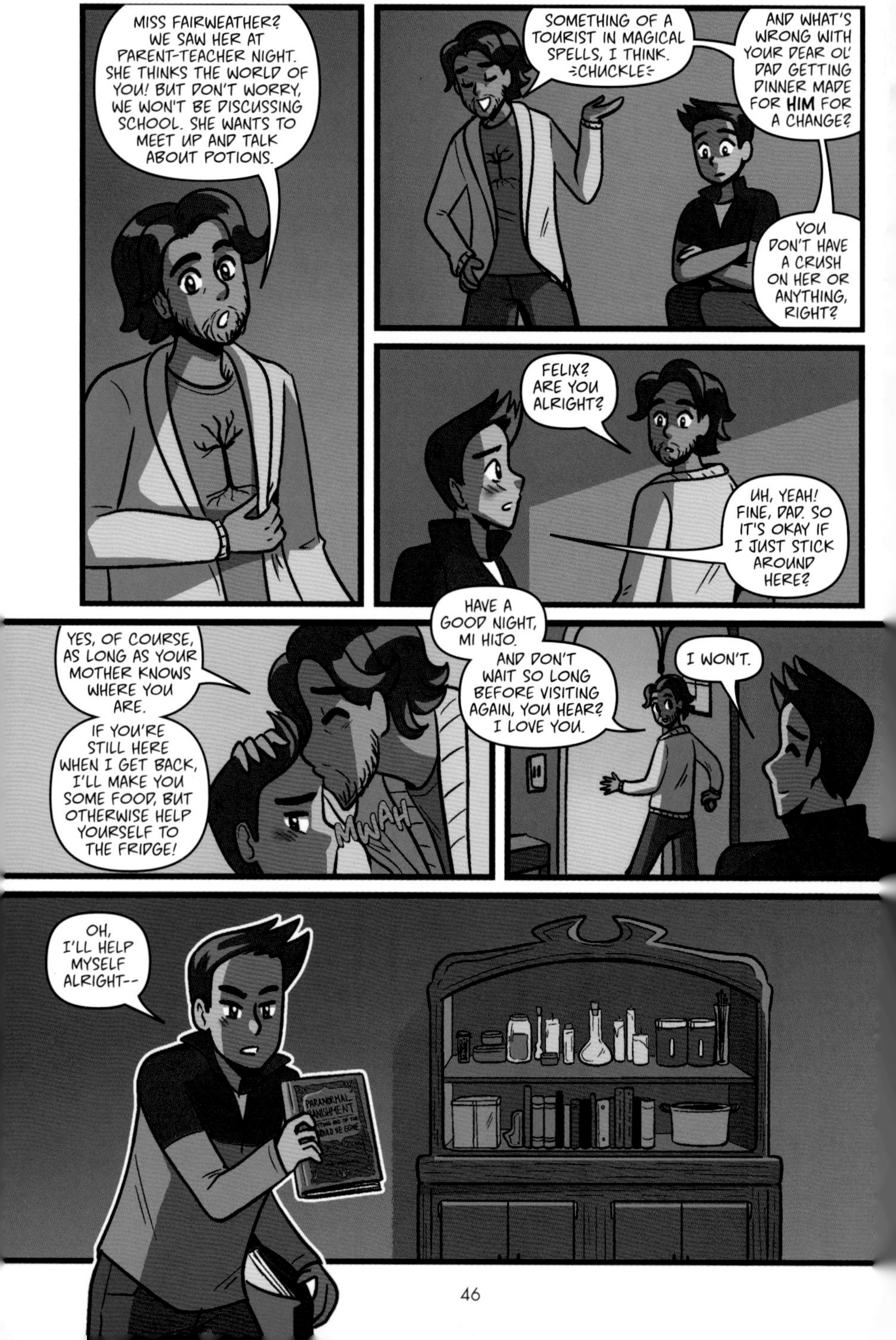
MISS FAIRWEATHER? WE SAW HER AT PARENT-TEACHER NIGHT. SHE THINKS THE WORLD OF YOU! BUT DON'T WORRY, WE WON'T BE DISCUSSING SCHOOL. SHE WANTS TO MEET UP AND TALK ABOUT POTIONS.
SOMETHING OF A TOURIST IN MAGICAL SPELLS, I THINK. ≈CHUCKLE≈
AND WHAT'S WRONG WITH YOUR DEAR OL' DAD GETTING DINNER MADE FOR **HIM** FOR A CHANGE?
YOU DON'T HAVE A CRUSH ON HER OR ANYTHING, RIGHT?
FELIX? ARE YOU ALRIGHT?
UH, YEAH! FINE, DAD. SO IT'S OKAY IF I JUST STICK AROUND HERE?
YES, OF COURSE, AS LONG AS YOUR MOTHER KNOWS WHERE YOU ARE.
IF YOU'RE STILL HERE WHEN I GET BACK, I'LL MAKE YOU SOME FOOD, BUT OTHERWISE HELP YOURSELF TO THE FRIDGE!
MWAH
HAVE A GOOD NIGHT, MI HIJO.
AND DON'T WAIT SO LONG BEFORE VISITING AGAIN, YOU HEAR? I LOVE YOU.
I WON'T.
OH, I'LL HELP MYSELF ALRIGHT--
PARANORMAL BANISHMENT

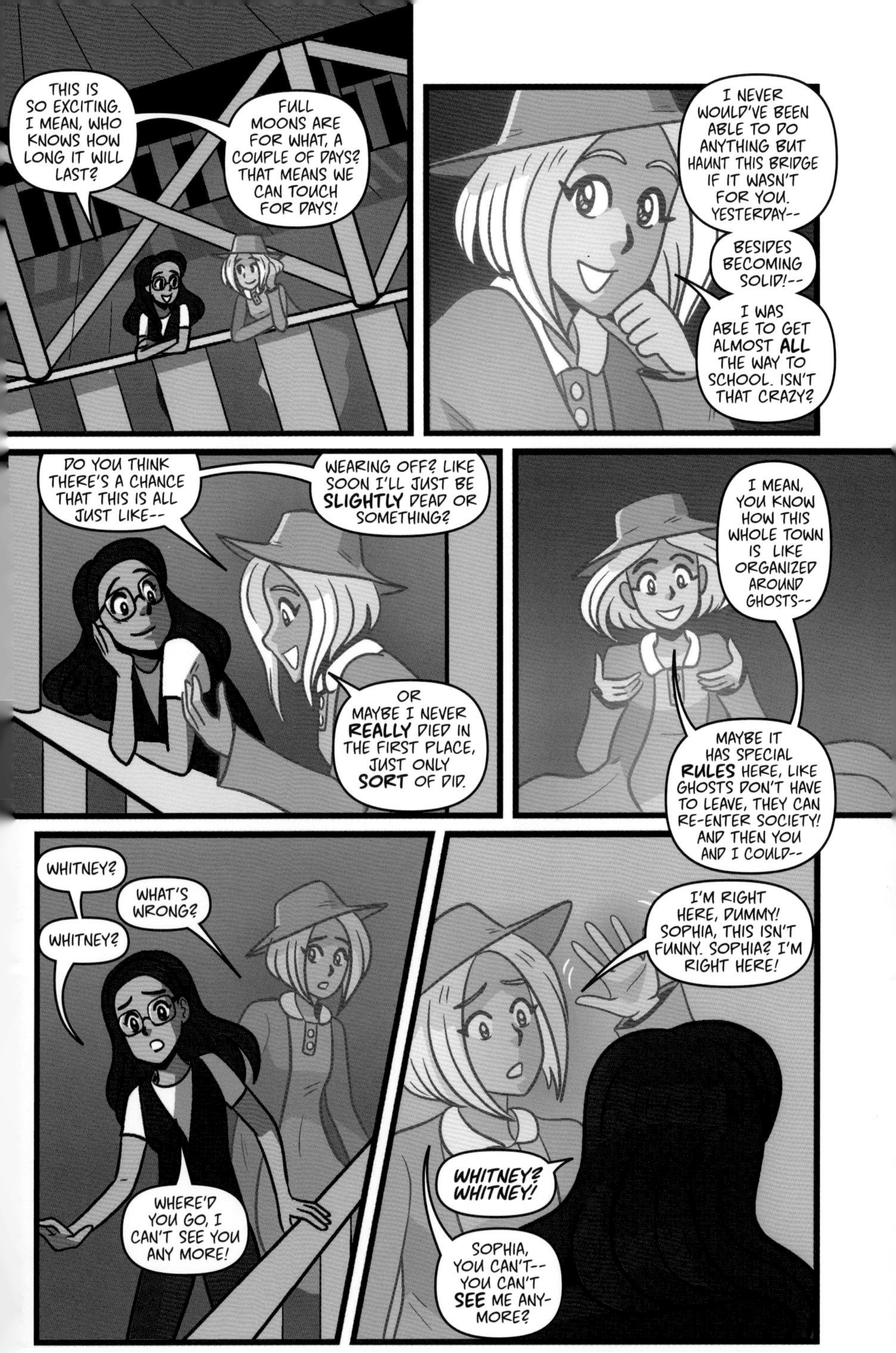
THIS IS SO EXCITING. I MEAN, WHO KNOWS HOW LONG IT WILL LAST?
FULL MOONS ARE FOR WHAT, A COUPLE OF DAYS? THAT MEANS WE CAN TOUCH FOR DAYS!
I NEVER WOULD'VE BEEN ABLE TO DO ANYTHING BUT HAUNT THIS BRIDGE IF IT WASN'T FOR YOU. YESTERDAY--
BESIDES BECOMING SOLID!--
I WAS ABLE TO GET ALMOST **ALL** THE WAY TO SCHOOL. ISN'T THAT CRAZY?
DO YOU THINK THERE'S A CHANCE THAT THIS IS ALL JUST LIKE--
WEARING OFF? LIKE SOON I'LL JUST BE **SLIGHTLY** DEAD OR SOMETHING?
OR MAYBE I NEVER **REALLY** DIED IN THE FIRST PLACE, JUST ONLY **SORT** OF DID.
I MEAN, YOU KNOW HOW THIS WHOLE TOWN IS LIKE ORGANIZED AROUND GHOSTS--
MAYBE IT HAS SPECIAL **RULES** HERE, LIKE GHOSTS DON'T HAVE TO LEAVE, THEY CAN RE-ENTER SOCIETY! AND THEN YOU AND I COULD--
WHITNEY?
WHAT'S WRONG?
WHITNEY?
WHERE'D YOU GO, I CAN'T SEE YOU ANY MORE!
I'M RIGHT HERE, DUMMY! SOPHIA, THIS ISN'T FUNNY. SOPHIA? I'M RIGHT HERE!
WHITNEY? WHITNEY!
SOPHIA, YOU CAN'T-- YOU CAN'T **SEE** ME ANY-MORE?

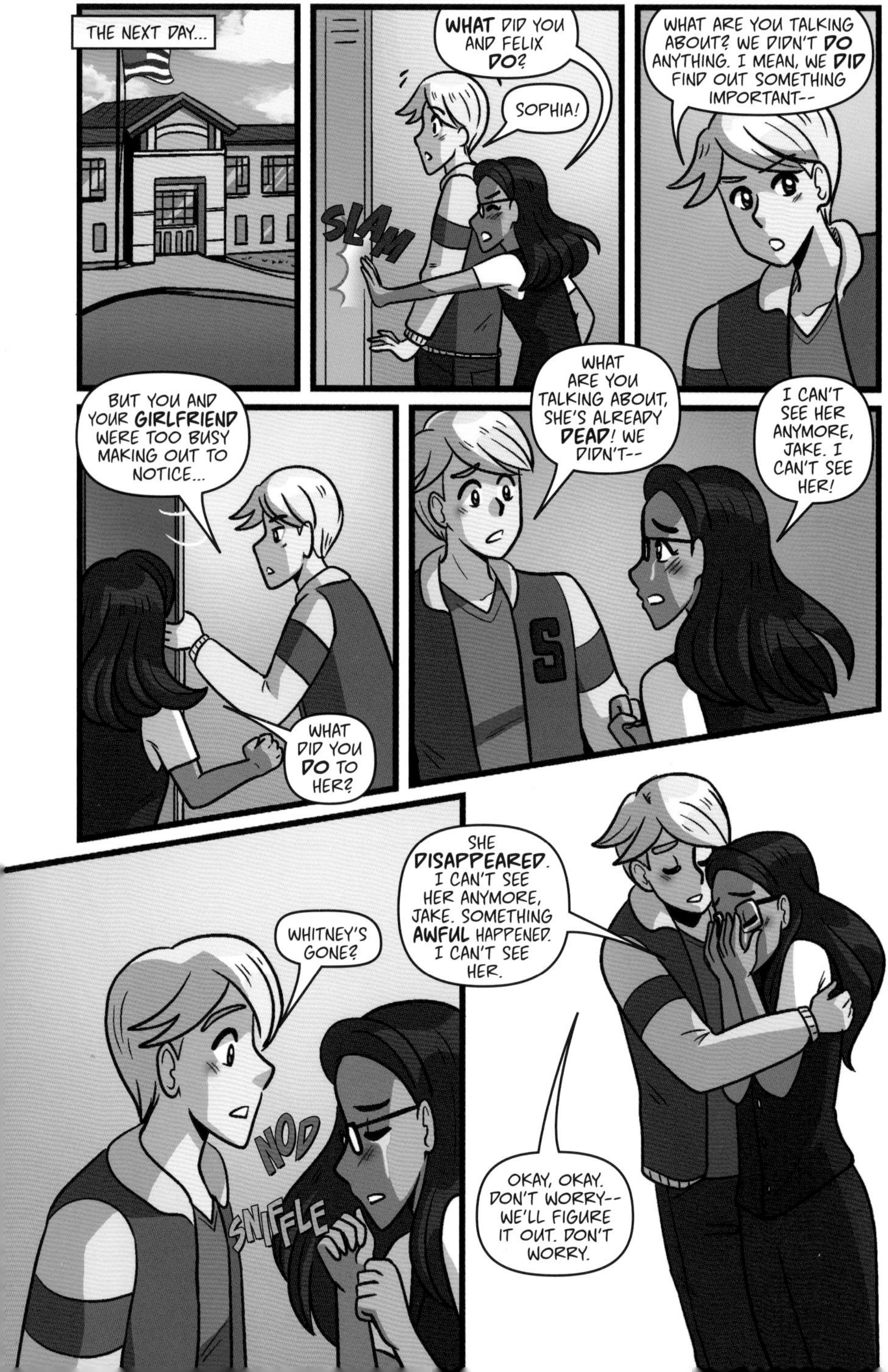

THE NEXT DAY...
WHAT DID YOU AND FELIX DO?
SOPHIA!
SLAM
WHAT ARE YOU TALKING ABOUT? WE DIDN'T DO ANYTHING. I MEAN, WE DID FIND OUT SOMETHING IMPORTANT--
BUT YOU AND YOUR GIRLFRIEND WERE TOO BUSY MAKING OUT TO NOTICE...
WHAT DID YOU DO TO HER?
WHAT ARE YOU TALKING ABOUT, SHE'S ALREADY DEAD! WE DIDN'T--
I CAN'T SEE HER ANYMORE, JAKE. I CAN'T SEE HER!
WHITNEY'S GONE?
NOD
SNIFFLE
SHE DISAPPEARED. I CAN'T SEE HER ANYMORE, JAKE. SOMETHING AWFUL HAPPENED. I CAN'T SEE HER.
OKAY, OKAY. DON'T WORRY-- WE'LL FIGURE IT OUT. DON'T WORRY.

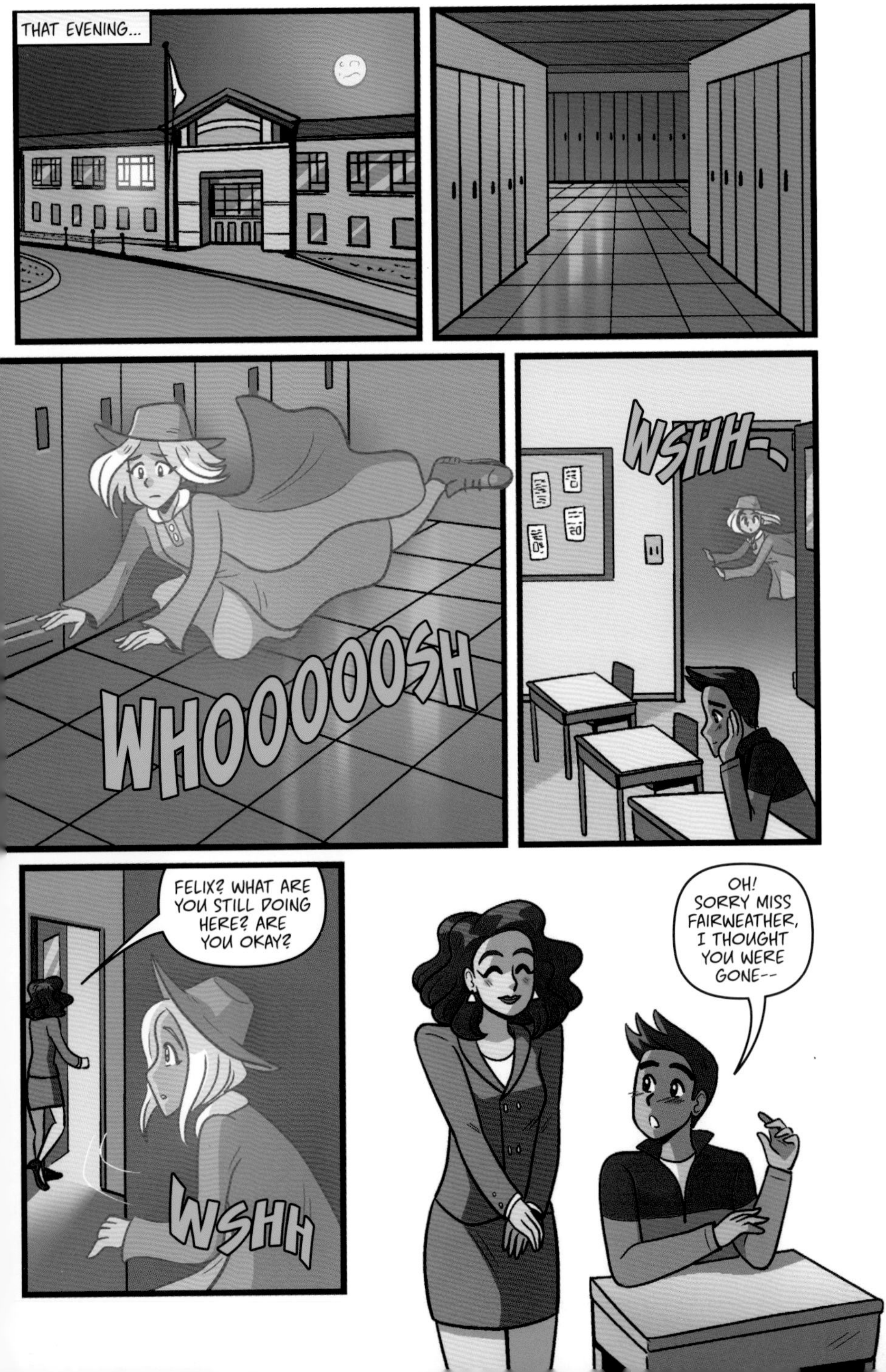
THAT EVENING...
WHOOOOOSH
WSHH--
FELIX? WHAT ARE YOU STILL DOING HERE? ARE YOU OKAY?
WSHH
OH! SORRY MISS FAIRWEATHER, I THOUGHT YOU WERE GONE--

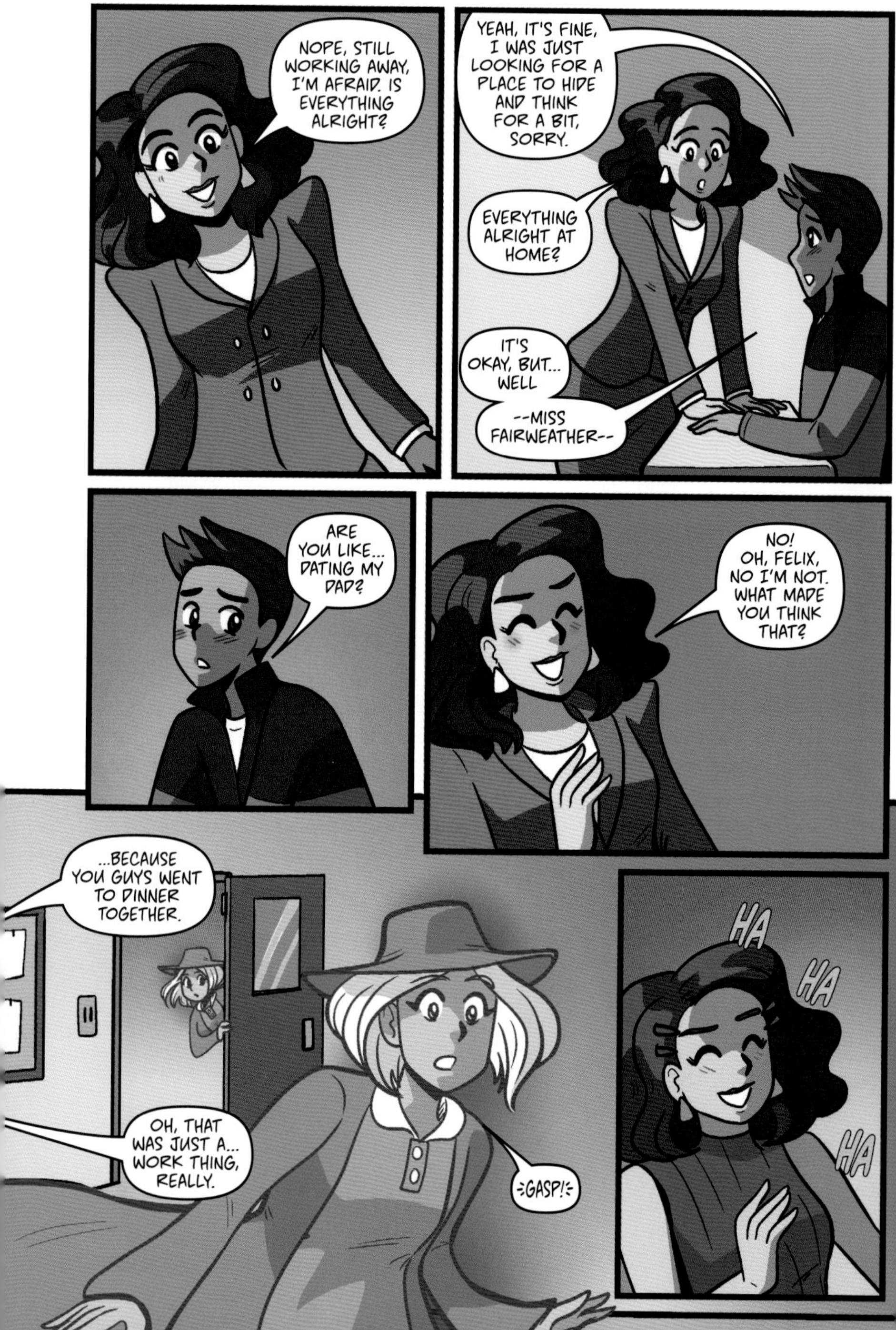
NOPE, STILL WORKING AWAY, I'M AFRAID. IS EVERYTHING ALRIGHT?
YEAH, IT'S FINE, I WAS JUST LOOKING FOR A PLACE TO HIDE AND THINK FOR A BIT, SORRY.
EVERYTHING ALRIGHT AT HOME?
IT'S OKAY, BUT... WELL
--MISS FAIRWEATHER--
ARE YOU LIKE... DATING MY DAD?
NO! OH, FELIX, NO I'M NOT. WHAT MADE YOU THINK THAT?
...BECAUSE YOU GUYS WENT TO DINNER TOGETHER.
OH, THAT WAS JUST A... WORK THING, REALLY.
GASP!
HA
HA
HA

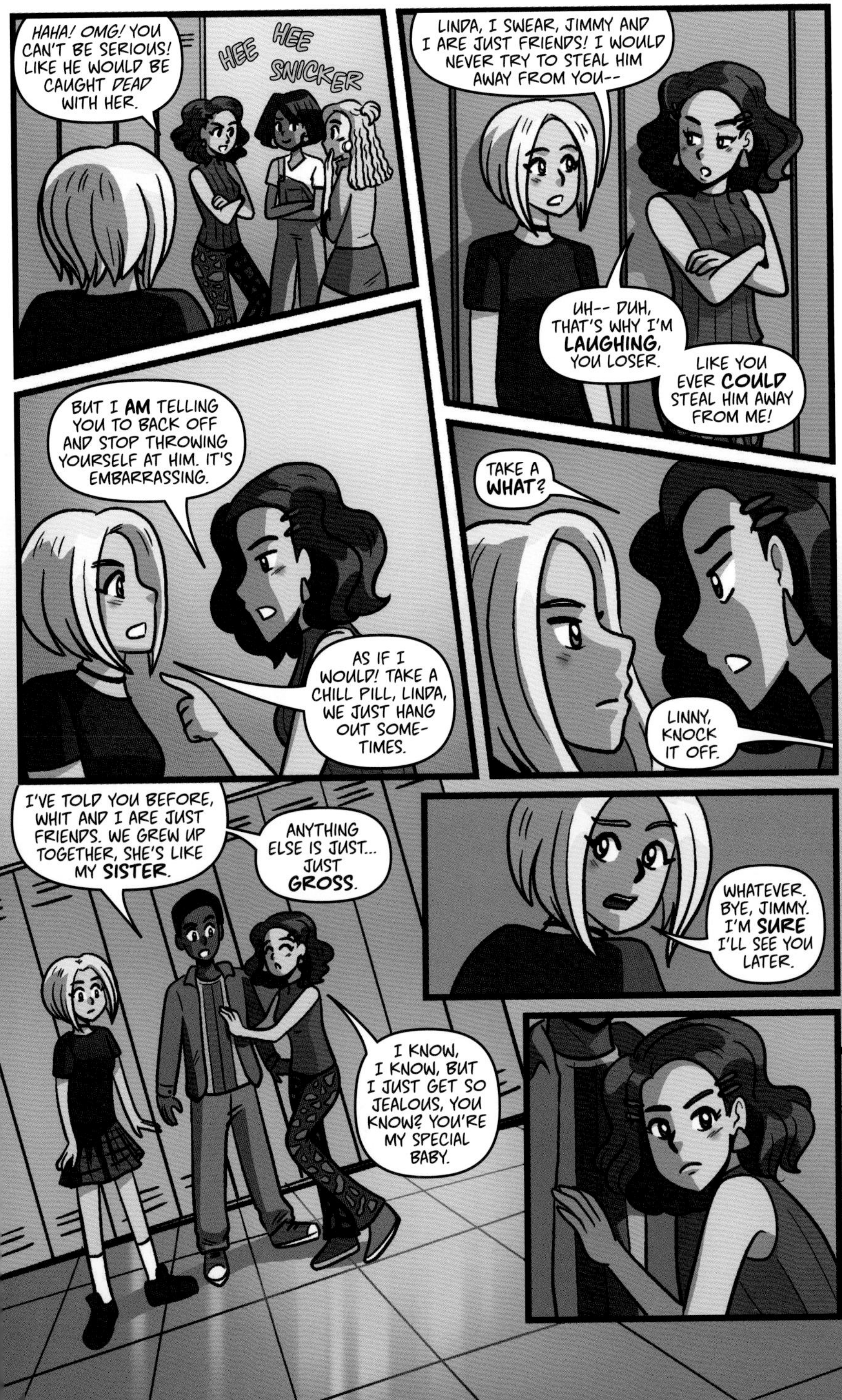
HAHA! OMG! YOU CAN'T BE SERIOUS! LIKE HE WOULD BE CAUGHT DEAD WITH HER.
HEE HEE
SNICKER
LINDA, I SWEAR, JIMMY AND I ARE JUST FRIENDS! I WOULD NEVER TRY TO STEAL HIM AWAY FROM YOU--
UH-- DUH, THAT'S WHY I'M LAUGHING, YOU LOSER.
LIKE YOU EVER COULD STEAL HIM AWAY FROM ME!
BUT I AM TELLING YOU TO BACK OFF AND STOP THROWING YOURSELF AT HIM. IT'S EMBARRASSING.
AS IF I WOULD! TAKE A CHILL PILL, LINDA, WE JUST HANG OUT SOME-TIMES.
TAKE A WHAT?
LINNY, KNOCK IT OFF.
I'VE TOLD YOU BEFORE, WHIT AND I ARE JUST FRIENDS. WE GREW UP TOGETHER, SHE'S LIKE MY SISTER.
ANYTHING ELSE IS JUST... JUST GROSS.
I KNOW, I KNOW, BUT I JUST GET SO JEALOUS, YOU KNOW? YOU'RE MY SPECIAL BABY.
WHATEVER. BYE, JIMMY. I'M SURE I'LL SEE YOU LATER.

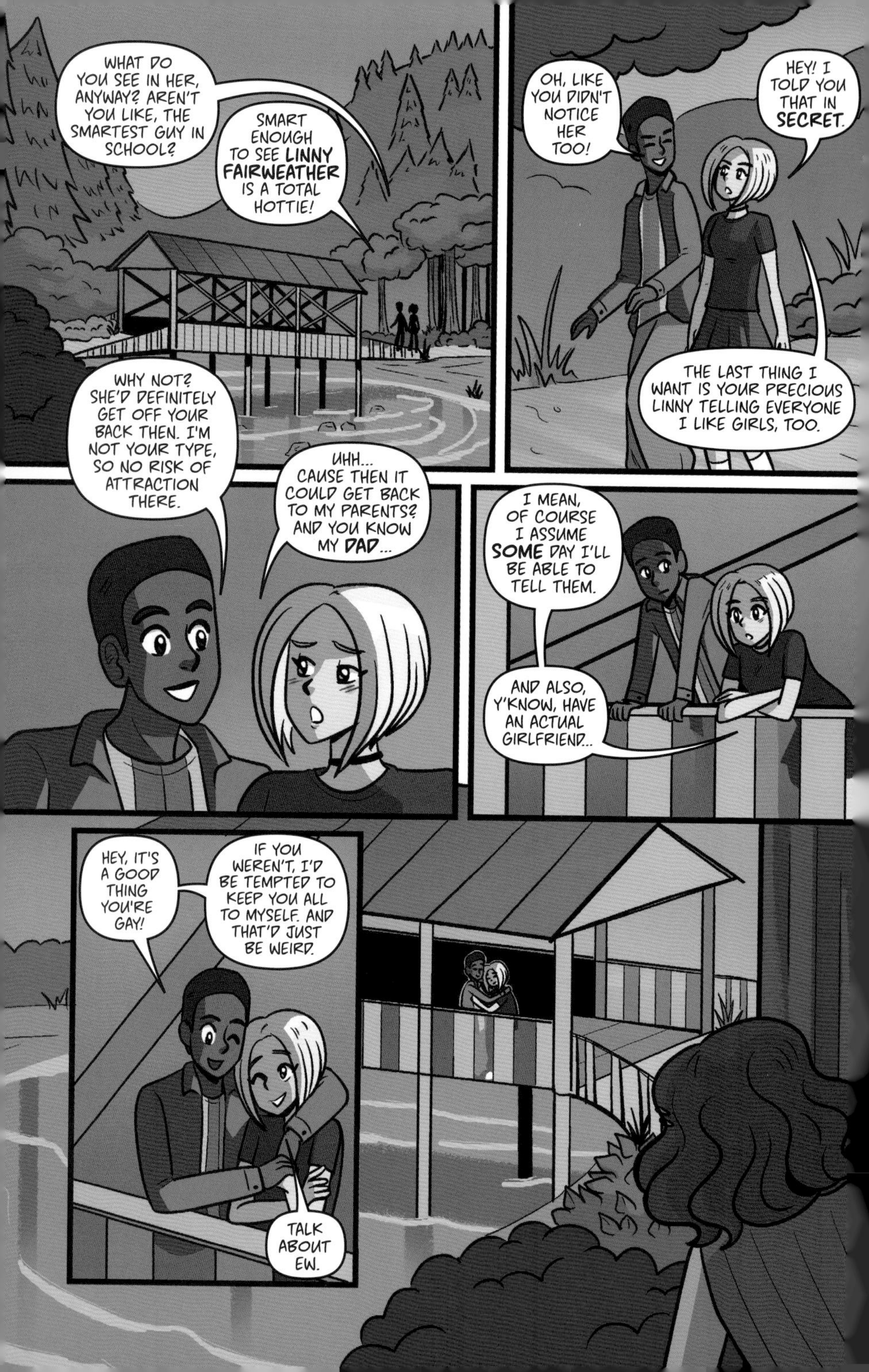
WHAT DO YOU SEE IN HER, ANYWAY? AREN'T YOU LIKE, THE SMARTEST GUY IN SCHOOL?
SMART ENOUGH TO SEE **LINNY FAIRWEATHER** IS A TOTAL HOTTIE!
OH, LIKE YOU DIDN'T NOTICE HER TOO!
HEY! I TOLD YOU THAT IN **SECRET**.
THE LAST THING I WANT IS YOUR PRECIOUS LINNY TELLING EVERYONE I LIKE GIRLS, TOO.
WHY NOT? SHE'D DEFINITELY GET OFF YOUR BACK THEN. I'M NOT YOUR TYPE, SO NO RISK OF ATTRACTION THERE.
UHH... CAUSE THEN IT COULD GET BACK TO MY PARENTS? AND YOU KNOW MY **DAD**...
I MEAN, OF COURSE I ASSUME **SOME** DAY I'LL BE ABLE TO TELL THEM.
AND ALSO, Y'KNOW, HAVE AN ACTUAL GIRLFRIEND...
HEY, IT'S A GOOD THING YOU'RE GAY!
IF YOU WEREN'T, I'D BE TEMPTED TO KEEP YOU ALL TO MYSELF. AND THAT'D JUST BE WEIRD.
TALK ABOUT EW.

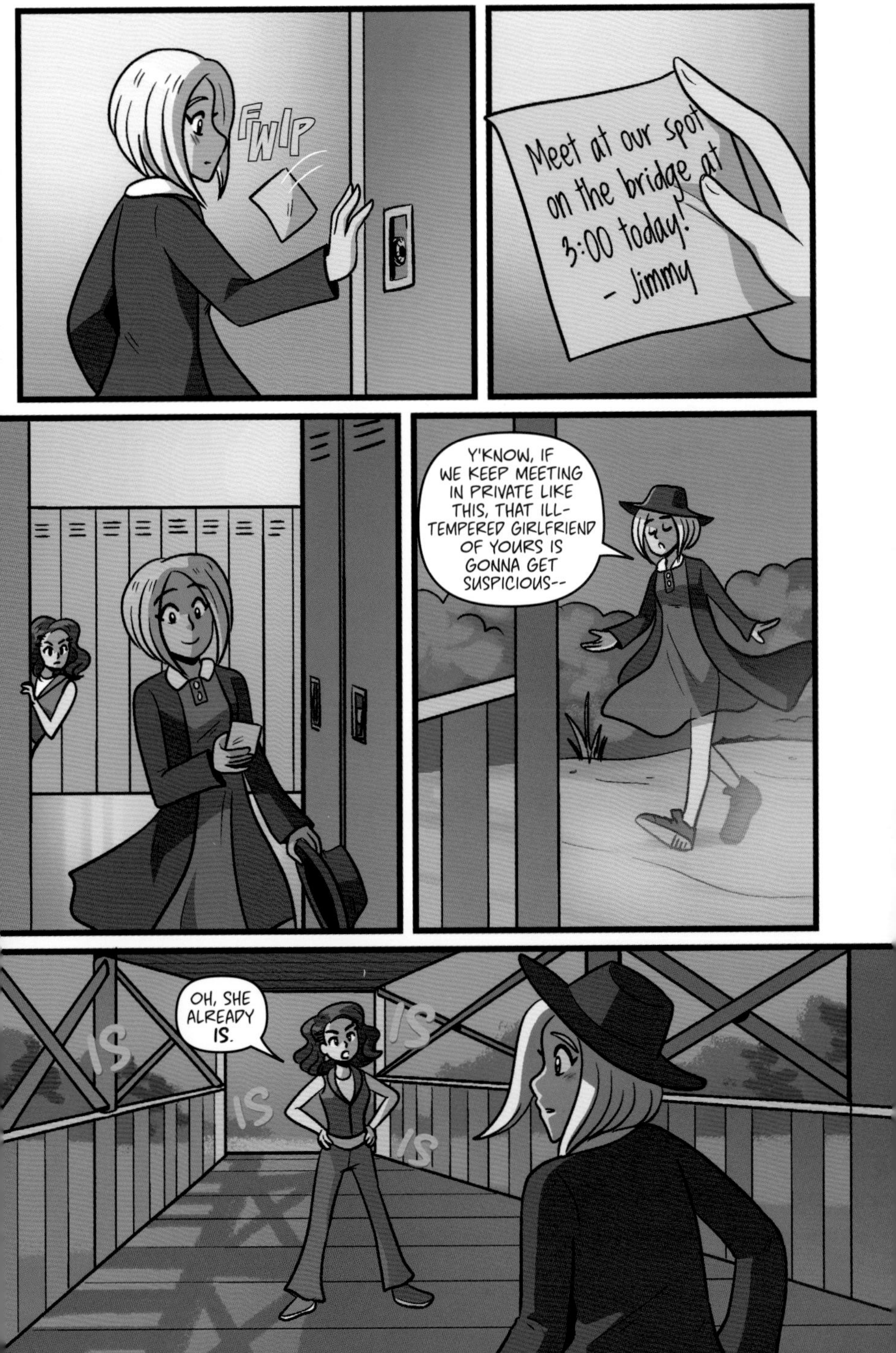
FWIP
Meet at our spot on the bridge at 3:00 today! - Jimmy
Y'KNOW, IF WE KEEP MEETING IN PRIVATE LIKE THIS, THAT ILL-TEMPERED GIRLFRIEND OF YOURS IS GONNA GET SUSPICIOUS--
OH, SHE ALREADY IS.
IS
IS
IS
IS

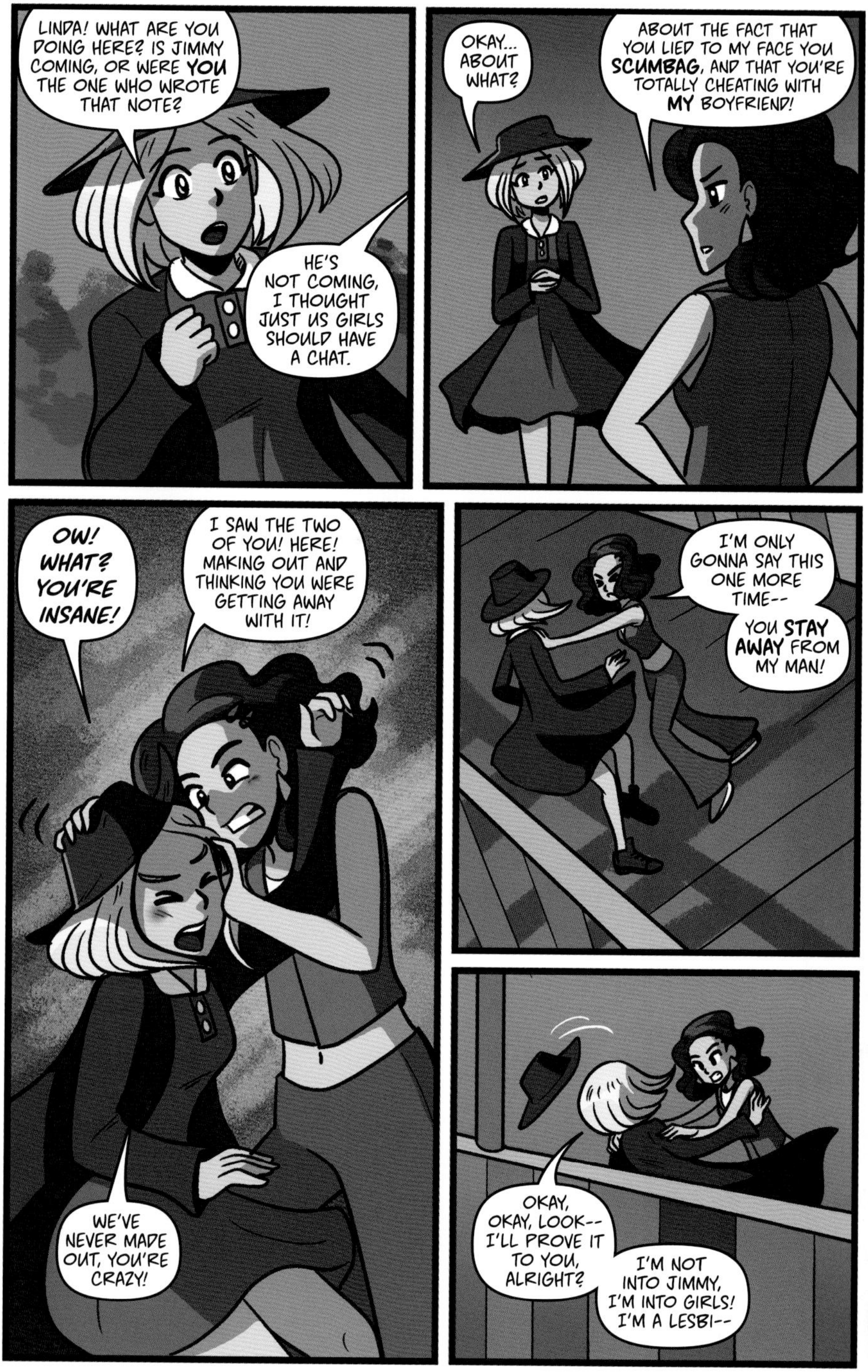
LINDA! WHAT ARE YOU DOING HERE? IS JIMMY COMING, OR WERE **YOU** THE ONE WHO WROTE THAT NOTE?
HE'S NOT COMING, I THOUGHT JUST US GIRLS SHOULD HAVE A CHAT.
OKAY... ABOUT WHAT?
ABOUT THE FACT THAT YOU LIED TO MY FACE YOU **SCUMBAG**, AND THAT YOU'RE TOTALLY CHEATING WITH **MY** BOYFRIEND!
OW! WHAT? YOU'RE INSANE!
I SAW THE TWO OF YOU! HERE! MAKING OUT AND THINKING YOU WERE GETTING AWAY WITH IT!
WE'VE NEVER MADE OUT, YOU'RE CRAZY!
I'M ONLY GONNA SAY THIS ONE MORE TIME--
YOU **STAY AWAY** FROM MY MAN!
OKAY, OKAY, LOOK-- I'LL PROVE IT TO YOU, ALRIGHT?
I'M NOT INTO JIMMY, I'M INTO GIRLS! I'M A LESBI--

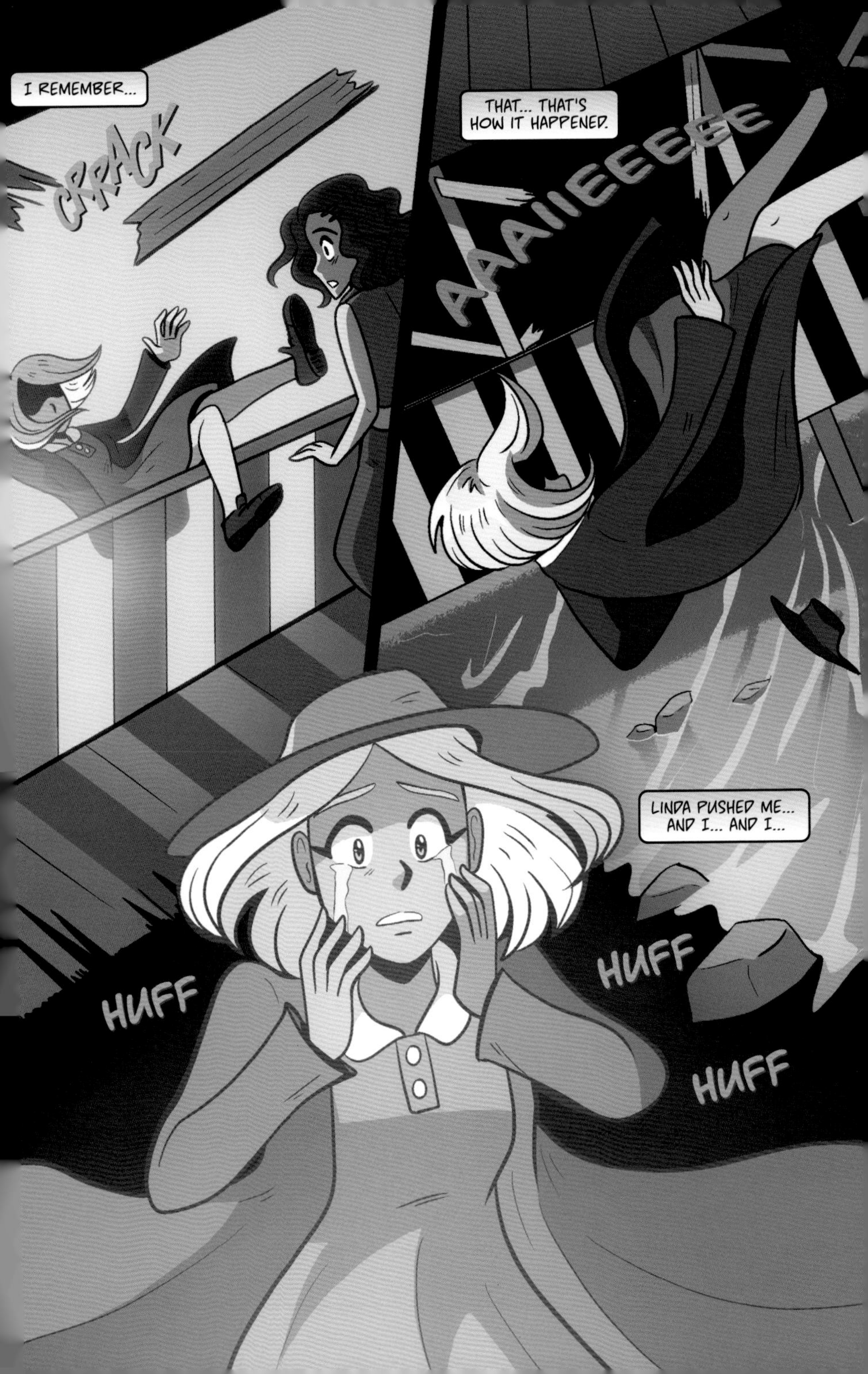
I REMEMBER...
CRACK
THAT... THAT'S HOW IT HAPPENED.
AAAIIEEEEEE
LINDA PUSHED ME... AND I... AND I...
HUFF
HUFF
HUFF

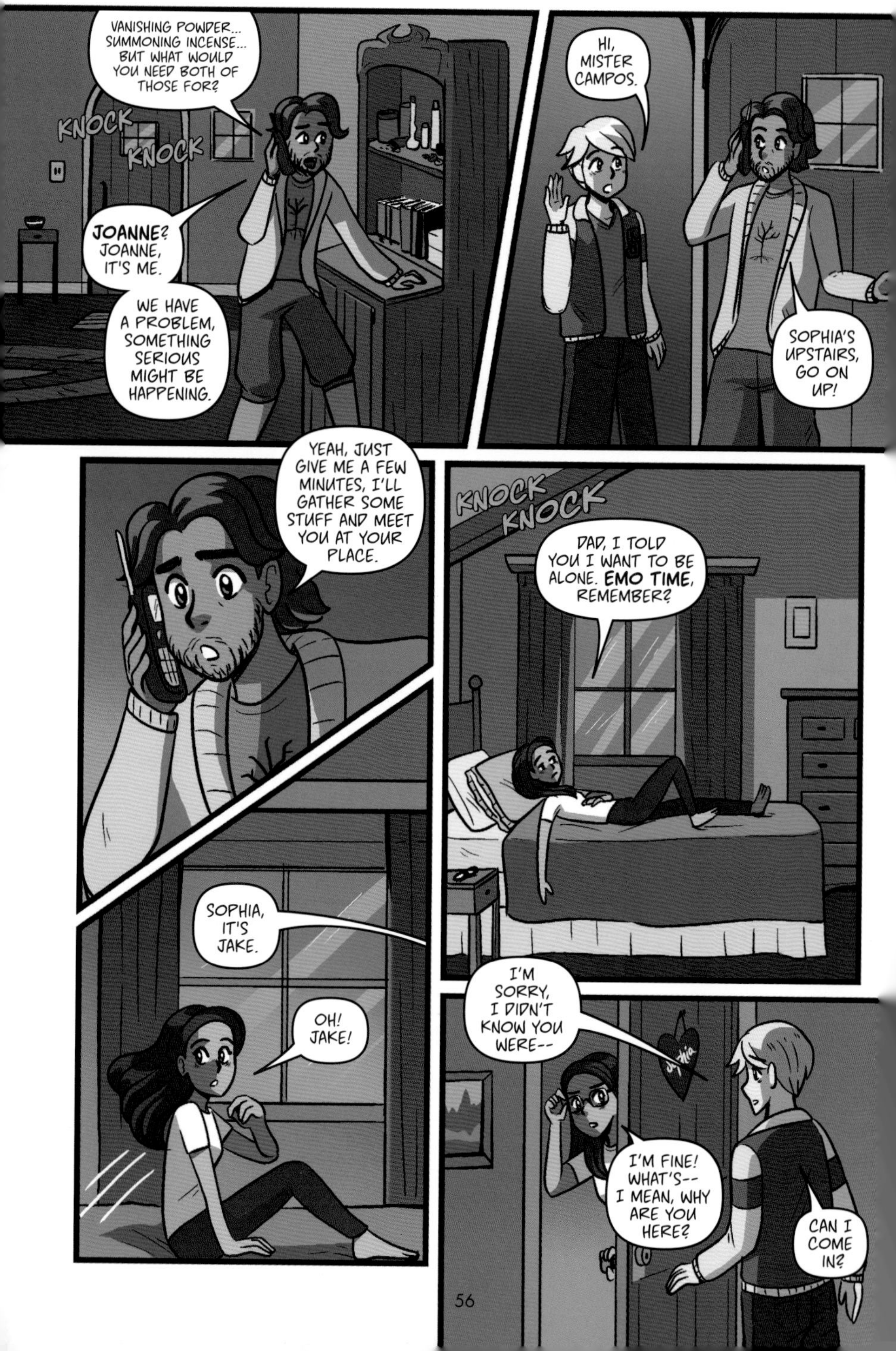
VANISHING POWDER... SUMMONING INCENSE... BUT WHAT WOULD YOU NEED BOTH OF THOSE FOR?
KNOCK KNOCK
JOANNE? JOANNE, IT'S ME.
WE HAVE A PROBLEM, SOMETHING SERIOUS MIGHT BE HAPPENING.
HI, MISTER CAMPOS.
SOPHIA'S UPSTAIRS, GO ON UP!
YEAH, JUST GIVE ME A FEW MINUTES, I'LL GATHER SOME STUFF AND MEET YOU AT YOUR PLACE.
KNOCK KNOCK
DAD, I TOLD YOU I WANT TO BE ALONE. EMO TIME, REMEMBER?
SOPHIA, IT'S JAKE.
OH! JAKE!
I'M SORRY, I DIDN'T KNOW YOU WERE--
I'M FINE! WHAT'S-- I MEAN, WHY ARE YOU HERE?
CAN I COME IN?

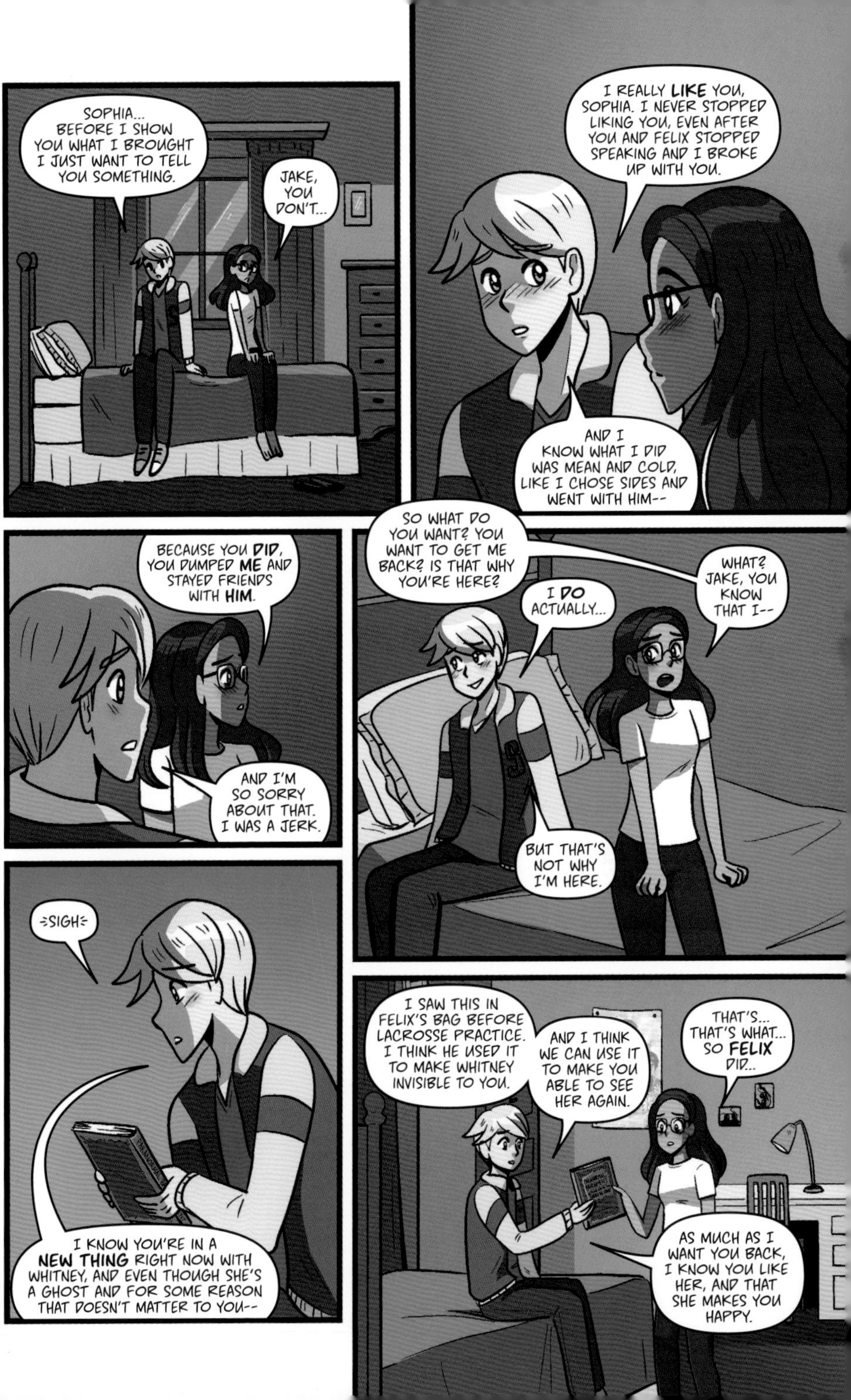
SOPHIA... BEFORE I SHOW YOU WHAT I BROUGHT I JUST WANT TO TELL YOU SOMETHING.
JAKE, YOU DON'T...
I REALLY **LIKE** YOU, SOPHIA. I NEVER STOPPED LIKING YOU, EVEN AFTER YOU AND FELIX STOPPED SPEAKING AND I BROKE UP WITH YOU.
AND I KNOW WHAT I DID WAS MEAN AND COLD, LIKE I CHOSE SIDES AND WENT WITH HIM--
BECAUSE YOU **DID**, YOU DUMPED **ME** AND STAYED FRIENDS WITH **HIM**.
AND I'M SO SORRY ABOUT THAT. I WAS A JERK.
SO WHAT DO YOU WANT? YOU WANT TO GET ME BACK? IS THAT WHY YOU'RE HERE?
I **DO** ACTUALLY...
WHAT? JAKE, YOU KNOW THAT I--
BUT THAT'S NOT WHY I'M HERE.
=SIGH=
I KNOW YOU'RE IN A **NEW THING** RIGHT NOW WITH WHITNEY, AND EVEN THOUGH SHE'S A GHOST AND FOR SOME REASON THAT DOESN'T MATTER TO YOU--
I SAW THIS IN FELIX'S BAG BEFORE LACROSSE PRACTICE. I THINK HE USED IT TO MAKE WHITNEY INVISIBLE TO YOU.
AND I THINK WE CAN USE IT TO MAKE YOU ABLE TO SEE HER AGAIN.
THAT'S... THAT'S WHAT... SO **FELIX** DID...
AS MUCH AS I WANT YOU BACK, I KNOW YOU LIKE HER, AND THAT SHE MAKES YOU HAPPY.

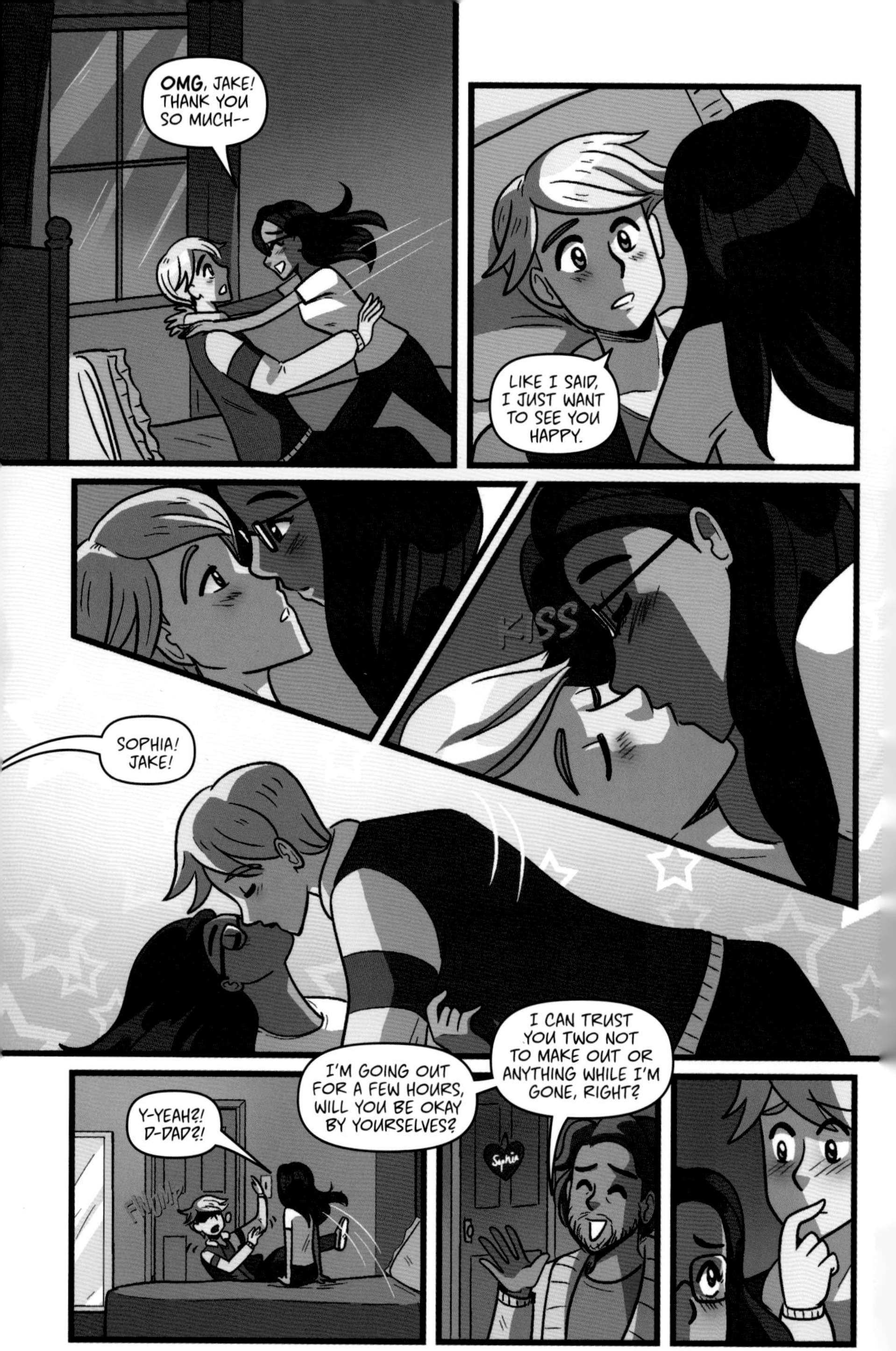
OMG, JAKE! THANK YOU SO MUCH--
LIKE I SAID, I JUST WANT TO SEE YOU HAPPY.
KISS
SOPHIA! JAKE!
Y-YEAH?! D-DAD?!
I'M GOING OUT FOR A FEW HOURS, WILL YOU BE OKAY BY YOURSELVES?
I CAN TRUST YOU TWO NOT TO MAKE OUT OR ANYTHING WHILE I'M GONE, RIGHT?
Sophia

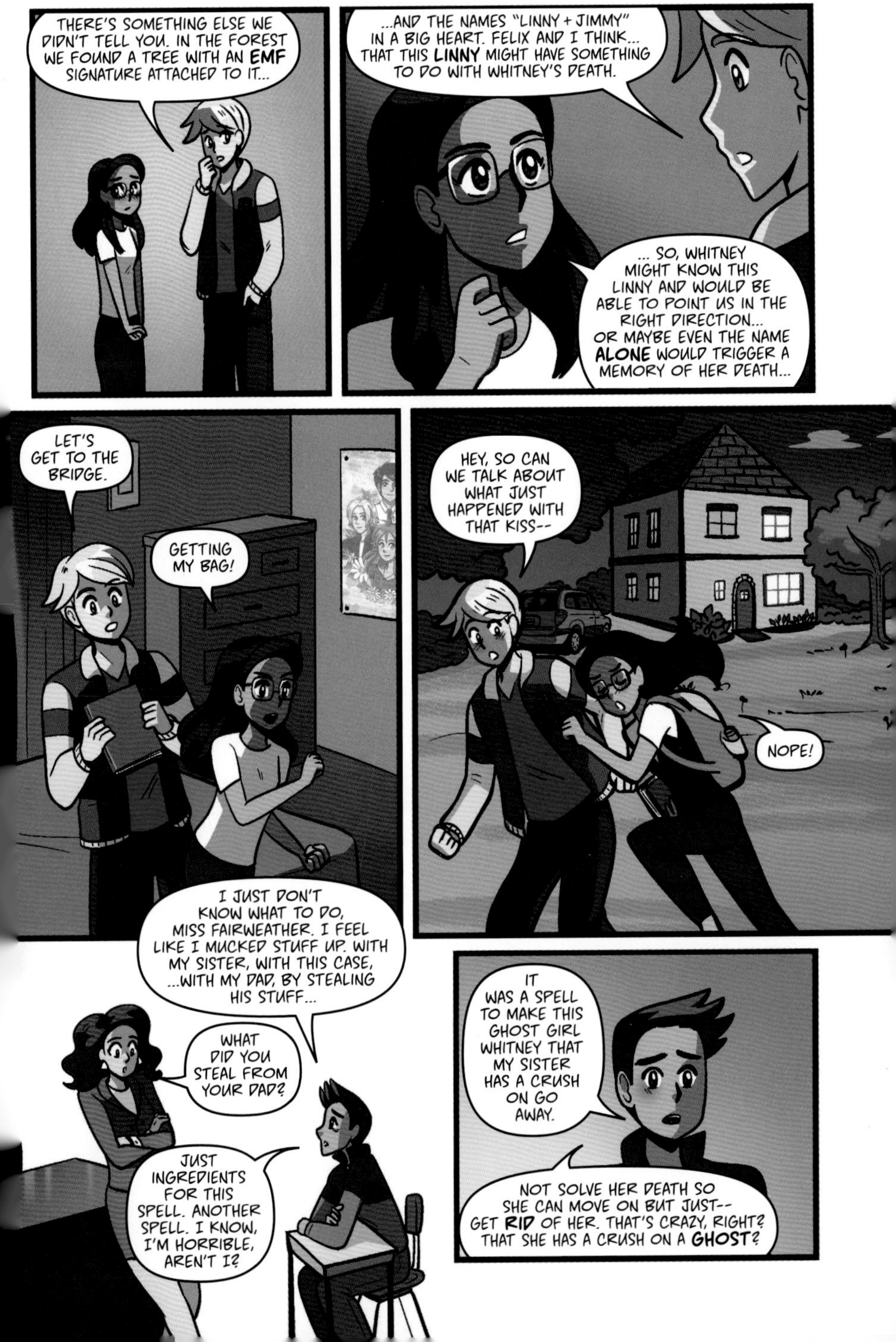
THERE'S SOMETHING ELSE WE DIDN'T TELL YOU. IN THE FOREST WE FOUND A TREE WITH AN **EMF** SIGNATURE ATTACHED TO IT...
...AND THE NAMES "LINNY + JIMMY" IN A BIG HEART. FELIX AND I THINK... THAT THIS **LINNY** MIGHT HAVE SOMETHING TO DO WITH WHITNEY'S DEATH.
... SO, WHITNEY MIGHT KNOW THIS LINNY AND WOULD BE ABLE TO POINT US IN THE RIGHT DIRECTION... OR MAYBE EVEN THE NAME **ALONE** WOULD TRIGGER A MEMORY OF HER DEATH...
LET'S GET TO THE BRIDGE.
GETTING MY BAG!
HEY, SO CAN WE TALK ABOUT WHAT JUST HAPPENED WITH THAT KISS--
NOPE!
I JUST DON'T KNOW WHAT TO DO, MISS FAIRWEATHER. I FEEL LIKE I MUCKED STUFF UP. WITH MY SISTER, WITH THIS CASE, ...WITH MY DAD, BY STEALING HIS STUFF...
WHAT DID YOU STEAL FROM YOUR DAD?
JUST INGREDIENTS FOR THIS SPELL. ANOTHER SPELL. I KNOW, I'M HORRIBLE, AREN'T I?
IT WAS A SPELL TO MAKE THIS GHOST GIRL WHITNEY THAT MY SISTER HAS A CRUSH ON GO AWAY.
NOT SOLVE HER DEATH SO SHE CAN MOVE ON BUT JUST-- GET **RID** OF HER. THAT'S CRAZY, RIGHT? THAT SHE HAS A CRUSH ON A **GHOST**?

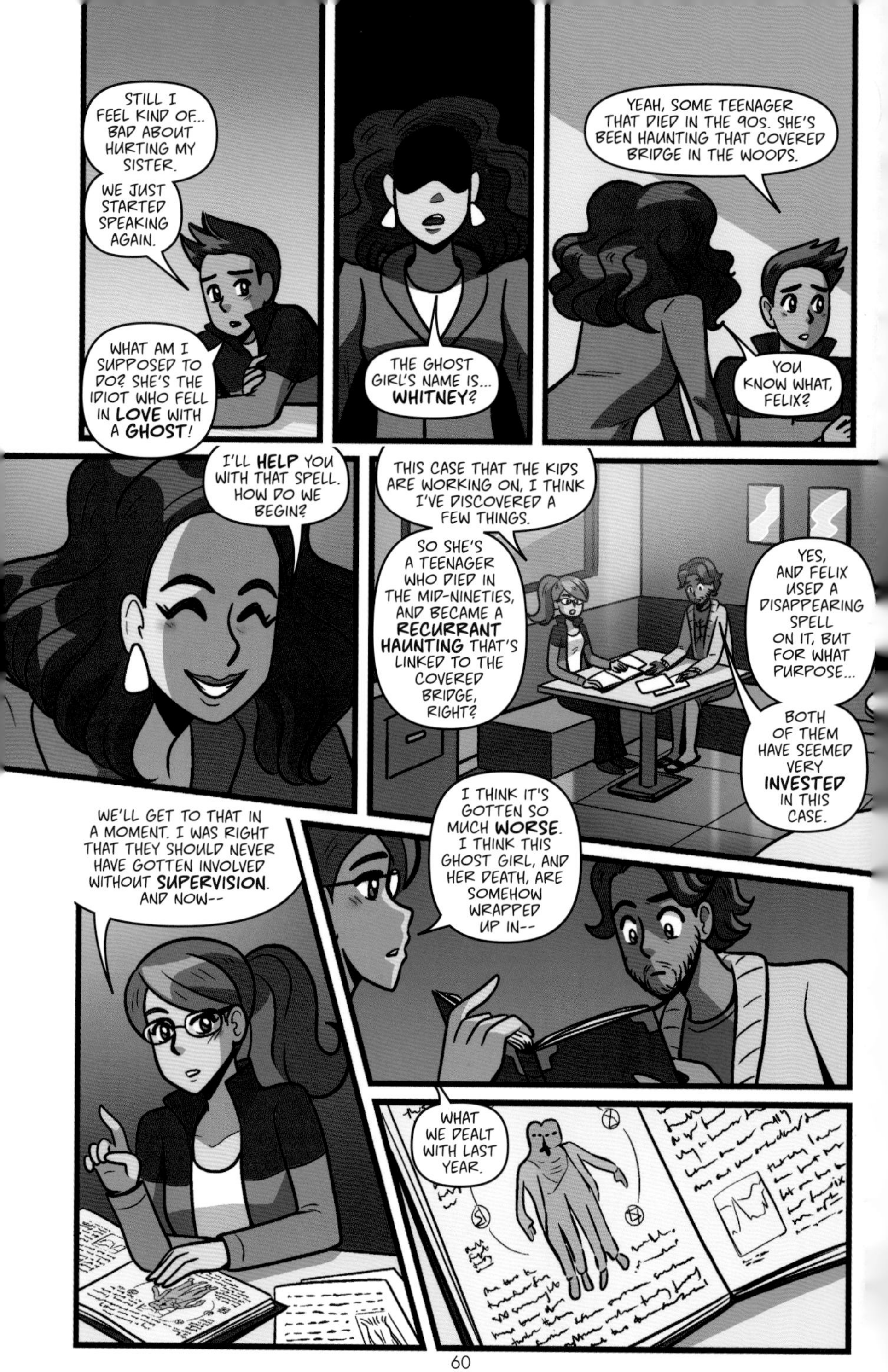
STILL I FEEL KIND OF... BAD ABOUT HURTING MY SISTER.
WE JUST STARTED SPEAKING AGAIN.
WHAT AM I SUPPOSED TO DO? SHE'S THE IDIOT WHO FELL IN LOVE WITH A GHOST!
THE GHOST GIRL'S NAME IS... WHITNEY?
YEAH, SOME TEENAGER THAT DIED IN THE 90s. SHE'S BEEN HAUNTING THAT COVERED BRIDGE IN THE WOODS.
YOU KNOW WHAT, FELIX?
I'LL HELP YOU WITH THAT SPELL. HOW DO WE BEGIN?
THIS CASE THAT THE KIDS ARE WORKING ON, I THINK I'VE DISCOVERED A FEW THINGS.
SO SHE'S A TEENAGER WHO DIED IN THE MID-NINETIES, AND BECAME A RECURRANT HAUNTING THAT'S LINKED TO THE COVERED BRIDGE, RIGHT?
YES, AND FELIX USED A DISAPPEARING SPELL ON IT, BUT FOR WHAT PURPOSE...
BOTH OF THEM HAVE SEEMED VERY INVESTED IN THIS CASE.
WE'LL GET TO THAT IN A MOMENT. I WAS RIGHT THAT THEY SHOULD NEVER HAVE GOTTEN INVOLVED WITHOUT SUPERVISION. AND NOW--
I THINK IT'S GOTTEN SO MUCH WORSE. I THINK THIS GHOST GIRL, AND HER DEATH, ARE SOMEHOW WRAPPED UP IN--
WHAT WE DEALT WITH LAST YEAR.

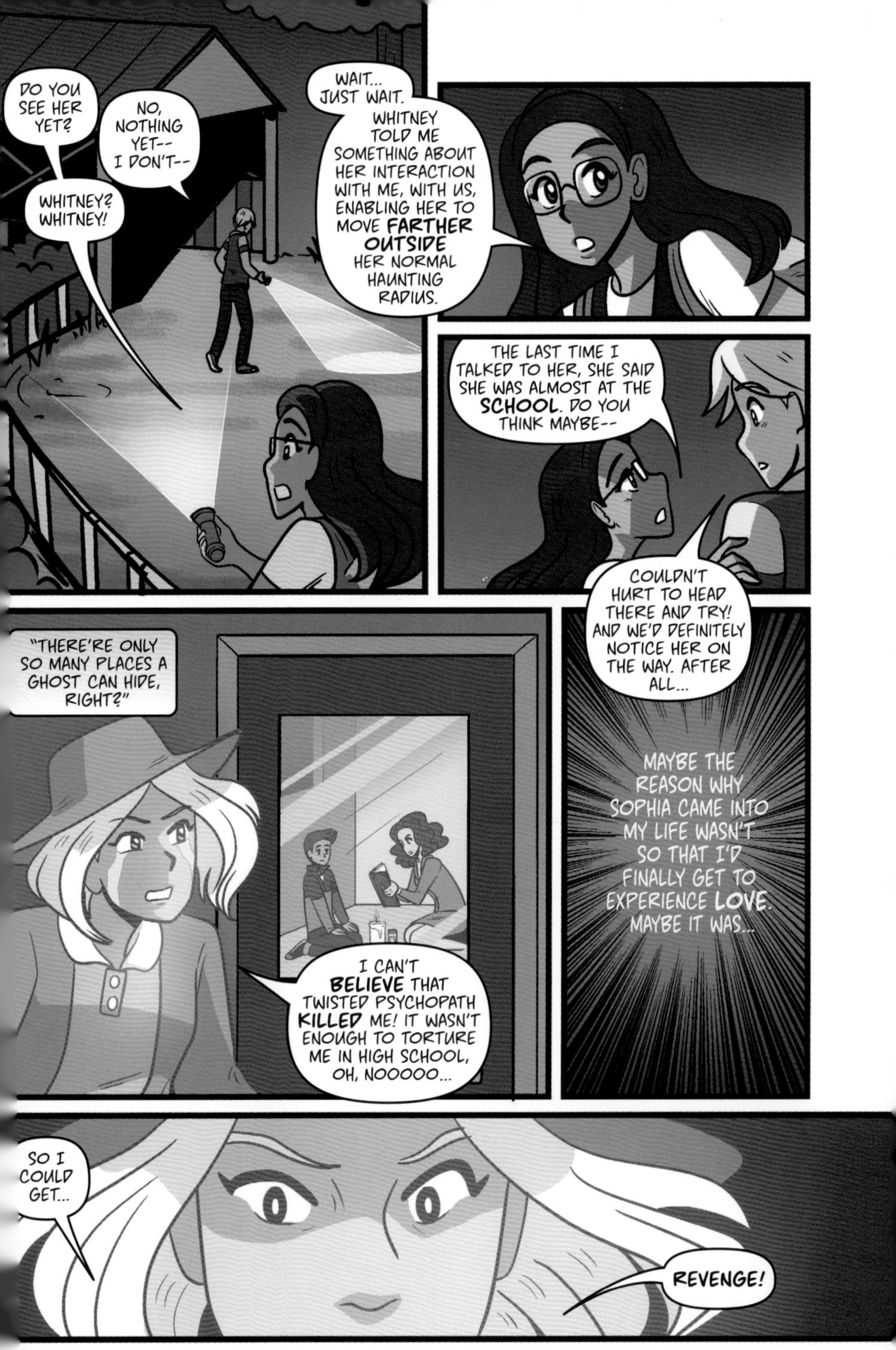
DO YOU SEE HER YET?
NO, NOTHING YET-- I DON'T--
WHITNEY? WHITNEY!
WAIT... JUST WAIT.
WHITNEY TOLD ME SOMETHING ABOUT HER INTERACTION WITH ME, WITH US, ENABLING HER TO MOVE **FARTHER OUTSIDE** HER NORMAL HAUNTING RADIUS.
THE LAST TIME I TALKED TO HER, SHE SAID SHE WAS ALMOST AT THE **SCHOOL**. DO YOU THINK MAYBE--
COULDN'T HURT TO HEAD THERE AND TRY! AND WE'D DEFINITELY NOTICE HER ON THE WAY. AFTER ALL...
"THERE'RE ONLY SO MANY PLACES A GHOST CAN HIDE, RIGHT?"
I CAN'T **BELIEVE** THAT TWISTED PSYCHOPATH **KILLED** ME! IT WASN'T ENOUGH TO TORTURE ME IN HIGH SCHOOL, OH, NOOOOO...
MAYBE THE REASON WHY SOPHIA CAME INTO MY LIFE WASN'T SO THAT I'D FINALLY GET TO EXPERIENCE **LOVE**. MAYBE IT WAS...
SO I COULD GET...
REVENGE!

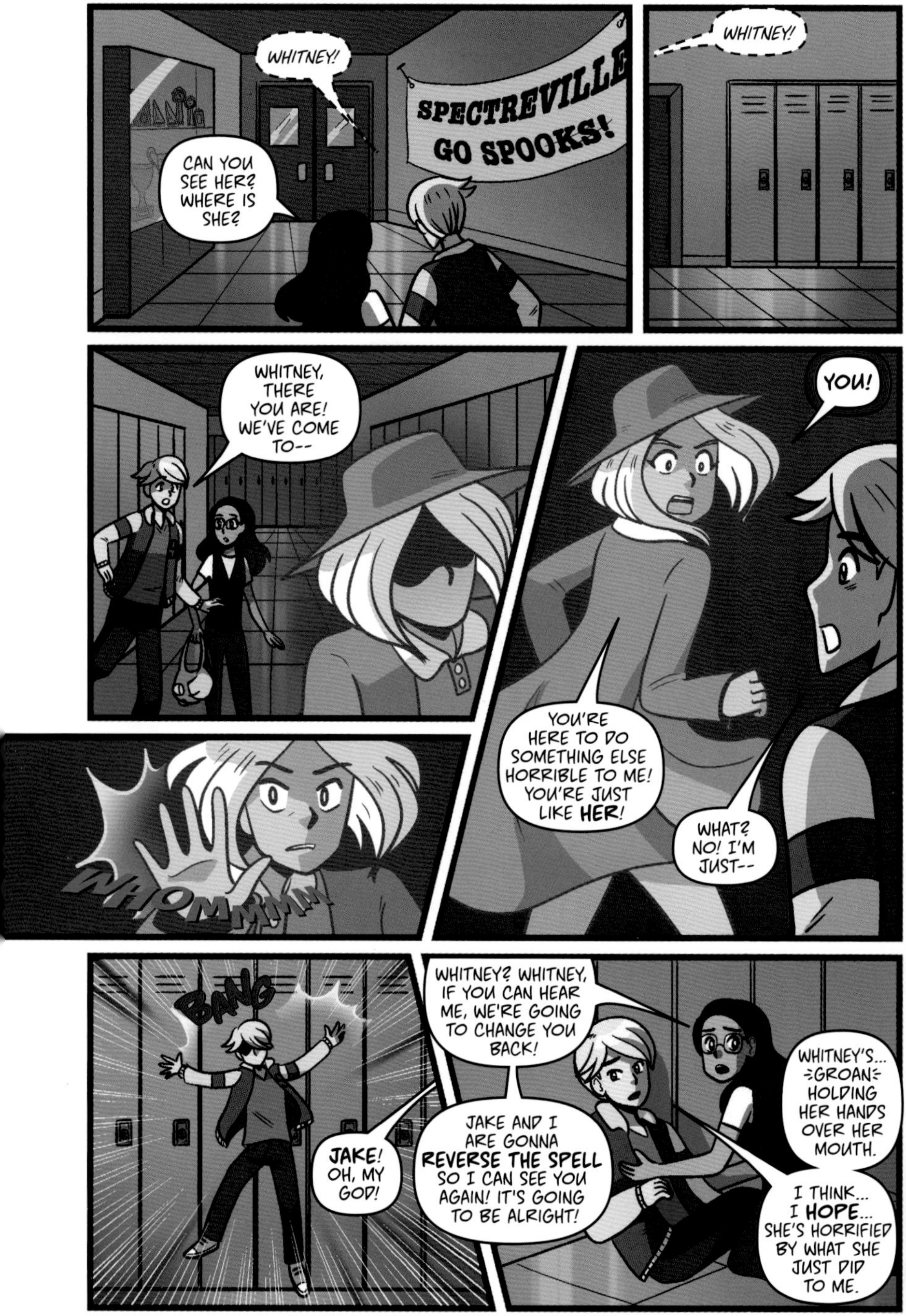
WHITNEY!
SPECTREVILLE GO SPOOKS!
CAN YOU SEE HER? WHERE IS SHE?
WHITNEY!
WHITNEY, THERE YOU ARE! WE'VE COME TO--
YOU!
YOU'RE HERE TO DO SOMETHING ELSE HORRIBLE TO ME! YOU'RE JUST LIKE HER!
WHAT? NO! I'M JUST--
WHOMMMM
BANG
JAKE! OH, MY GOD!
WHITNEY? WHITNEY, IF YOU CAN HEAR ME, WE'RE GOING TO CHANGE YOU BACK!
JAKE AND I ARE GONNA REVERSE THE SPELL SO I CAN SEE YOU AGAIN! IT'S GOING TO BE ALRIGHT!
WHITNEY'S... GROAN HOLDING HER HANDS OVER HER MOUTH.
I THINK... I HOPE... SHE'S HORRIFIED BY WHAT SHE JUST DID TO ME.

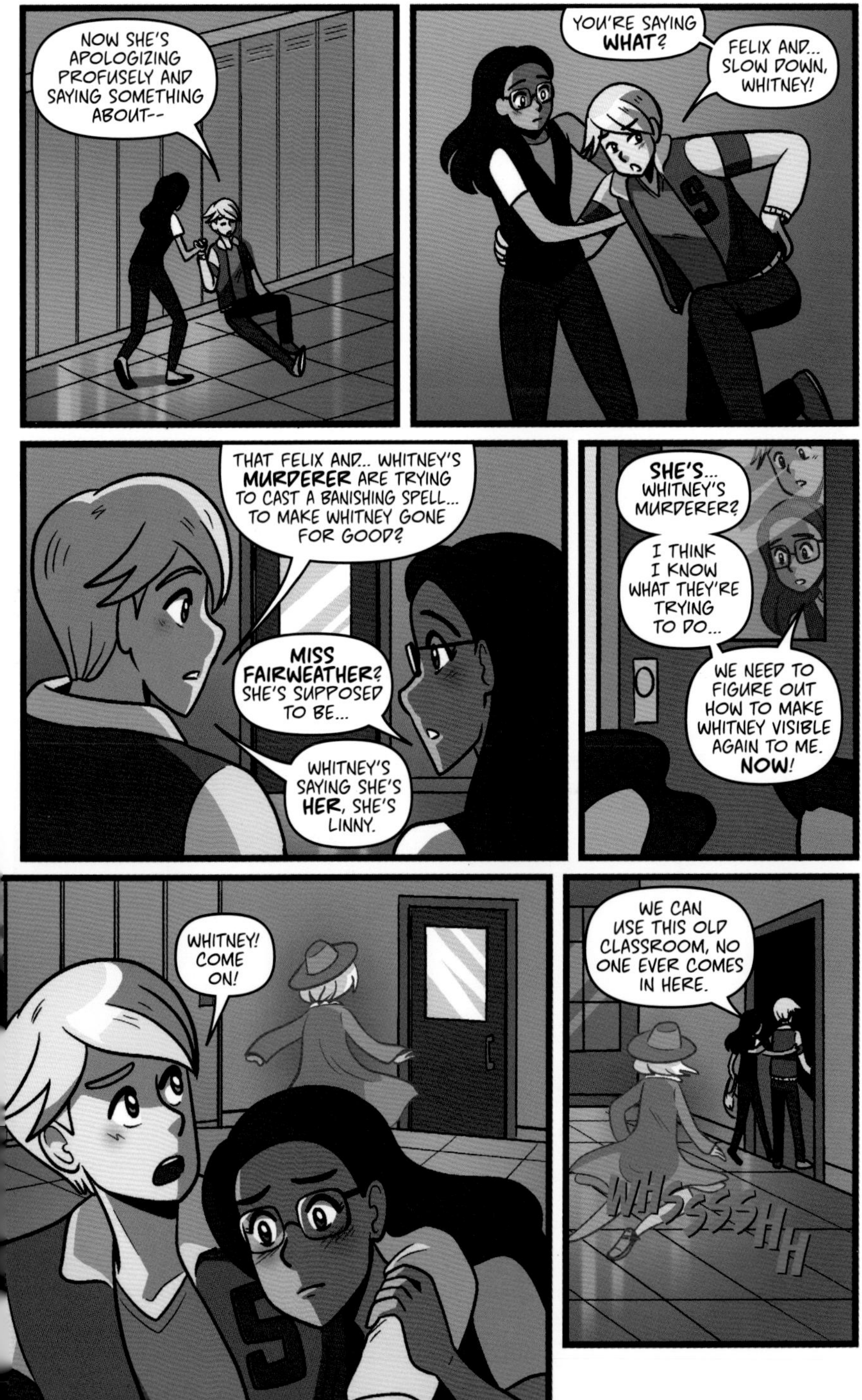
NOW SHE'S APOLOGIZING PROFUSELY AND SAYING SOMETHING ABOUT--
YOU'RE SAYING WHAT?
FELIX AND... SLOW DOWN, WHITNEY!
THAT FELIX AND... WHITNEY'S MURDERER ARE TRYING TO CAST A BANISHING SPELL... TO MAKE WHITNEY GONE FOR GOOD?
MISS FAIRWEATHER? SHE'S SUPPOSED TO BE...
WHITNEY'S SAYING SHE'S HER, SHE'S LINNY.
SHE'S... WHITNEY'S MURDERER?
I THINK I KNOW WHAT THEY'RE TRYING TO DO...
WE NEED TO FIGURE OUT HOW TO MAKE WHITNEY VISIBLE AGAIN TO ME. NOW!
WHITNEY! COME ON!
WE CAN USE THIS OLD CLASSROOM, NO ONE EVER COMES IN HERE.
WHSSSSHH

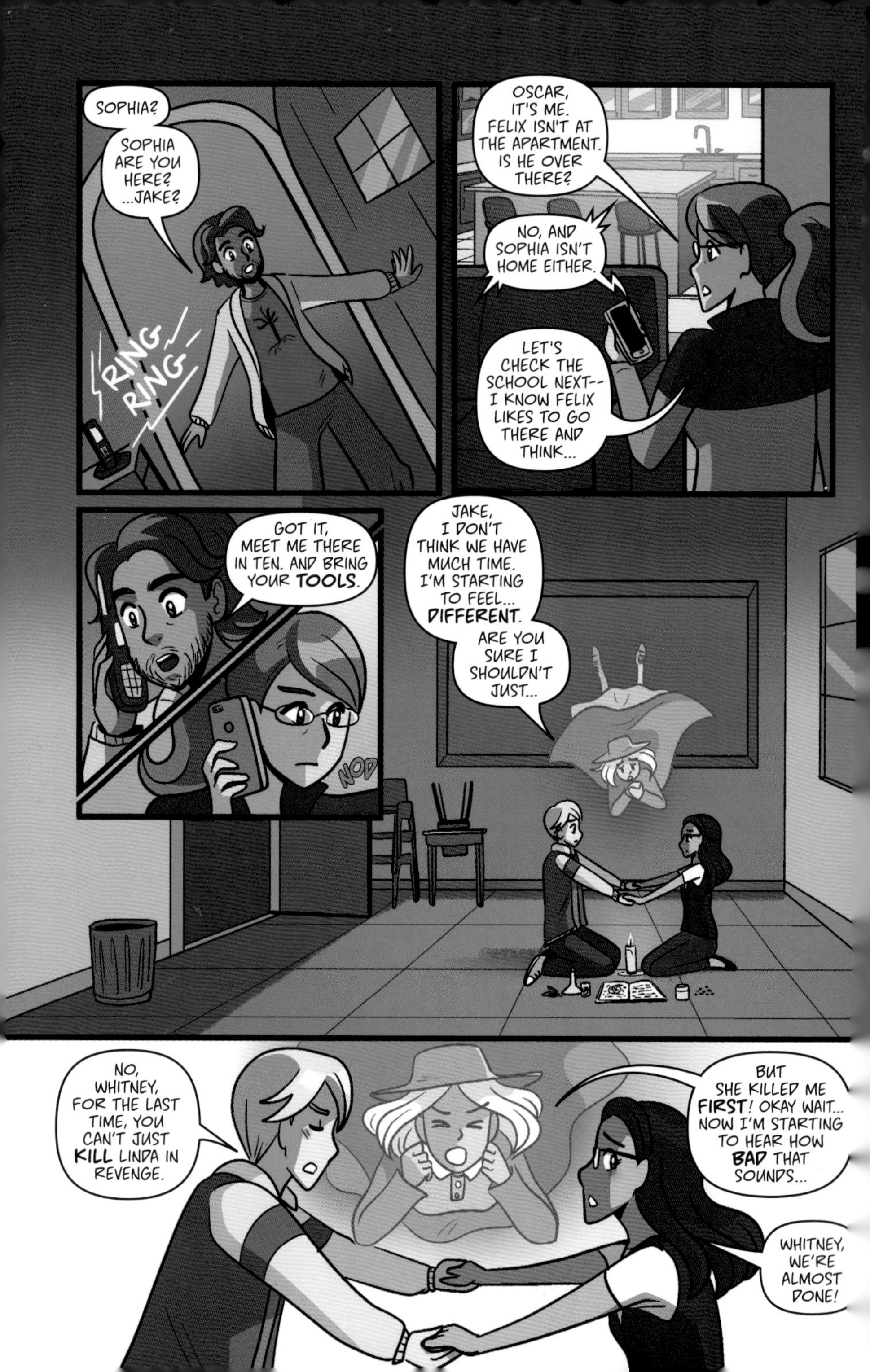
SOPHIA?
SOPHIA ARE YOU HERE? ...JAKE?
RING RING
OSCAR, IT'S ME. FELIX ISN'T AT THE APARTMENT. IS HE OVER THERE?
NO, AND SOPHIA ISN'T HOME EITHER.
LET'S CHECK THE SCHOOL NEXT-- I KNOW FELIX LIKES TO GO THERE AND THINK...
GOT IT, MEET ME THERE IN TEN. AND BRING YOUR TOOLS.
NOD
JAKE, I DON'T THINK WE HAVE MUCH TIME. I'M STARTING TO FEEL... DIFFERENT.
ARE YOU SURE I SHOULDN'T JUST...
NO, WHITNEY, FOR THE LAST TIME, YOU CAN'T JUST KILL LINDA IN REVENGE.
BUT SHE KILLED ME FIRST! OKAY WAIT... NOW I'M STARTING TO HEAR HOW BAD THAT SOUNDS...
WHITNEY, WE'RE ALMOST DONE!

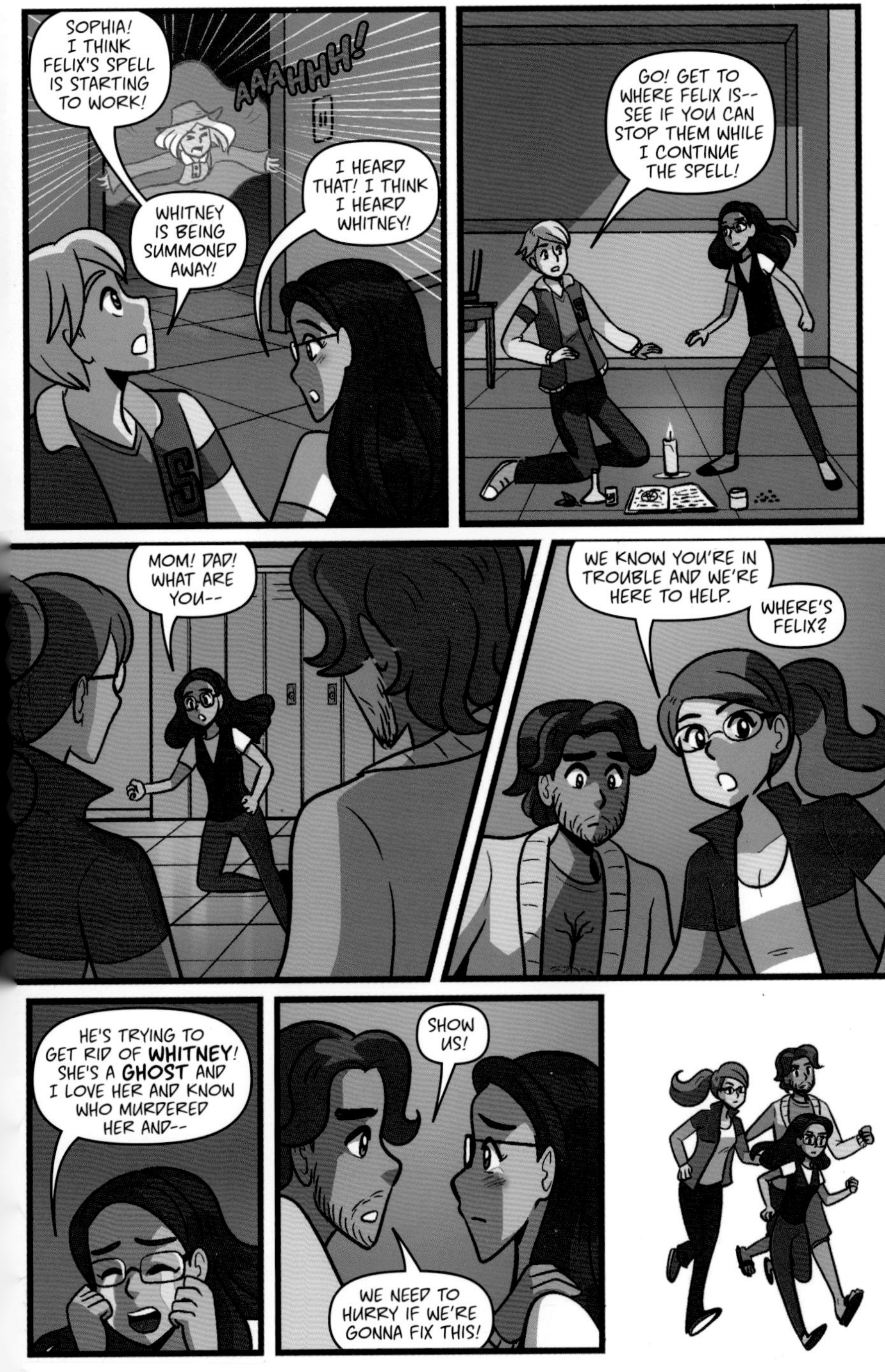
SOPHIA! I THINK FELIX'S SPELL IS STARTING TO WORK!
AAAHHHH!
WHITNEY IS BEING SUMMONED AWAY!
I HEARD THAT! I THINK I HEARD WHITNEY!
GO! GET TO WHERE FELIX IS-- SEE IF YOU CAN STOP THEM WHILE I CONTINUE THE SPELL!
MOM! DAD! WHAT ARE YOU--
WE KNOW YOU'RE IN TROUBLE AND WE'RE HERE TO HELP.
WHERE'S FELIX?
HE'S TRYING TO GET RID OF **WHITNEY**! SHE'S A **GHOST** AND I LOVE HER AND KNOW WHO MURDERED HER AND--
SHOW US!
WE NEED TO HURRY IF WE'RE GONNA FIX THIS!

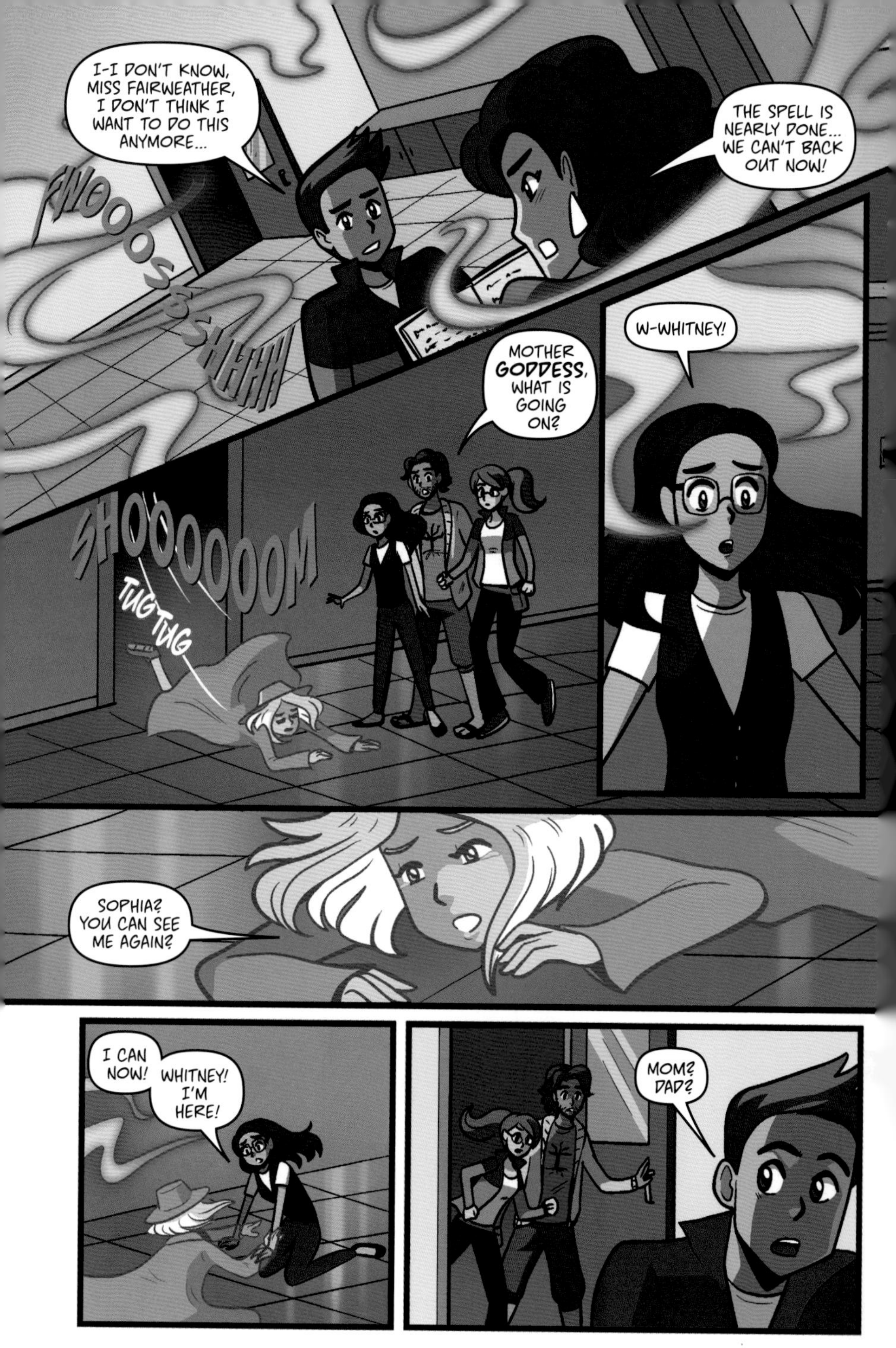
I-I DON'T KNOW, MISS FAIRWEATHER, I DON'T THINK I WANT TO DO THIS ANYMORE...
THE SPELL IS NEARLY DONE... WE CAN'T BACK OUT NOW!
FWOOOSSSHHHH
MOTHER GODDESS, WHAT IS GOING ON?
SHOOOOOOOM
TUG TUG
W-WHITNEY!
SOPHIA? YOU CAN SEE ME AGAIN?
I CAN NOW!
WHITNEY! I'M HERE!
MOM? DAD?

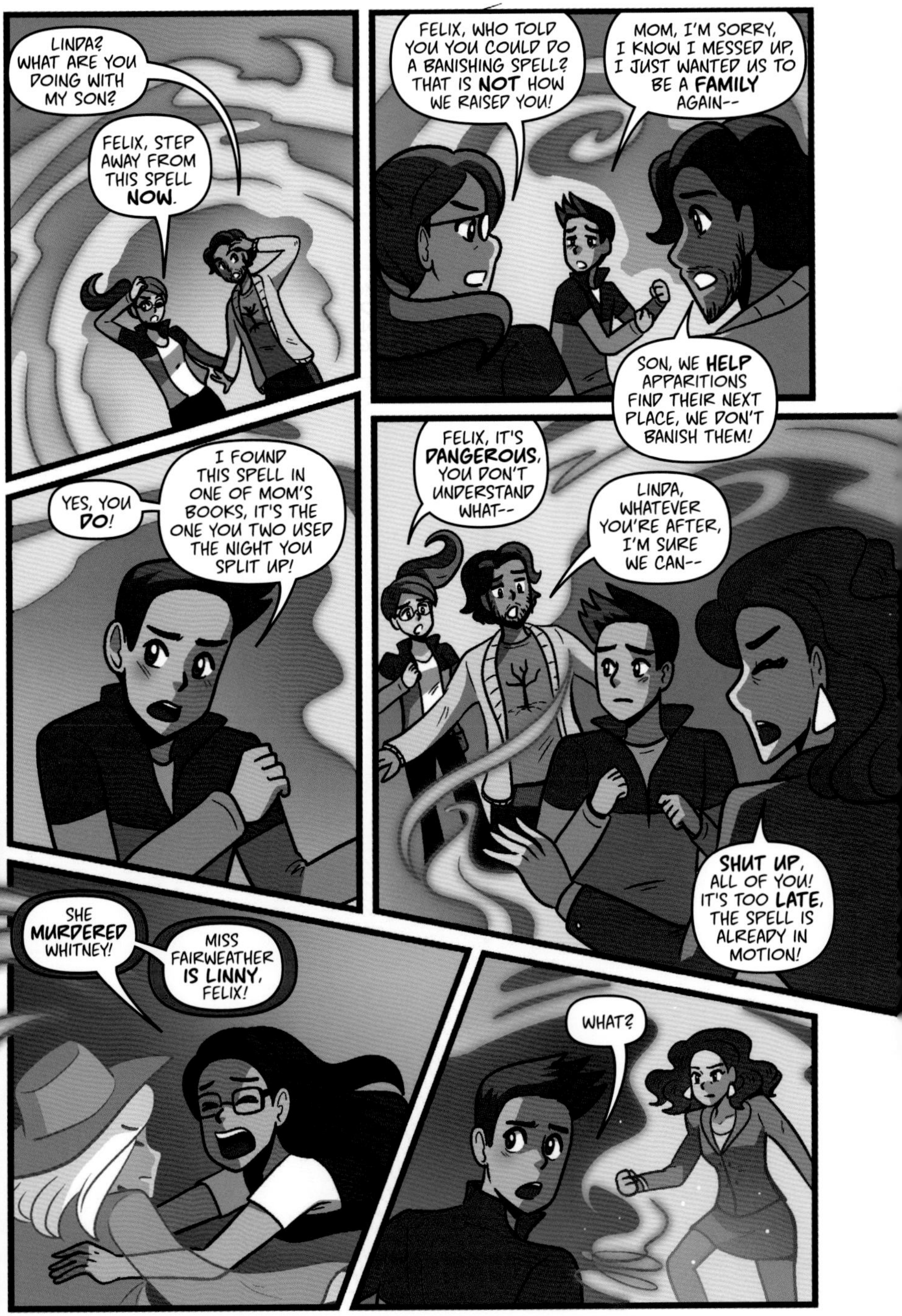
LINDA? WHAT ARE YOU DOING WITH MY SON?
FELIX, STEP AWAY FROM THIS SPELL **NOW**.
FELIX, WHO TOLD YOU YOU COULD DO A BANISHING SPELL? THAT IS **NOT** HOW WE RAISED YOU!
MOM, I'M SORRY, I KNOW I MESSED UP, I JUST WANTED US TO BE A **FAMILY** AGAIN--
SON, WE **HELP** APPARITIONS FIND THEIR NEXT PLACE, WE DON'T BANISH THEM!
YES, YOU **DO**!
I FOUND THIS SPELL IN ONE OF MOM'S BOOKS, IT'S THE ONE YOU TWO USED THE NIGHT YOU SPLIT UP!
FELIX, IT'S **DANGEROUS**, YOU DON'T UNDERSTAND WHAT--
LINDA, WHATEVER YOU'RE AFTER, I'M SURE WE CAN--
SHUT UP, ALL OF YOU! IT'S TOO **LATE**, THE SPELL IS ALREADY IN MOTION!
SHE **MURDERED** WHITNEY!
MISS FAIRWEATHER **IS LINNY**, FELIX!
WHAT?

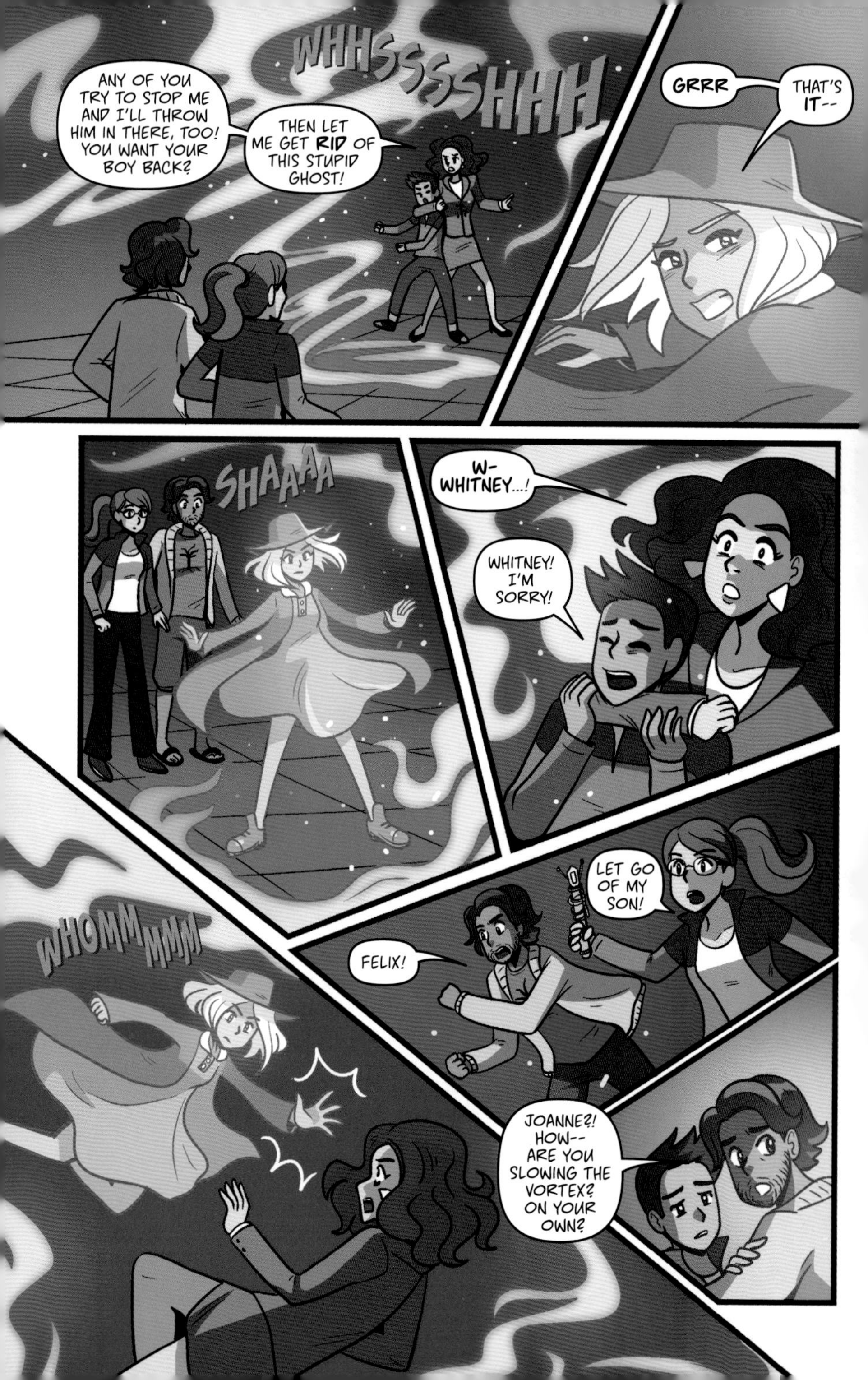
WHHSSSSSHHH
ANY OF YOU TRY TO STOP ME AND I'LL THROW HIM IN THERE, TOO! YOU WANT YOUR BOY BACK?
THEN LET ME GET **RID** OF THIS STUPID GHOST!
GRRR
THAT'S **IT**--
SHAAAA
W- WHITNEY...!
WHITNEY! I'M SORRY!
LET GO OF MY SON!
FELIX!
WHOMMMMM
JOANNE?! HOW-- ARE YOU SLOWING THE VORTEX? ON YOUR OWN?

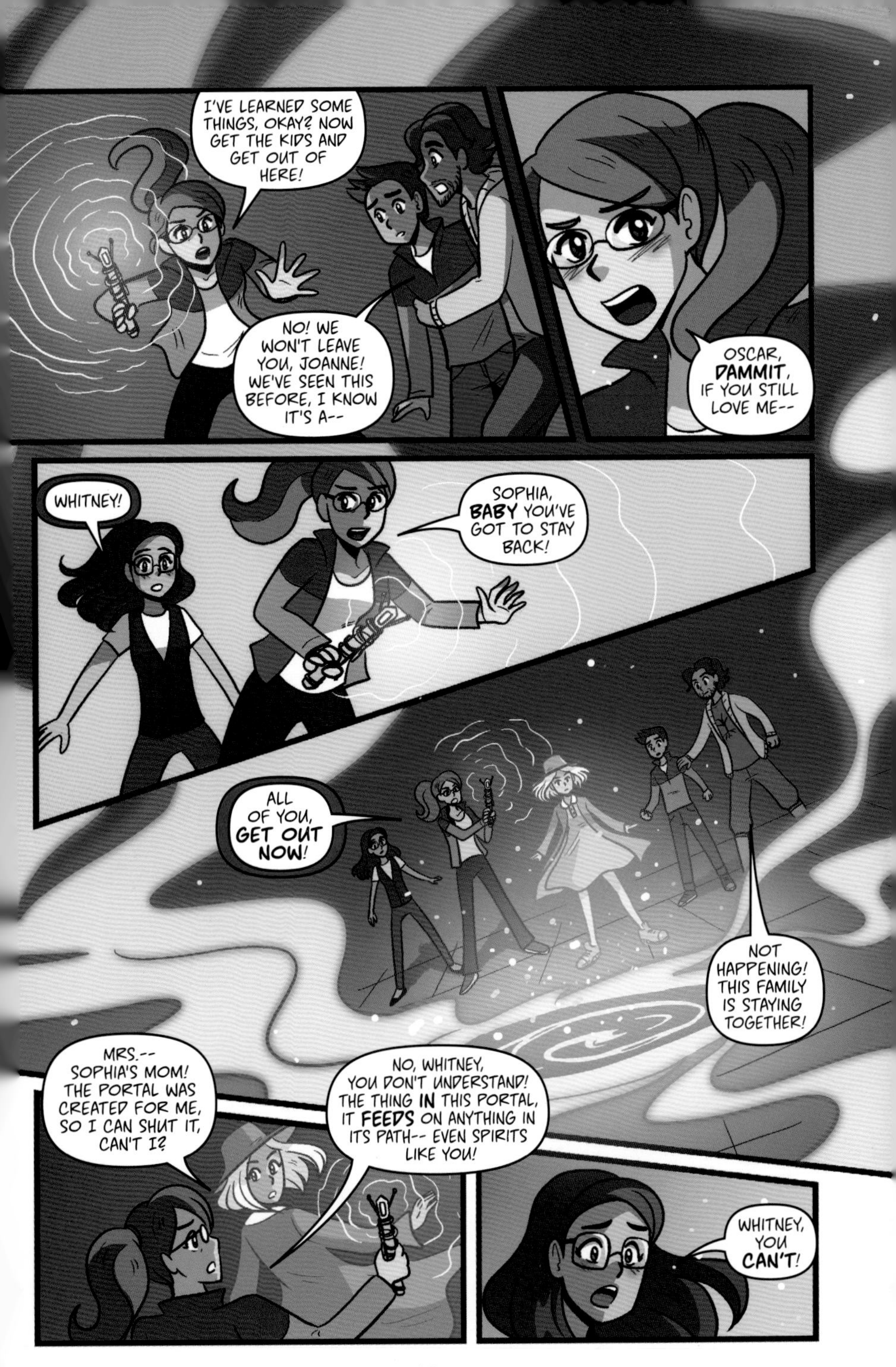
I'VE LEARNED SOME THINGS, OKAY? NOW GET THE KIDS AND GET OUT OF HERE!
NO! WE WON'T LEAVE YOU, JOANNE! WE'VE SEEN THIS BEFORE, I KNOW IT'S A--
OSCAR, DAMMIT, IF YOU STILL LOVE ME--
WHITNEY!
SOPHIA, BABY YOU'VE GOT TO STAY BACK!
ALL OF YOU, GET OUT NOW!
NOT HAPPENING! THIS FAMILY IS STAYING TOGETHER!
MRS.-- SOPHIA'S MOM! THE PORTAL WAS CREATED FOR ME, SO I CAN SHUT IT, CAN'T I?
NO, WHITNEY, YOU DON'T UNDERSTAND! THE THING IN THIS PORTAL, IT FEEDS ON ANYTHING IN ITS PATH-- EVEN SPIRITS LIKE YOU!
WHITNEY, YOU CAN'T!

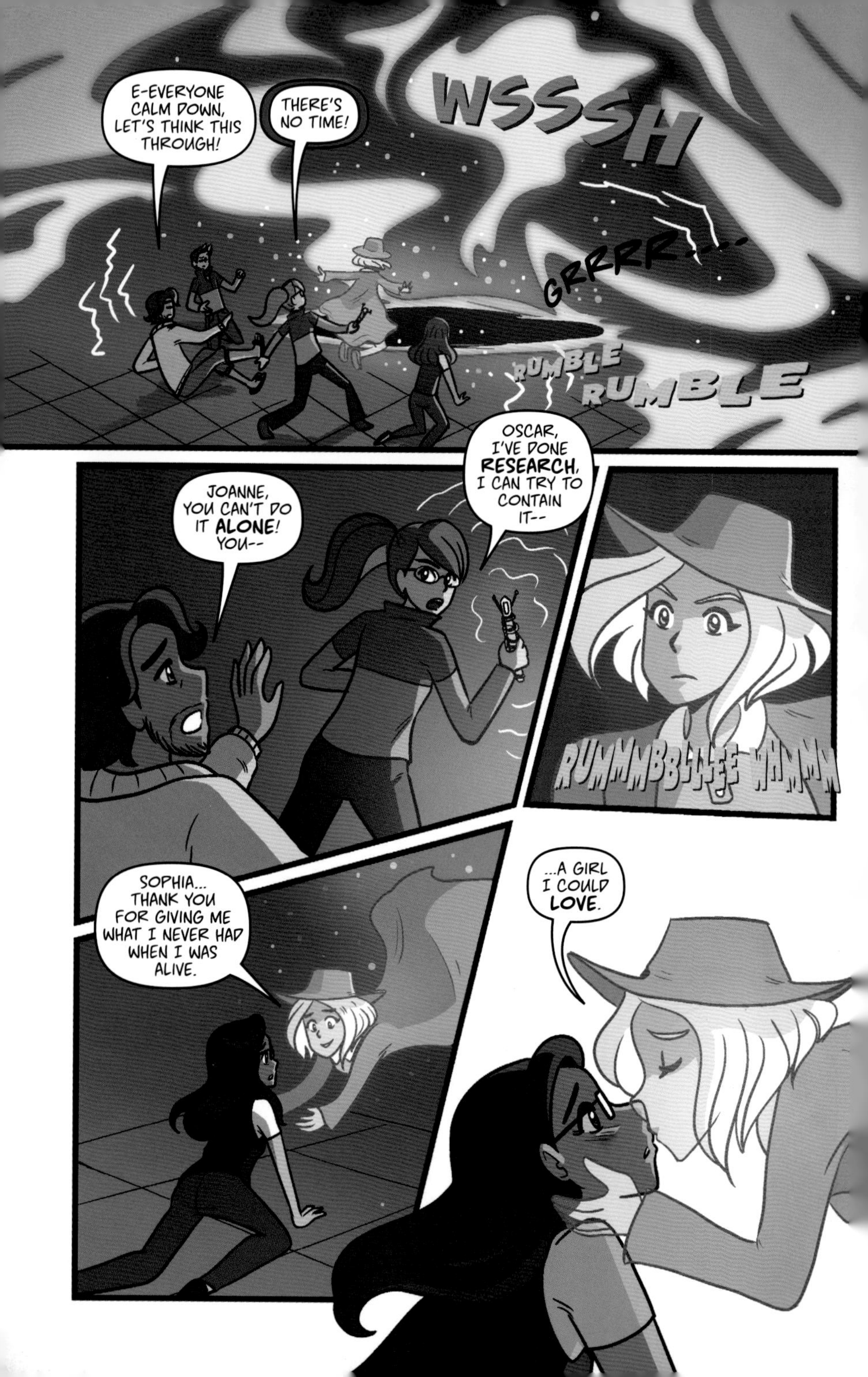
E-EVERYONE CALM DOWN, LET'S THINK THIS THROUGH!
THERE'S NO TIME!
WSSSH
GRRRR....
RUMBLE RUMBLE
JOANNE, YOU CAN'T DO IT **ALONE**! YOU--
OSCAR, I'VE DONE **RESEARCH**, I CAN TRY TO CONTAIN IT--
RUMMMBBLLEE WHMMM
SOPHIA... THANK YOU FOR GIVING ME WHAT I NEVER HAD WHEN I WAS ALIVE.
...A GIRL I COULD **LOVE**.

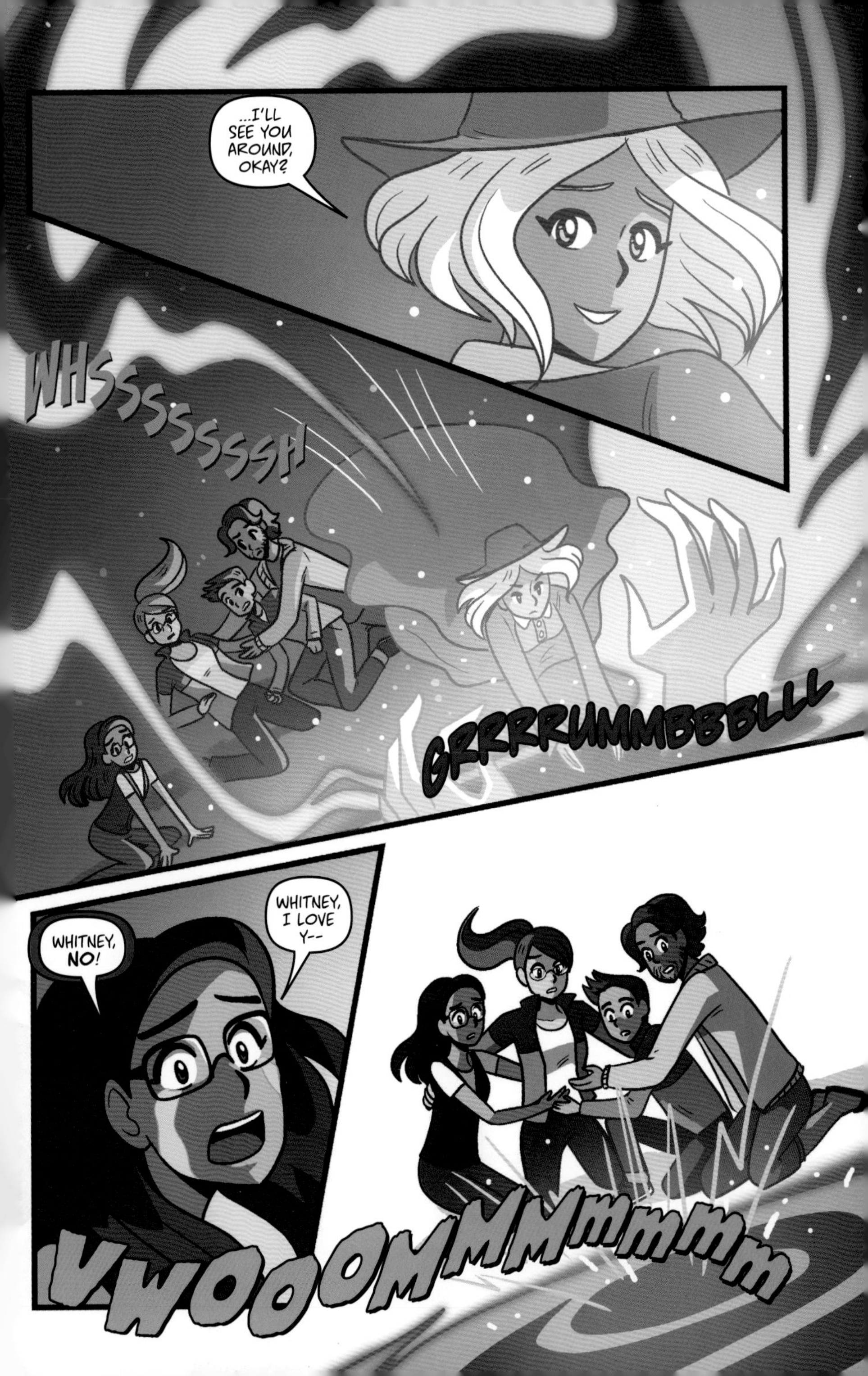

...I'LL SEE YOU AROUND, OKAY?
WHSSSSSSSSH
GRRRRUMMBBBLLL
WHITNEY, NO!
WHITNEY, I LOVE Y--
VWOOOOMMMMMMMM

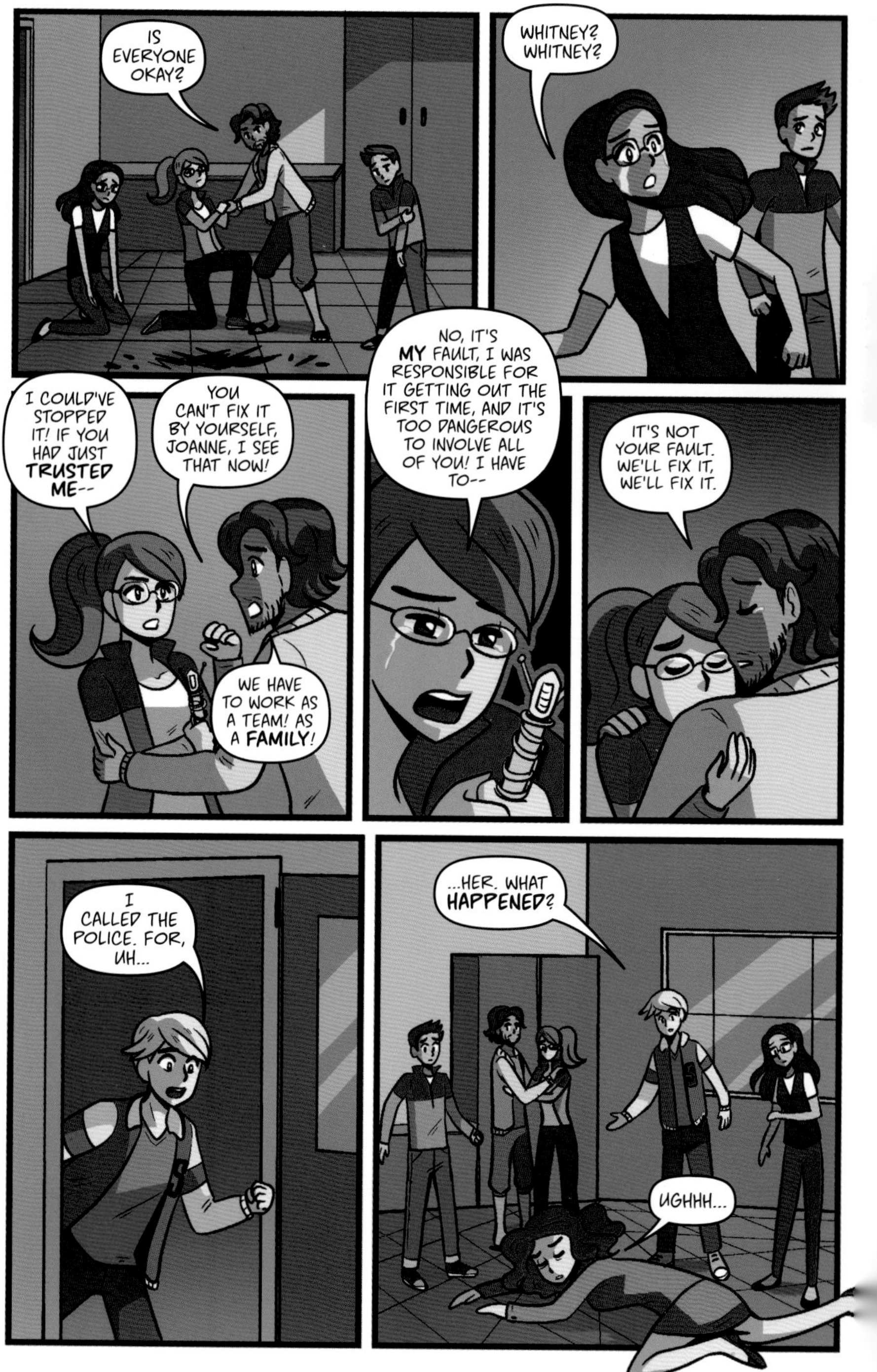
IS EVERYONE OKAY?
WHITNEY? WHITNEY?
I COULD'VE STOPPED IT! IF YOU HAD JUST **TRUSTED** **ME**--
YOU CAN'T FIX IT BY YOURSELF, JOANNE, I SEE THAT NOW!
WE HAVE TO WORK AS A TEAM! AS A **FAMILY**!
NO, IT'S **MY** FAULT, I WAS RESPONSIBLE FOR IT GETTING OUT THE FIRST TIME, AND IT'S TOO DANGEROUS TO INVOLVE ALL OF YOU! I HAVE TO--
IT'S NOT YOUR FAULT. WE'LL FIX IT, WE'LL FIX IT.
I CALLED THE POLICE. FOR, UH...
...HER. WHAT **HAPPENED**?
UGHHH...

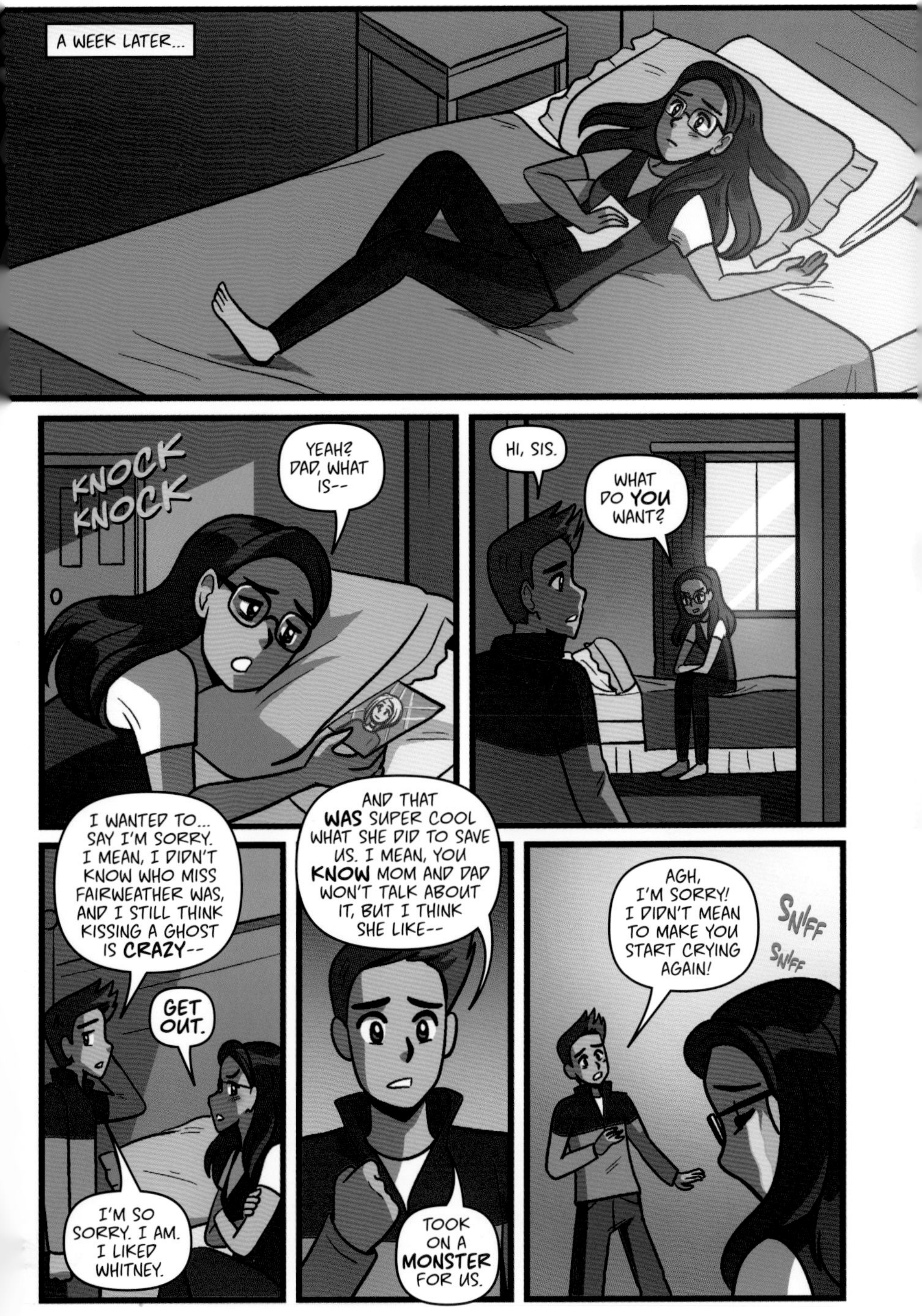
A WEEK LATER...
KNOCK KNOCK
YEAH? DAD, WHAT IS--
HI, SIS.
WHAT DO YOU WANT?
I WANTED TO... SAY I'M SORRY. I MEAN, I DIDN'T KNOW WHO MISS FAIRWEATHER WAS, AND I STILL THINK KISSING A GHOST IS CRAZY--
GET OUT.
I'M SO SORRY. I AM. I LIKED WHITNEY.
AND THAT WAS SUPER COOL WHAT SHE DID TO SAVE US. I MEAN, YOU KNOW MOM AND DAD WON'T TALK ABOUT IT, BUT I THINK SHE LIKE--
TOOK ON A MONSTER FOR US.
AGH, I'M SORRY! I DIDN'T MEAN TO MAKE YOU START CRYING AGAIN!
SNIFF
SNIFF

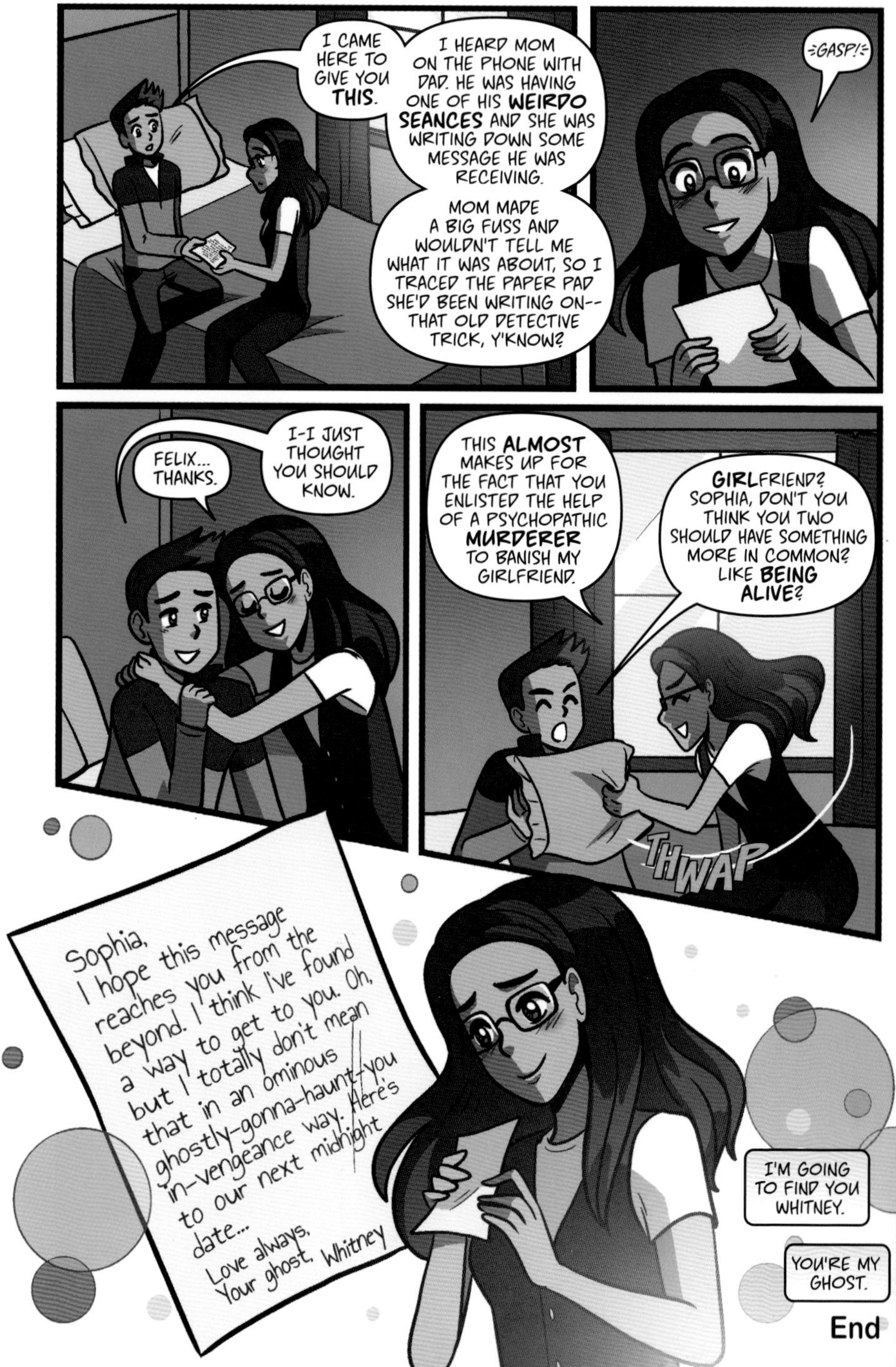
I CAME HERE TO GIVE YOU **THIS**.
I HEARD MOM ON THE PHONE WITH DAD. HE WAS HAVING ONE OF HIS **WEIRDO SEANCES** AND SHE WAS WRITING DOWN SOME MESSAGE HE WAS RECEIVING.
MOM MADE A BIG FUSS AND WOULDN'T TELL ME WHAT IT WAS ABOUT, SO I TRACED THE PAPER PAD SHE'D BEEN WRITING ON--THAT OLD DETECTIVE TRICK, Y'KNOW?
GASP!
FELIX... THANKS.
I-I JUST THOUGHT YOU SHOULD KNOW.
THIS **ALMOST** MAKES UP FOR THE FACT THAT YOU ENLISTED THE HELP OF A PSYCHOPATHIC **MURDERER** TO BANISH MY GIRLFRIEND.
GIRLFRIEND? SOPHIA, DON'T YOU THINK YOU TWO SHOULD HAVE SOMETHING MORE IN COMMON? LIKE **BEING ALIVE**?
THWAP
Sophia,
I hope this message reaches you from the beyond. I think I've found a way to get to you. Oh, but I totally don't mean that in an ominous ghostly-gonna-haunt-you in-vengeance way. Here's to our next midnight date...
Love always,
Your ghost, Whitney
I'M GOING TO FIND YOU WHITNEY.
YOU'RE MY GHOST.
End

charmz chat

My first crush was in Middle School, I think. I was about twelve and before then, I hadn't really thought about that kind of thing at all. I was a lot more interested in reading, drawing, watching movies and writing little stories.

Of course, my first crush wasn't on a real person, it was on a movie character. I would get butterflies thinking about them and wondered what it would be like to get to know them. I knew they were imaginary, of course, but it was still fun to wonder. Plus it was safer than a real person, who might not like me back. I was pretty shy back then.

As I got older I got braver about being myself and telling people I cared about that I care about them. Sure, sometimes it didn't work out. But I've never regretted being honest about my feelings or telling people what they mean to me.

One of the things I love most about all the Charmz books is that our characters are willing to put themselves out there and, even though they might get hurt, they experience a lot of joy and sweetness and love as well. Like when the heroine in CHLOE meets a new boy on a class trip and has to tell him they're just friends. Or when Crimson in STITCHED realizes she's hurting people she's caring about and has to make amends. Whether it's the high adventure of SCARLET ROSE or the mystery in GFFs: GHOST FRIENDS FOREVER, our girls never give up. Even when they're nervous or scared, these characters learn a lot about themselves and try to be the best friends and people they can. They make mistakes, like everyone does, but they learn from that and grow.

Life can be pretty weird and complicated sometimes, but we're always better off being ourselves. Doing the right thing can be hard, but when we do, we make a little bit of a difference in the world. We make things better for the people we care about and that often matters more than we know.

I hope you're all enjoying the Charmz books as much as we are making them. Never stop being yourselves!

-Mariah

STAY IN TOUCH!

EMAIL: mariah@papercutz.com
WEB: papercutz.com
INSTAGRAM: @papercutzgn
TWITTER: @papercutzgn
FACEBOOK: PAPERCUTZGRAPHICNOVELS
FAN MAIL: Papercutz, 160 Broadway, Suite 700,
             East Wing, New York, NY 10038

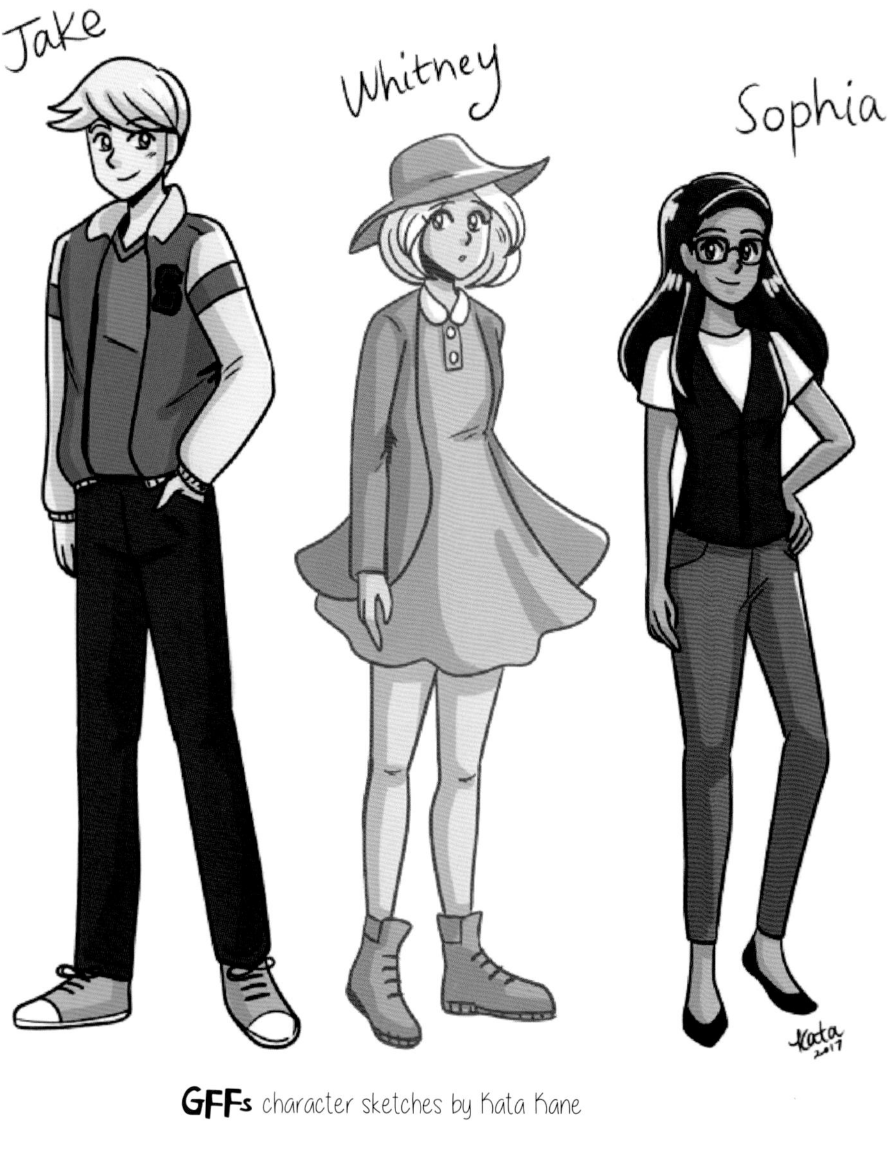
Jake
Whitney
Sophia
Kata
2017

GFFs character sketches by Kata Kane

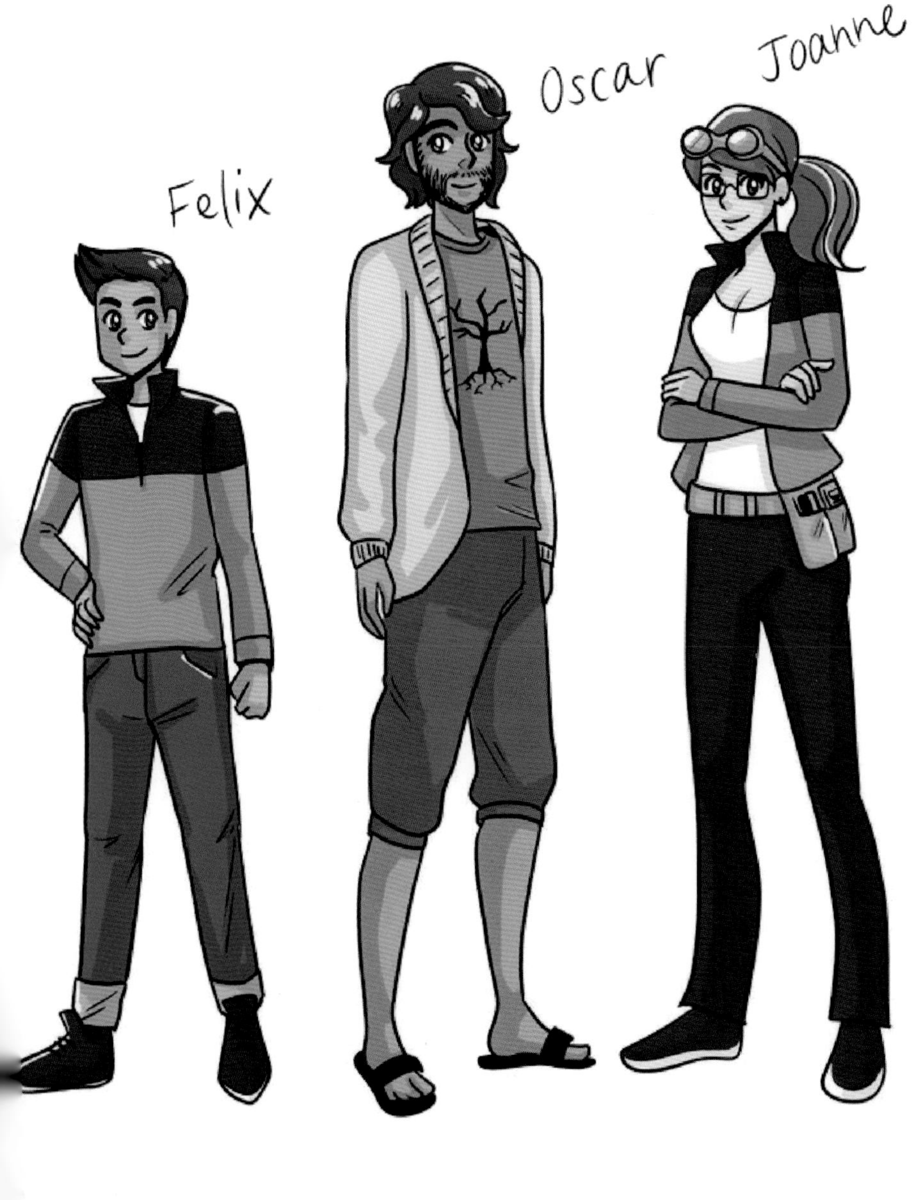
Felix
Oscar
Joanne

Enjoy this preview of STITCHED #1
"The First Day Of The Rest Of Her Life," another Charmz title!

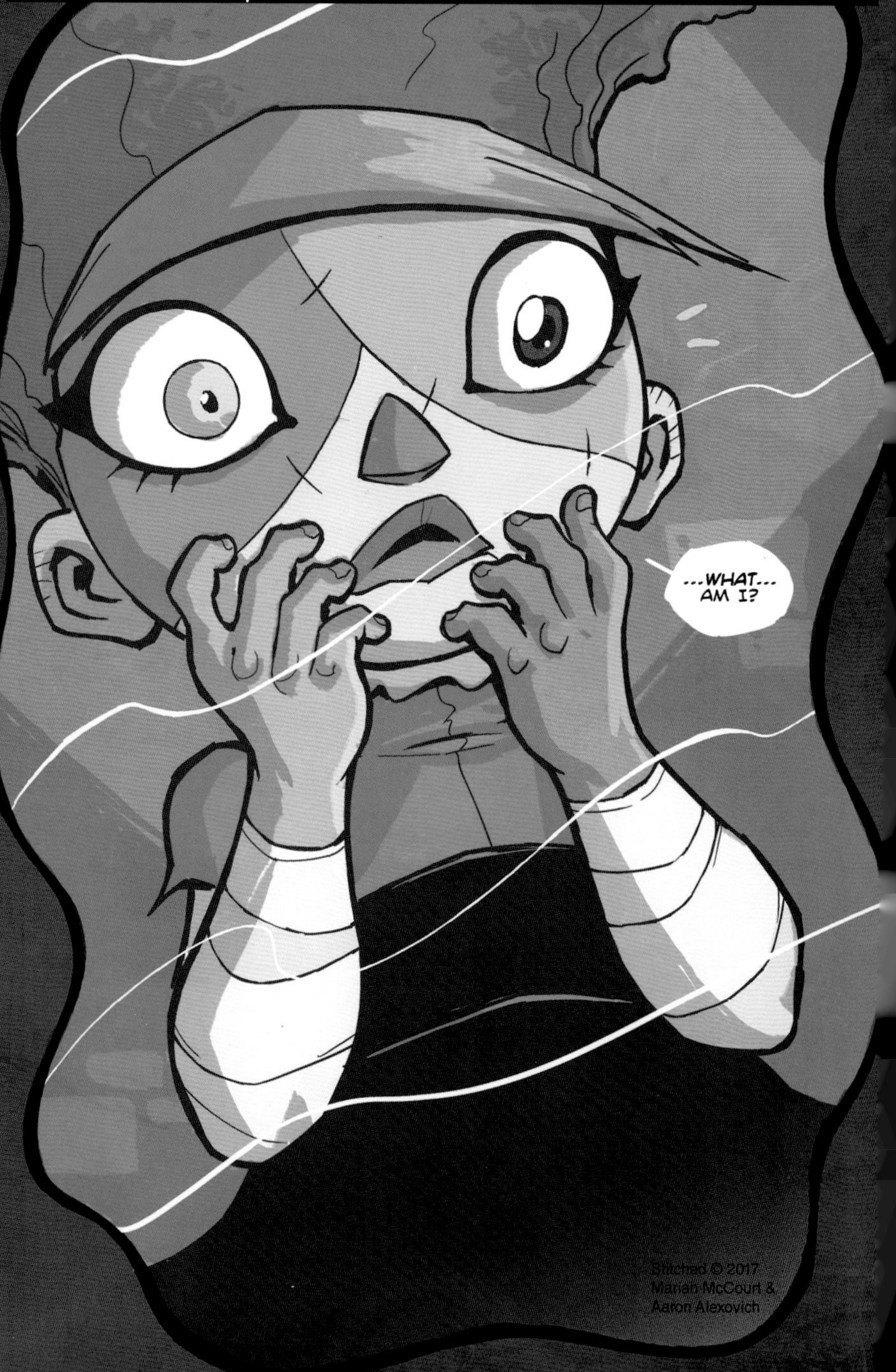

...WHAT... AM I?

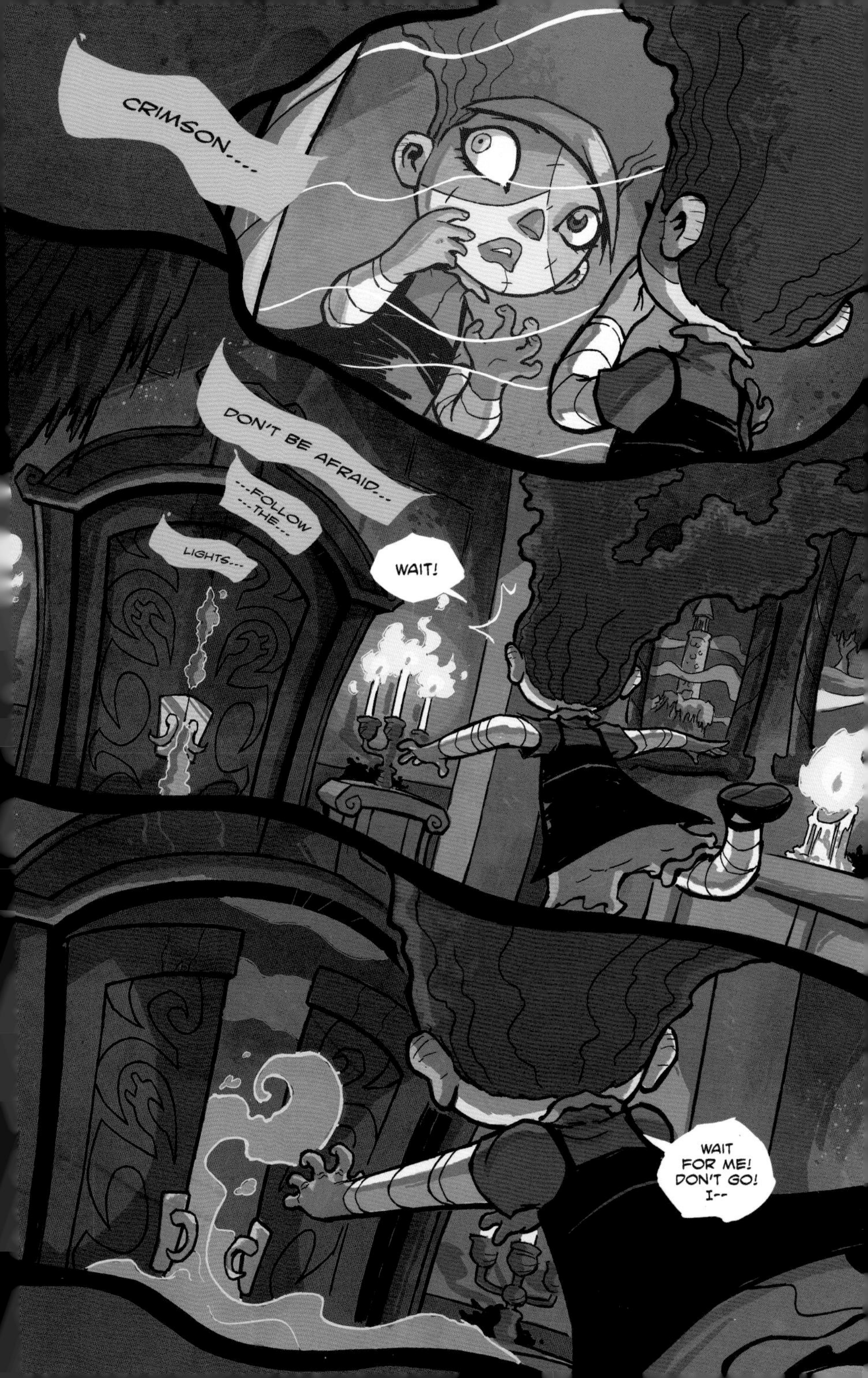
CRIMSON....
DON'T BE AFRAID...
...FOLLOW ...THE...
LIGHTS...
WAIT!
WAIT FOR ME! DON'T GO! I--

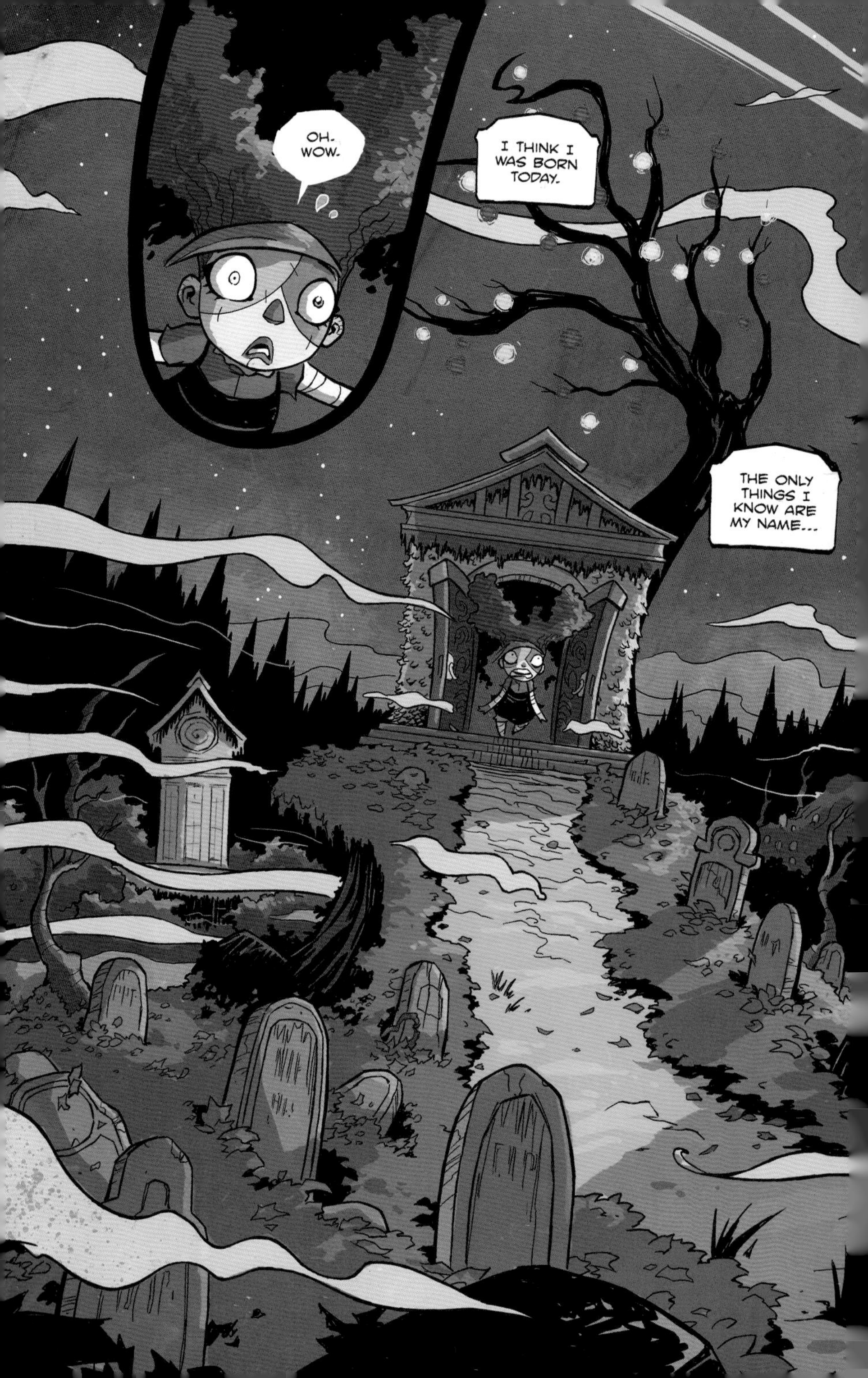
OH. WOW.
I THINK I WAS BORN TODAY.
THE ONLY THINGS I KNOW ARE MY NAME...

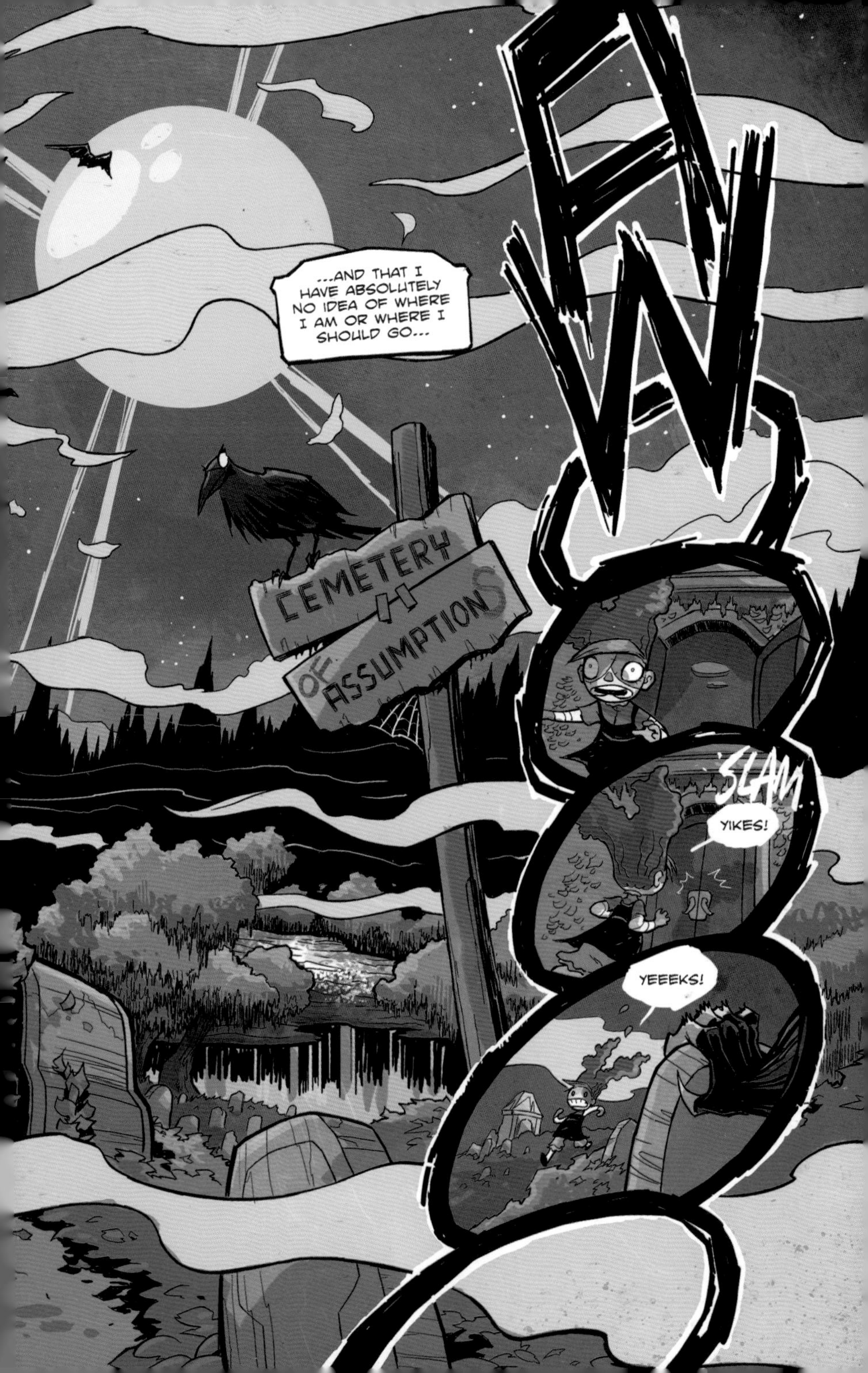
...AND THAT I HAVE ABSOLUTELY NO IDEA OF WHERE I AM OR WHERE I SHOULD GO...
CEMETERY OF ASSUMPTIONS
FWOOSH
SLAM
YIKES!
YEEEKS!

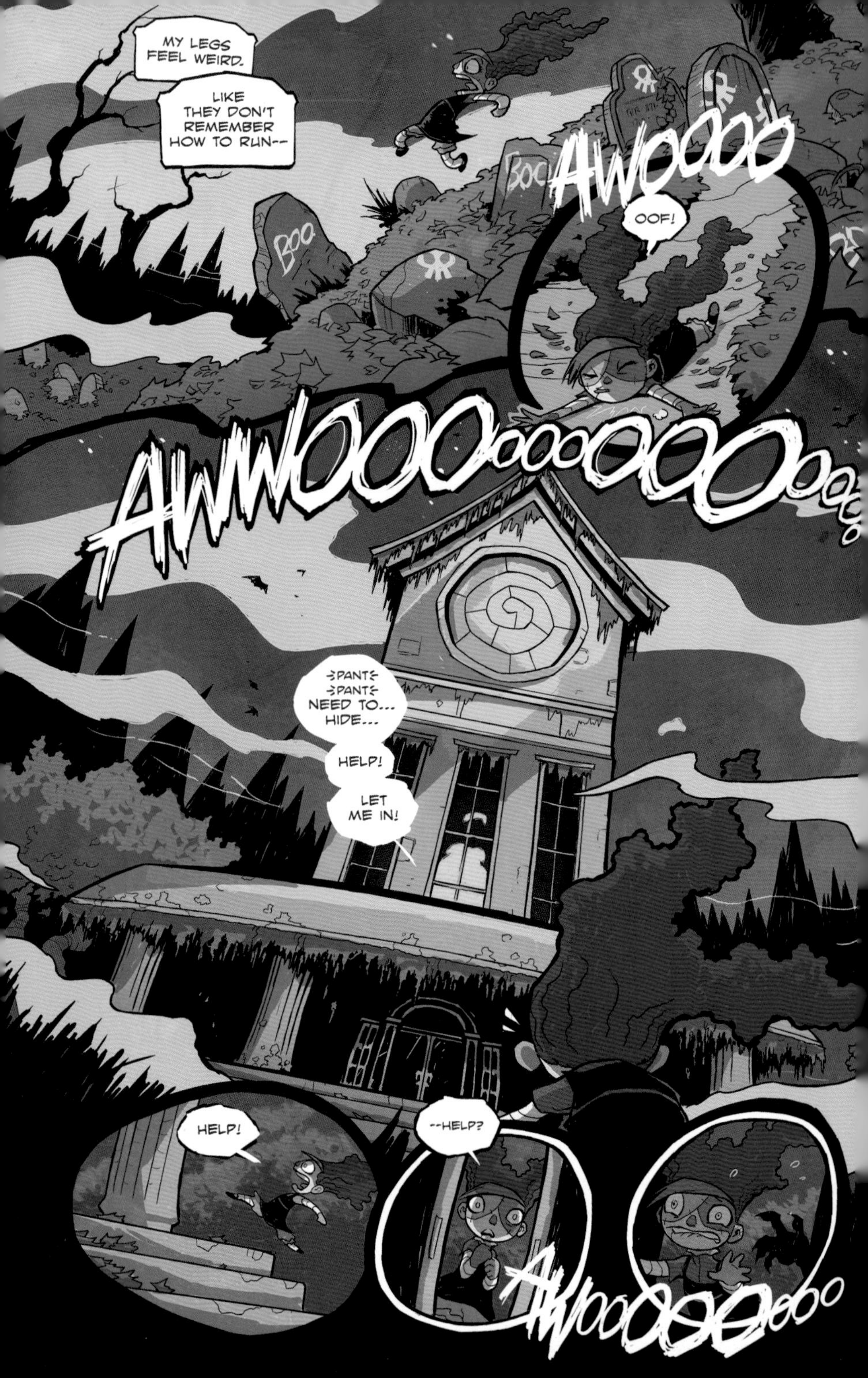
MY LEGS FEEL WEIRD.
LIKE THEY DON'T REMEMBER HOW TO RUN--
AWOOOO
OOF!
AWWOOOooooOOOOooo
≠PANT≠ ≠PANT≠ NEED TO... HIDE...
HELP!
LET ME IN!
HELP!
--HELP?
AWOOOOOOoo

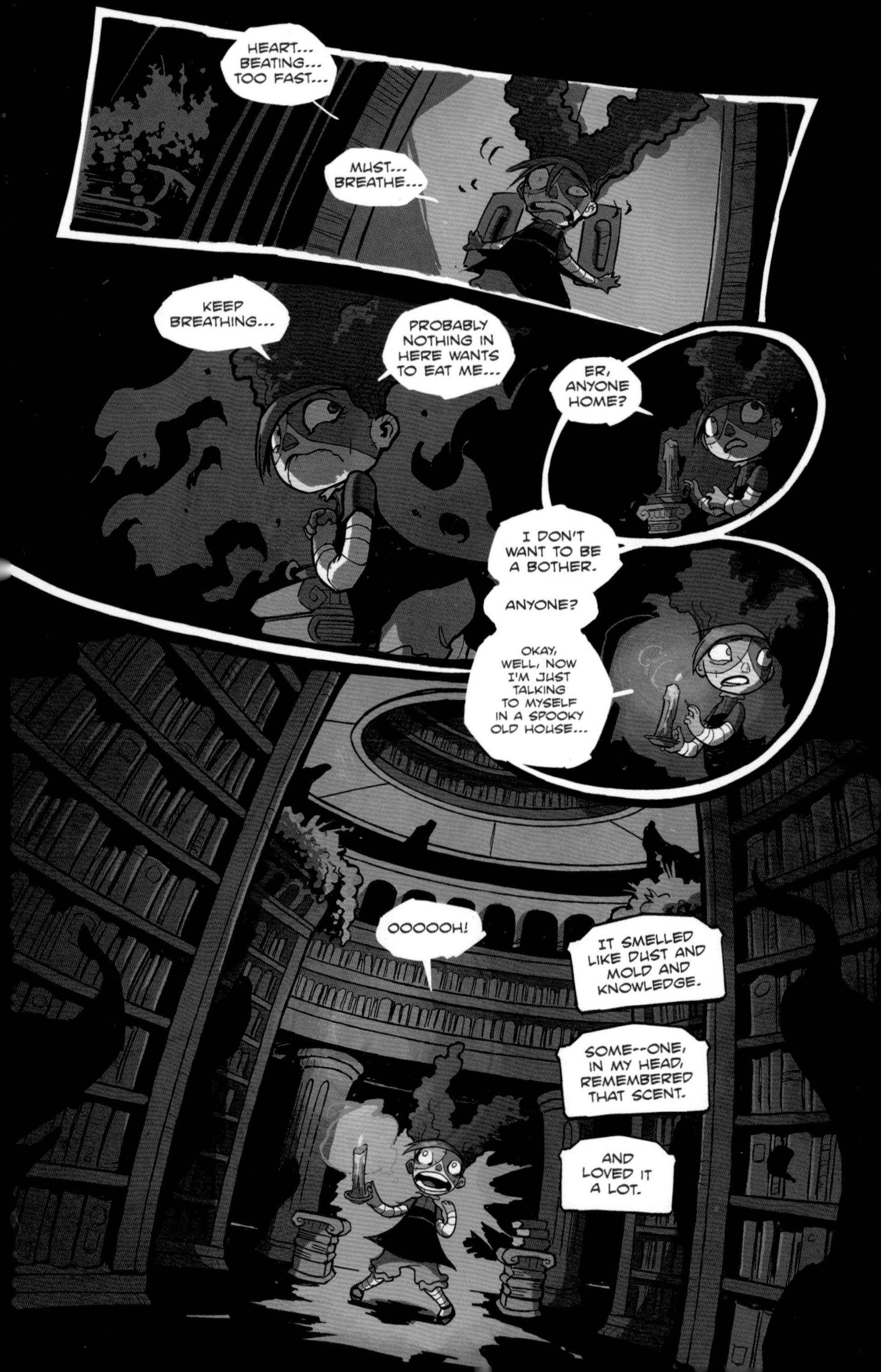
HEART... BEATING... TOO FAST...
MUST... BREATHE...
KEEP BREATHING...
PROBABLY NOTHING IN HERE WANTS TO EAT ME...
ER, ANYONE HOME?
I DON'T WANT TO BE A BOTHER.
ANYONE?
OKAY, WELL, NOW I'M JUST TALKING TO MYSELF IN A SPOOKY OLD HOUSE...
OOOOOH!
IT SMELLED LIKE DUST AND MOLD AND KNOWLEDGE.
SOME--ONE, IN MY HEAD, REMEMBERED THAT SCENT.
AND LOVED IT A LOT.

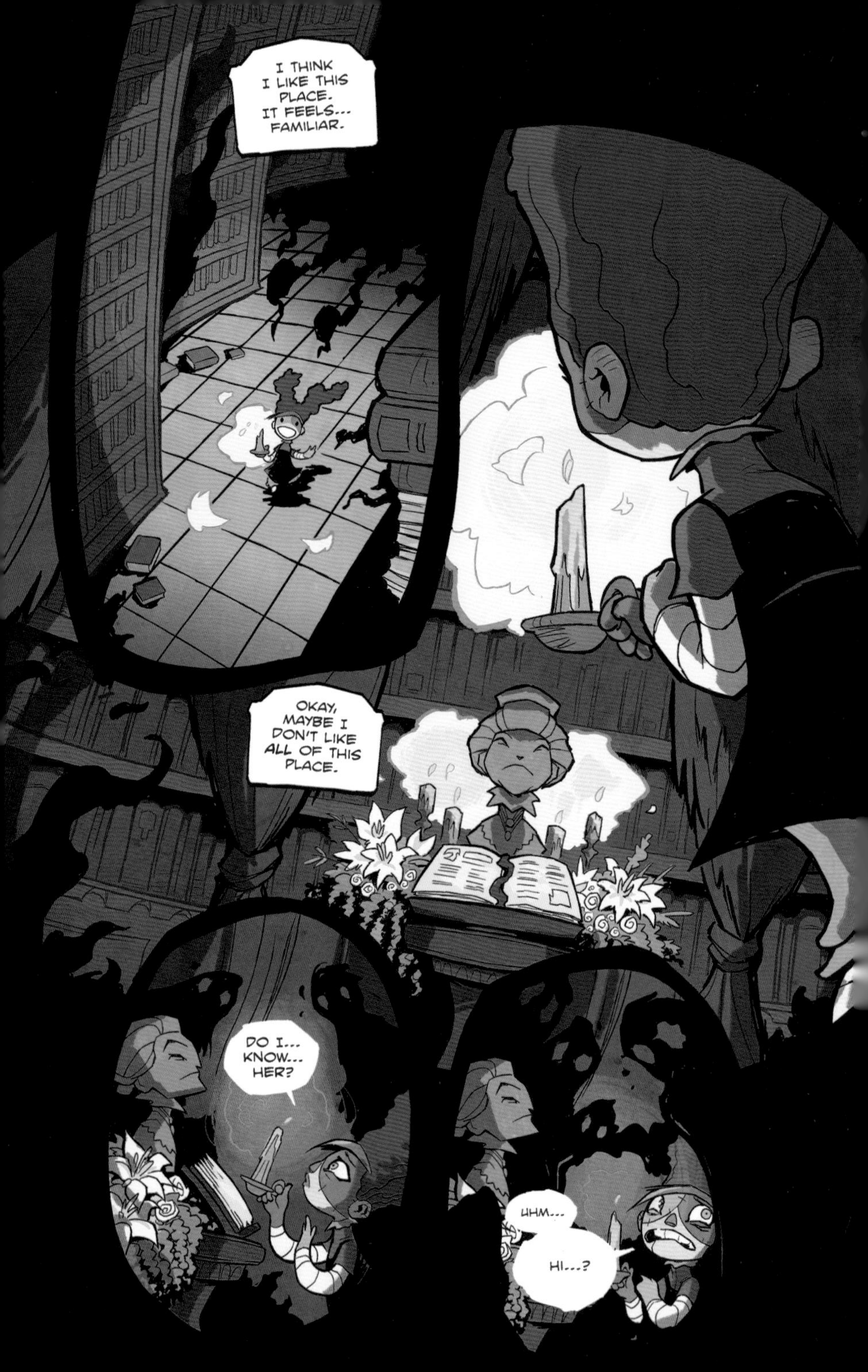
I THINK I LIKE THIS PLACE. IT FEELS... FAMILIAR.
OKAY, MAYBE I DON'T LIKE ALL OF THIS PLACE.
DO I... KNOW... HER?
UHM...
HI...?

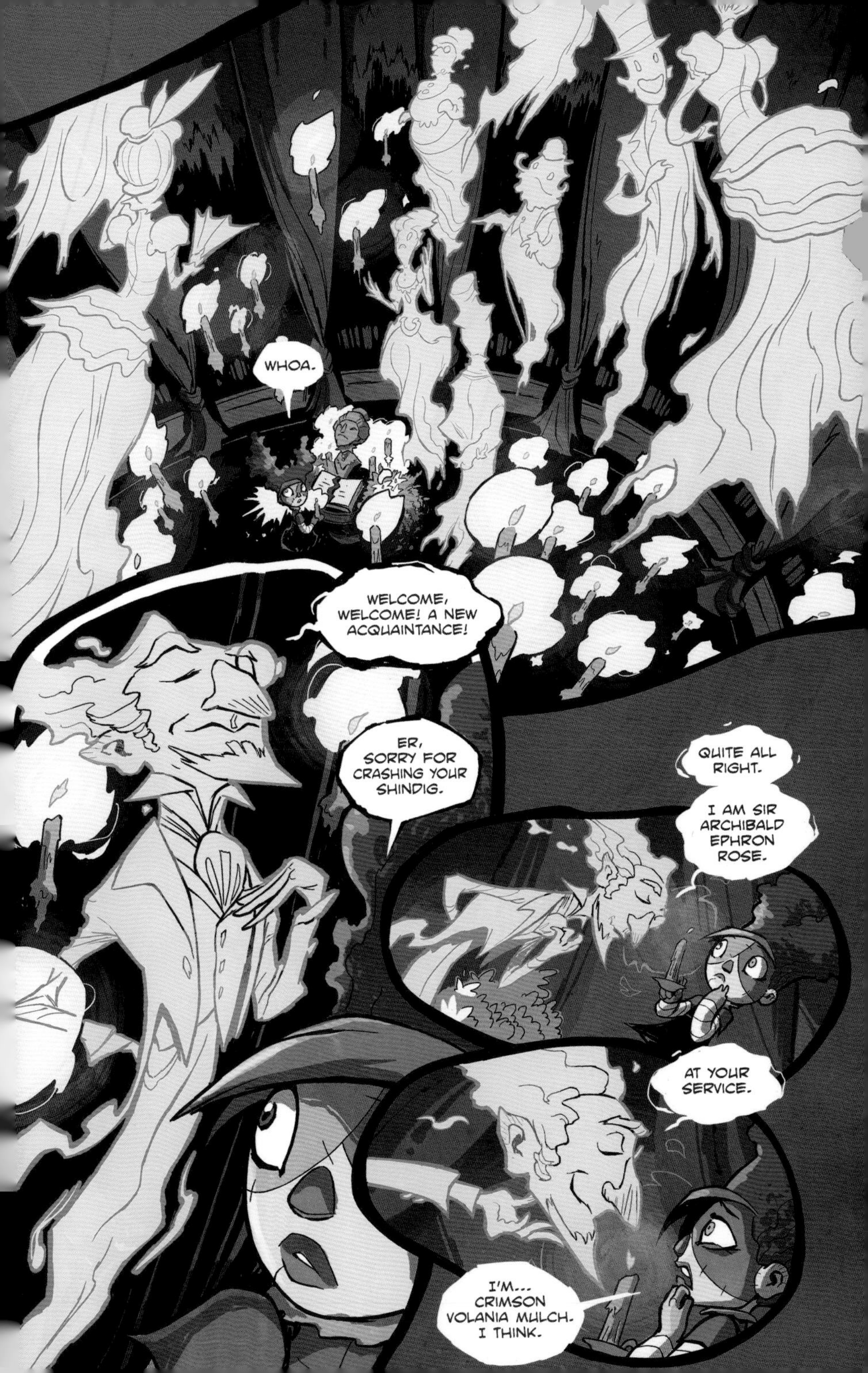
WHOA.
WELCOME, WELCOME! A NEW ACQUAINTANCE!
ER, SORRY FOR CRASHING YOUR SHINDIG.
QUITE ALL RIGHT.
I AM SIR ARCHIBALD EPHRON ROSE.
AT YOUR SERVICE.
I'M... CRIMSON VOLANIA MULCH. I THINK.

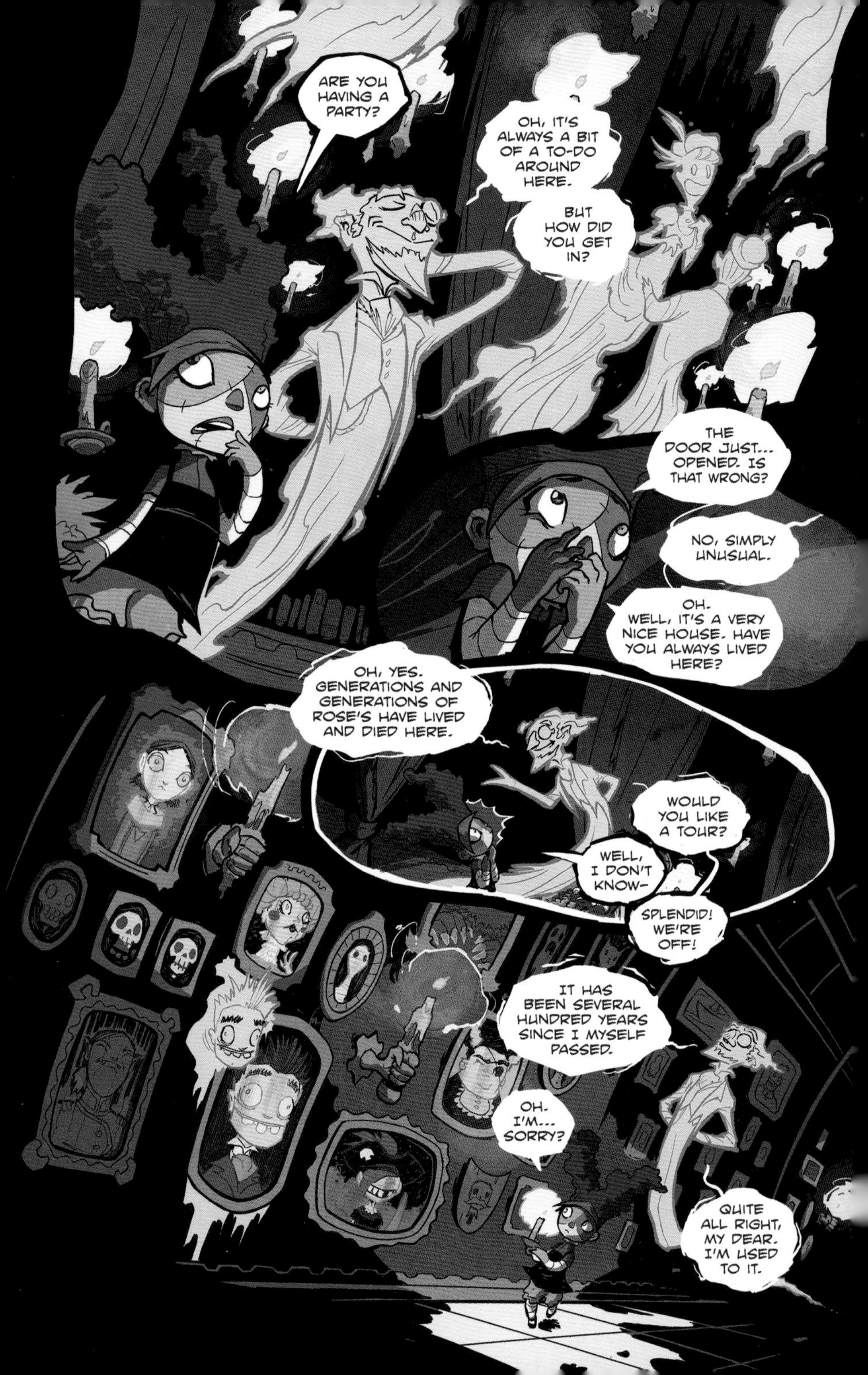
ARE YOU HAVING A PARTY?
OH, IT'S ALWAYS A BIT OF A TO-DO AROUND HERE.
BUT HOW DID YOU GET IN?
THE DOOR JUST... OPENED. IS THAT WRONG?
NO, SIMPLY UNUSUAL.
OH. WELL, IT'S A VERY NICE HOUSE. HAVE YOU ALWAYS LIVED HERE?
OH, YES. GENERATIONS AND GENERATIONS OF ROSE'S HAVE LIVED AND DIED HERE.
WOULD YOU LIKE A TOUR?
WELL, I DON'T KNOW-
SPLENDID! WE'RE OFF!
IT HAS BEEN SEVERAL HUNDRED YEARS SINCE I MYSELF PASSED.
OH. I'M... SORRY?
QUITE ALL RIGHT, MY DEAR. I'M USED TO IT.

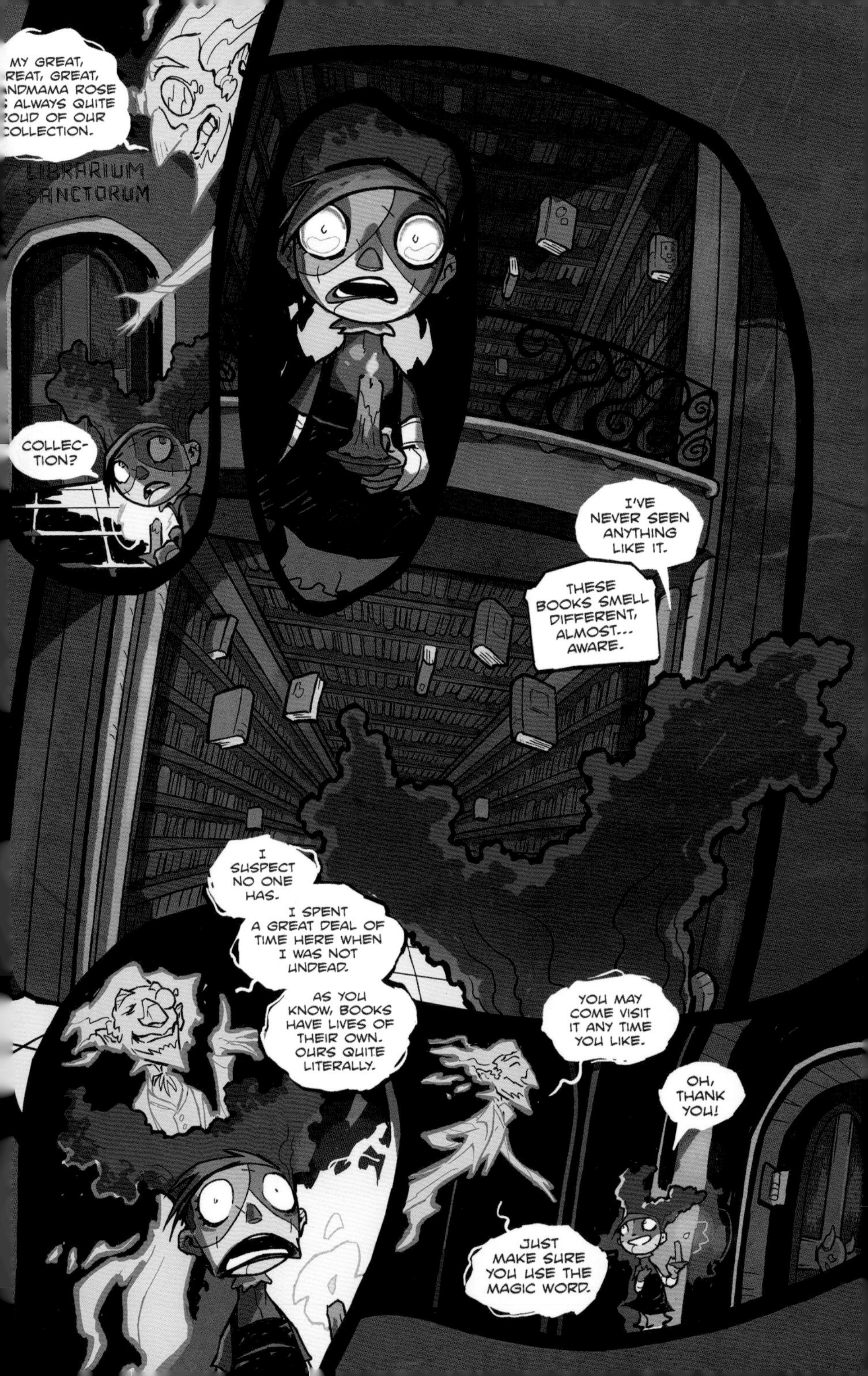
MY GREAT, REAT, GREAT, ANDMAMA ROSE S ALWAYS QUITE ROUD OF OUR COLLECTION.
LIBRARIUM SANCTORUM
COLLEC-TION?
I'VE NEVER SEEN ANYTHING LIKE IT.
THESE BOOKS SMELL DIFFERENT, ALMOST... AWARE.
I SUSPECT NO ONE HAS.
I SPENT A GREAT DEAL OF TIME HERE WHEN I WAS NOT UNDEAD.
AS YOU KNOW, BOOKS HAVE LIVES OF THEIR OWN. OURS QUITE LITERALLY.
YOU MAY COME VISIT IT ANY TIME YOU LIKE.
OH, THANK YOU!
JUST MAKE SURE YOU USE THE MAGIC WORD.

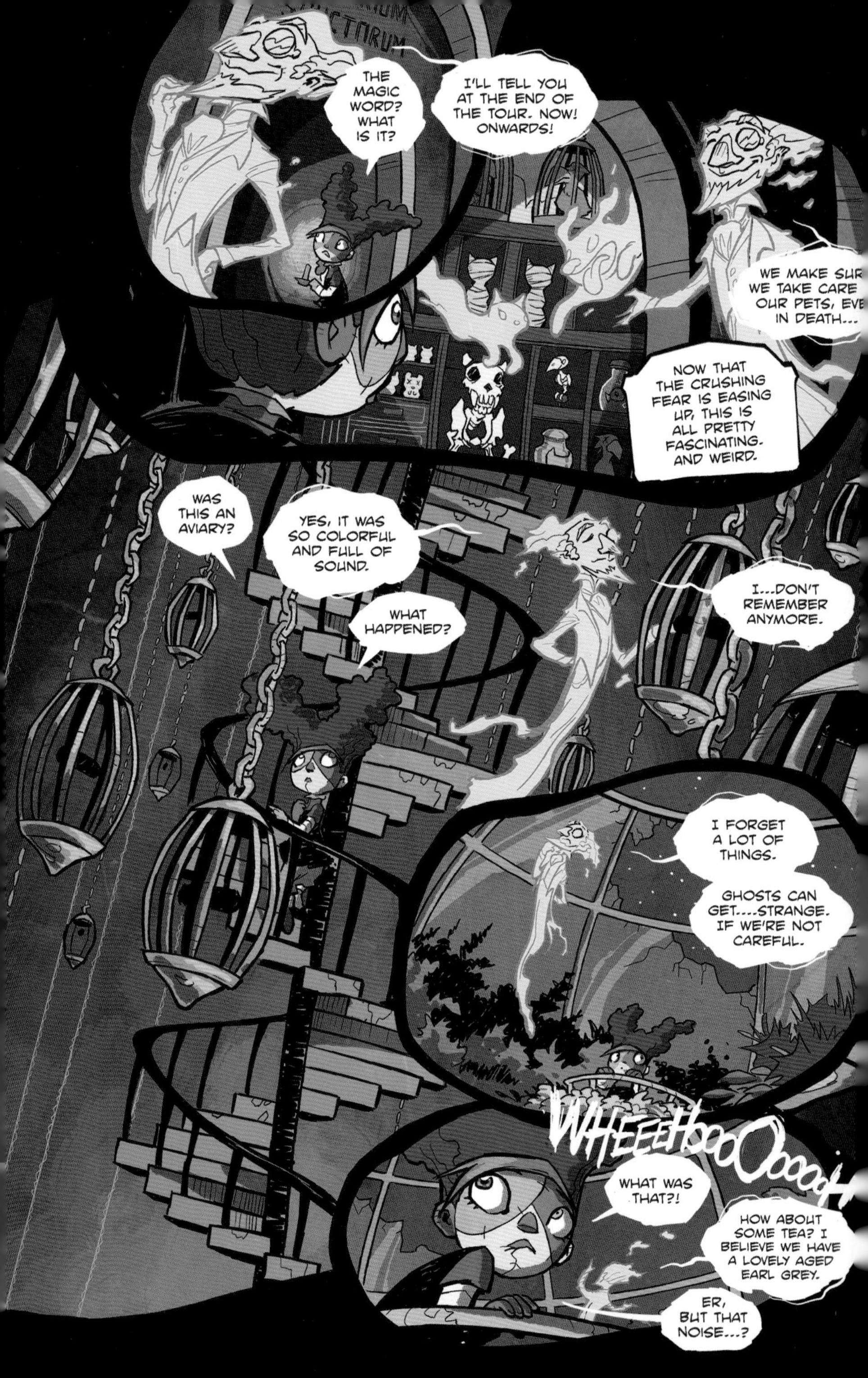
THE MAGIC WORD? WHAT IS IT?
I'LL TELL YOU AT THE END OF THE TOUR. NOW! ONWARDS!
WE MAKE SUR WE TAKE CARE OUR PETS, EVE IN DEATH...
NOW THAT THE CRUSHING FEAR IS EASING UP, THIS IS ALL PRETTY FASCINATING. AND WEIRD.
WAS THIS AN AVIARY?
YES, IT WAS SO COLORFUL AND FULL OF SOUND.
WHAT HAPPENED?
I...DON'T REMEMBER ANYMORE.
I FORGET A LOT OF THINGS.
GHOSTS CAN GET....STRANGE. IF WE'RE NOT CAREFUL.
WHEEEHoooOoooh
WHAT WAS THAT?!
HOW ABOUT SOME TEA? I BELIEVE WE HAVE A LOVELY AGED EARL GREY.
ER, BUT THAT NOISE...?

Don't miss STITCHED #1
"The First Day Of The Rest Of Her Life,"
available now!

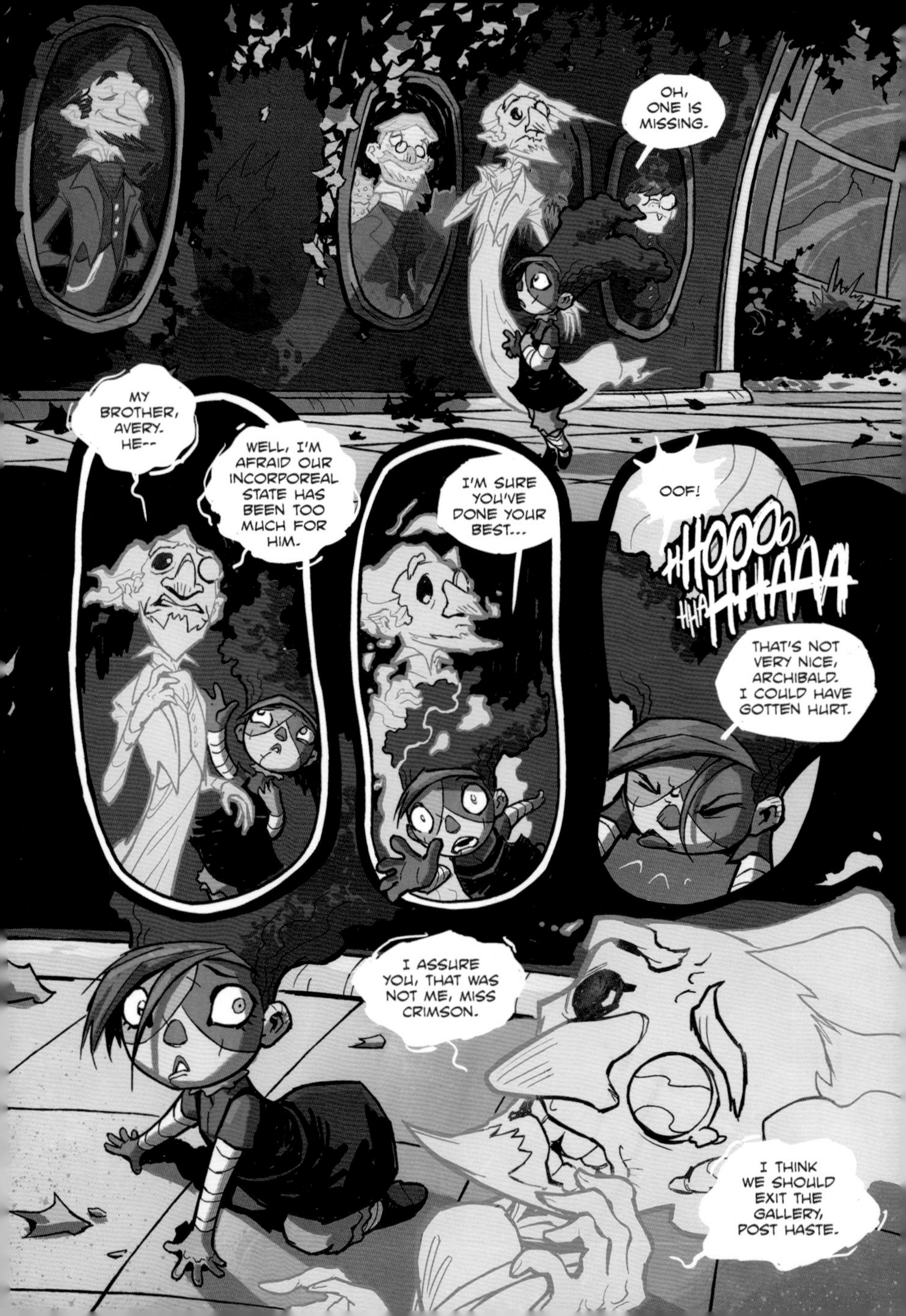
OH, ONE IS MISSING.
MY BROTHER, AVERY. HE--
WELL, I'M AFRAID OUR INCORPOREAL STATE HAS BEEN TOO MUCH FOR HIM.
I'M SURE YOU'VE DONE YOUR BEST...
OOF!
HHOOO HHAHHAAA
THAT'S NOT VERY NICE, ARCHIBALD. I COULD HAVE GOTTEN HURT.
I ASSURE YOU, THAT WAS NOT ME, MISS CRIMSON.
I THINK WE SHOULD EXIT THE GALLERY, POST HASTE.

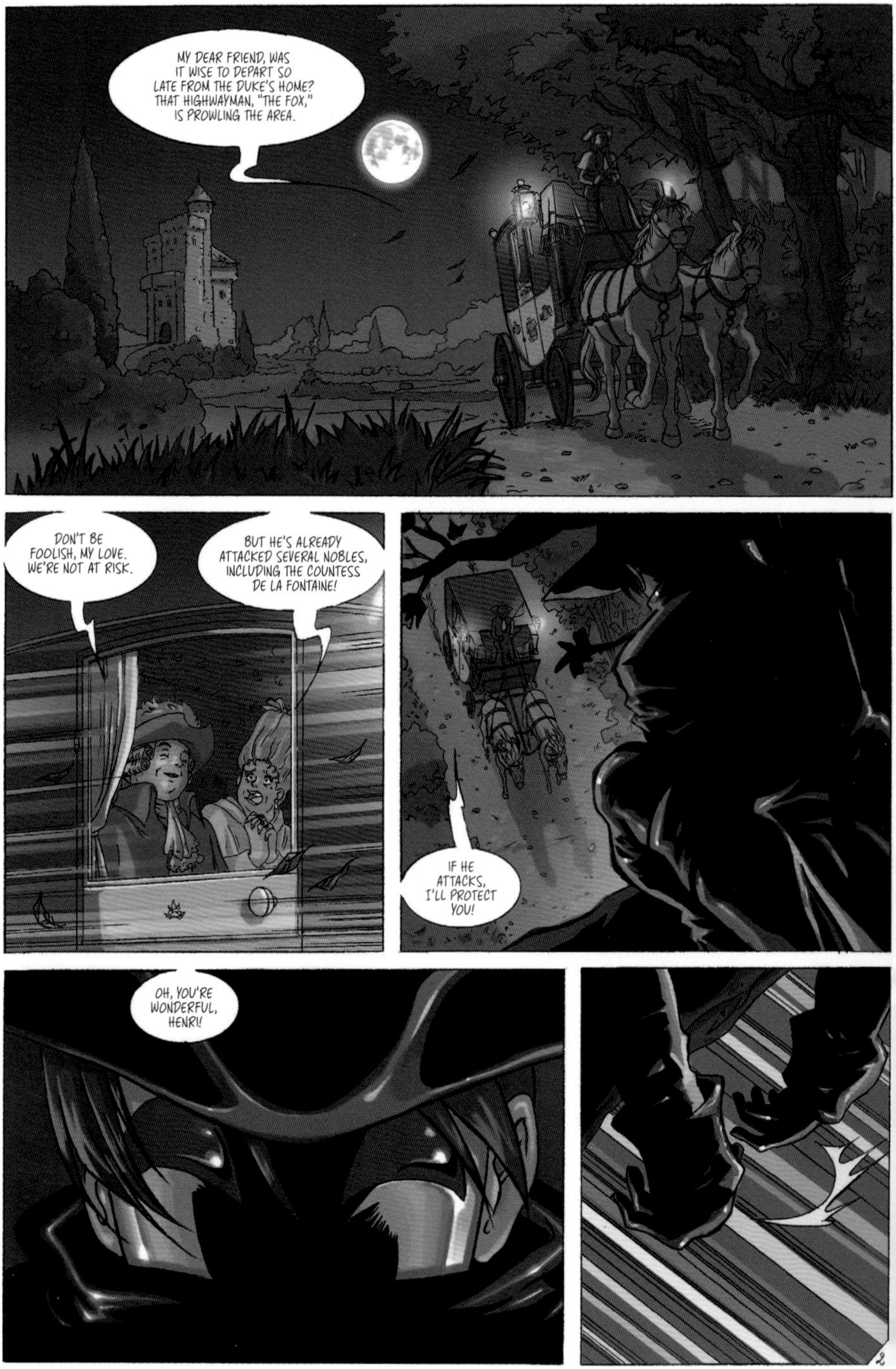

MY DEAR FRIEND, WAS IT WISE TO DEPART SO LATE FROM THE DUKE'S HOME? THAT HIGHWAYMAN, "THE FOX," IS PROWLING THE AREA.
DON'T BE FOOLISH, MY LOVE. WE'RE NOT AT RISK.
BUT HE'S ALREADY ATTACKED SEVERAL NOBLES, INCLUDING THE COUNTESS DE LA FONTAINE!
IF HE ATTACKS, I'LL PROTECT YOU!
OH, YOU'RE WONDERFUL, HENRI!

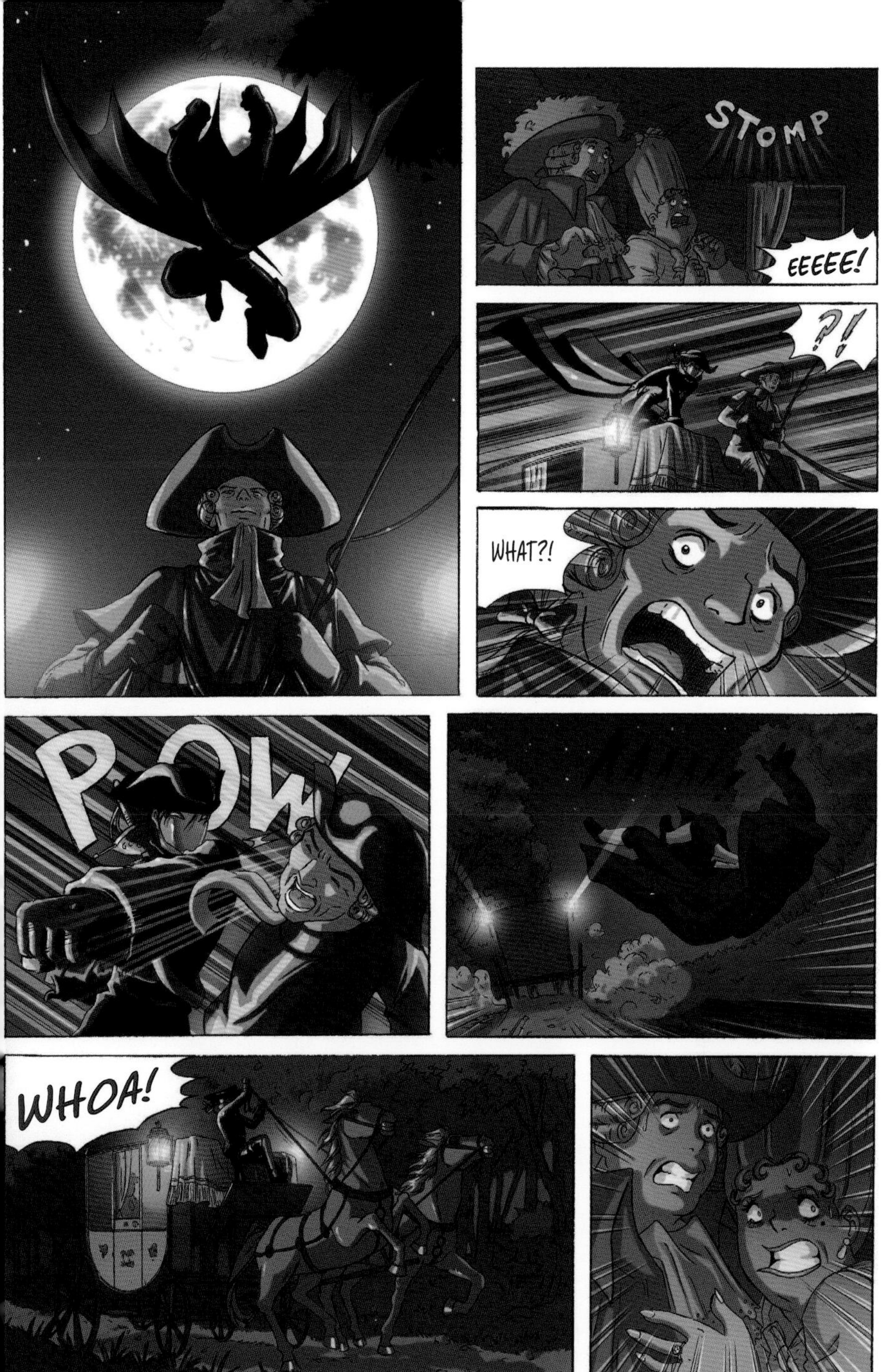
STOMP
EEEEE!
?!
WHAT?!
POW
WHOA!
3

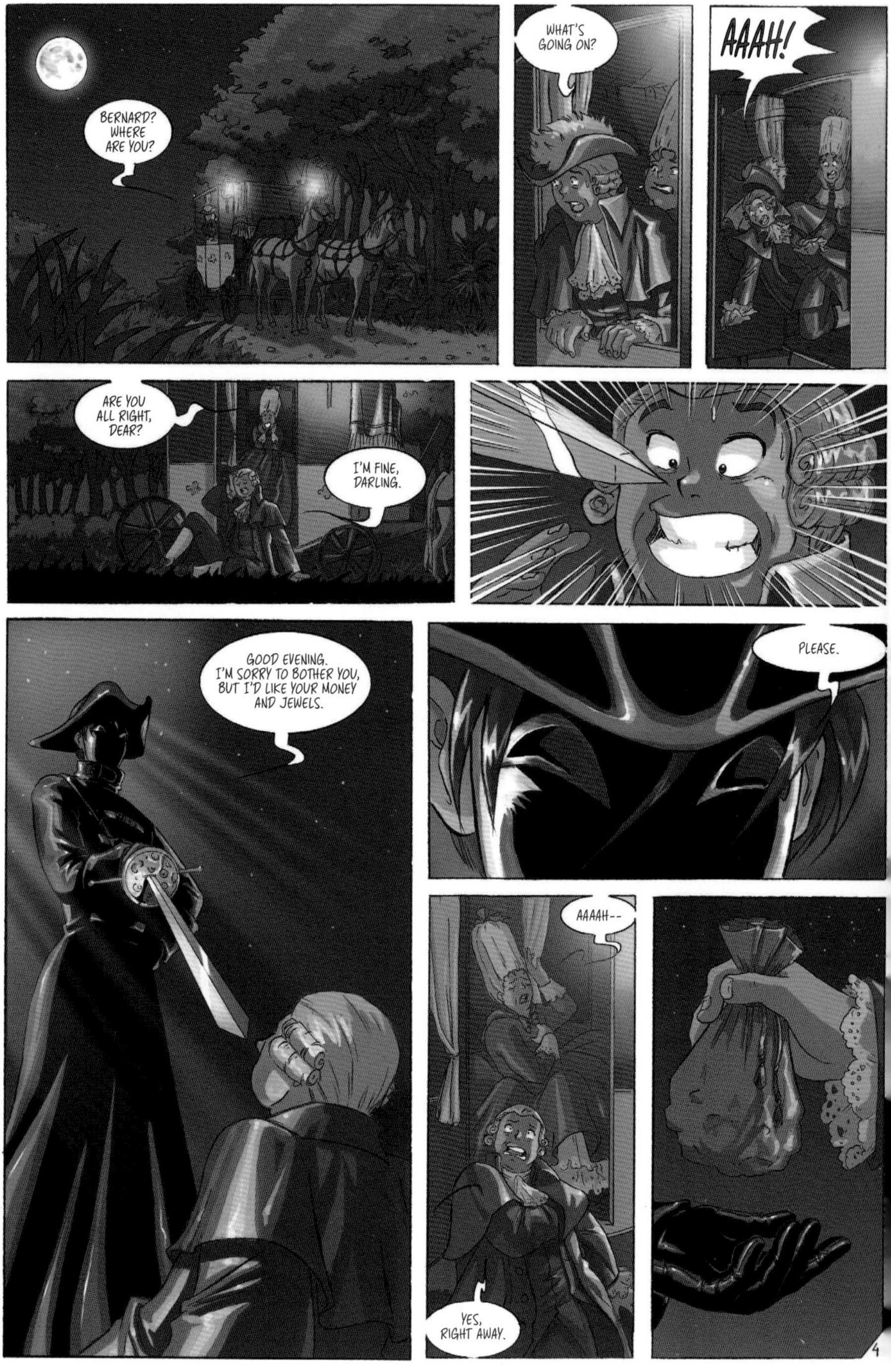
BERNARD? WHERE ARE YOU?
WHAT'S GOING ON?
AAAH!
ARE YOU ALL RIGHT, DEAR?
I'M FINE, DARLING.
GOOD EVENING. I'M SORRY TO BOTHER YOU, BUT I'D LIKE YOUR MONEY AND JEWELS.
PLEASE.
AAAAH--
YES, RIGHT AWAY.
4

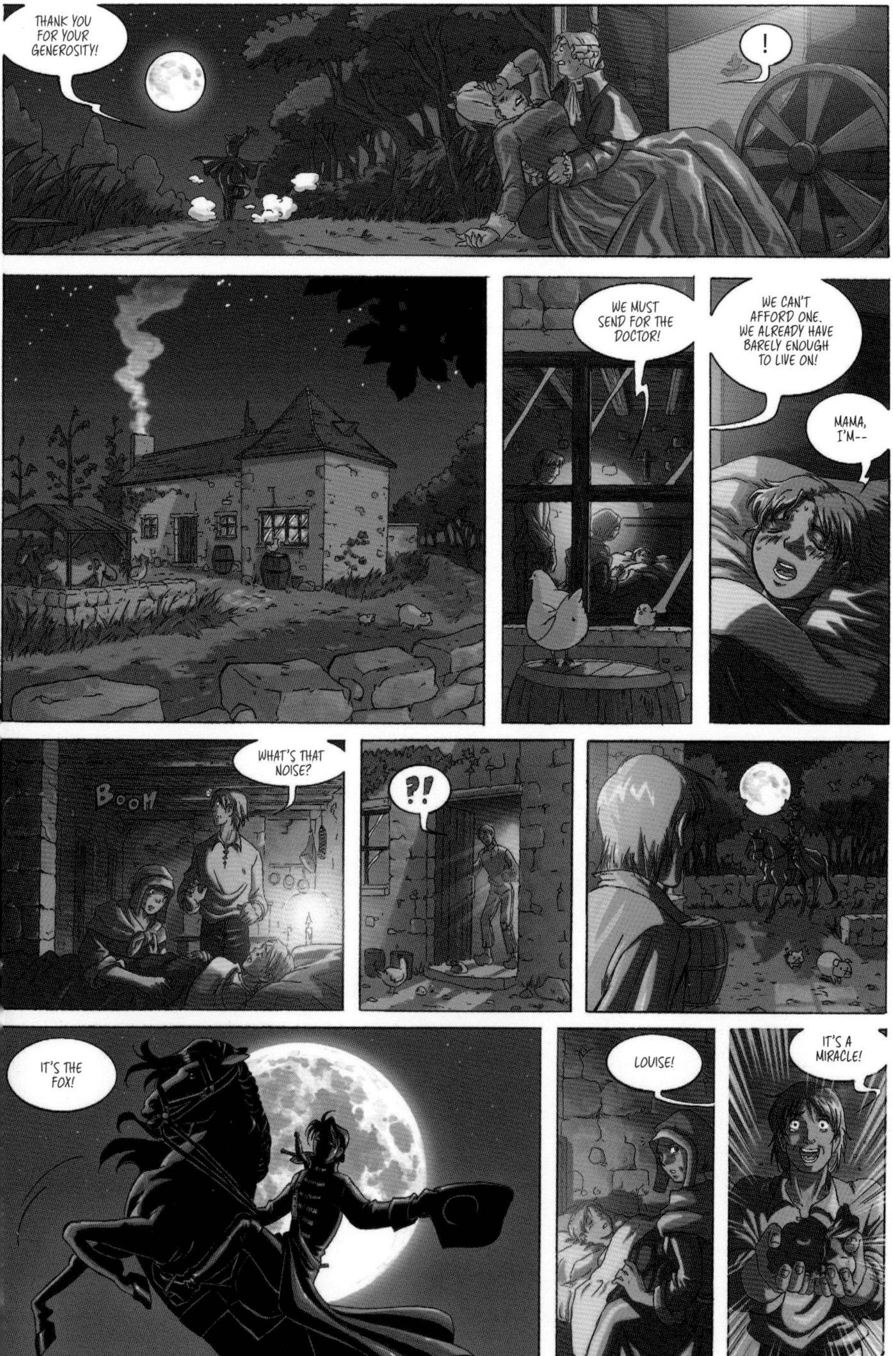
THANK YOU FOR YOUR GENEROSITY!
!
WE MUST SEND FOR THE DOCTOR!
WE CAN'T AFFORD ONE. WE ALREADY HAVE BARELY ENOUGH TO LIVE ON!
MAMA, I'M--
BOOM
WHAT'S THAT NOISE?
?!
IT'S THE FOX!
LOUISE!
IT'S A MIRACLE!
5

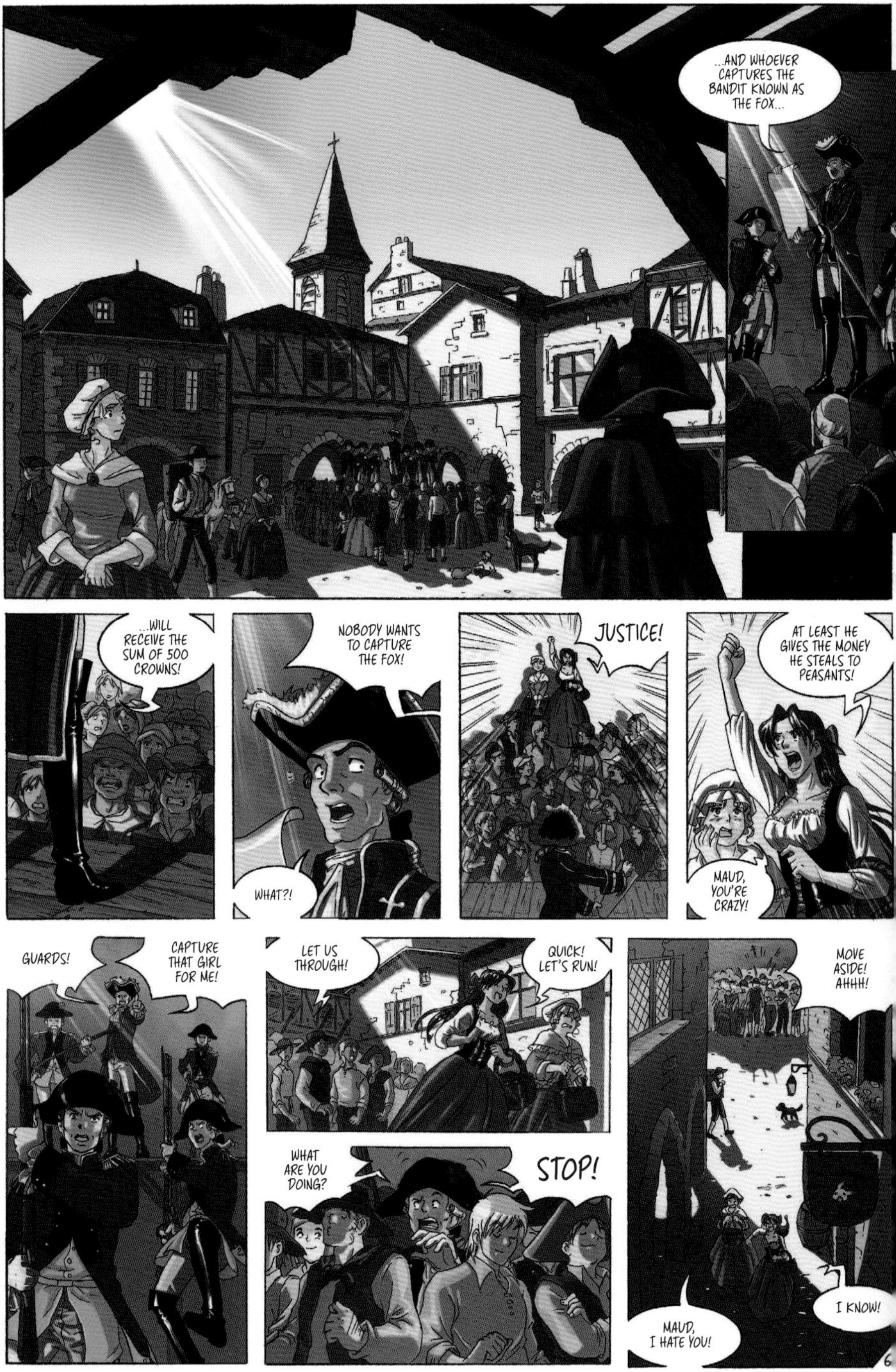
...AND WHOEVER CAPTURES THE BANDIT KNOWN AS THE FOX...
...WILL RECEIVE THE SUM OF 500 CROWNS!
NOBODY WANTS TO CAPTURE THE FOX!
WHAT?!
JUSTICE!
AT LEAST HE GIVES THE MONEY HE STEALS TO PEASANTS!
MAUD, YOU'RE CRAZY!
GUARDS!
CAPTURE THAT GIRL FOR ME!
LET US THROUGH!
QUICK! LET'S RUN!
WHAT ARE YOU DOING?
STOP!
MOVE ASIDE! AHHH!
MAUD, I HATE YOU!
I KNOW!
6

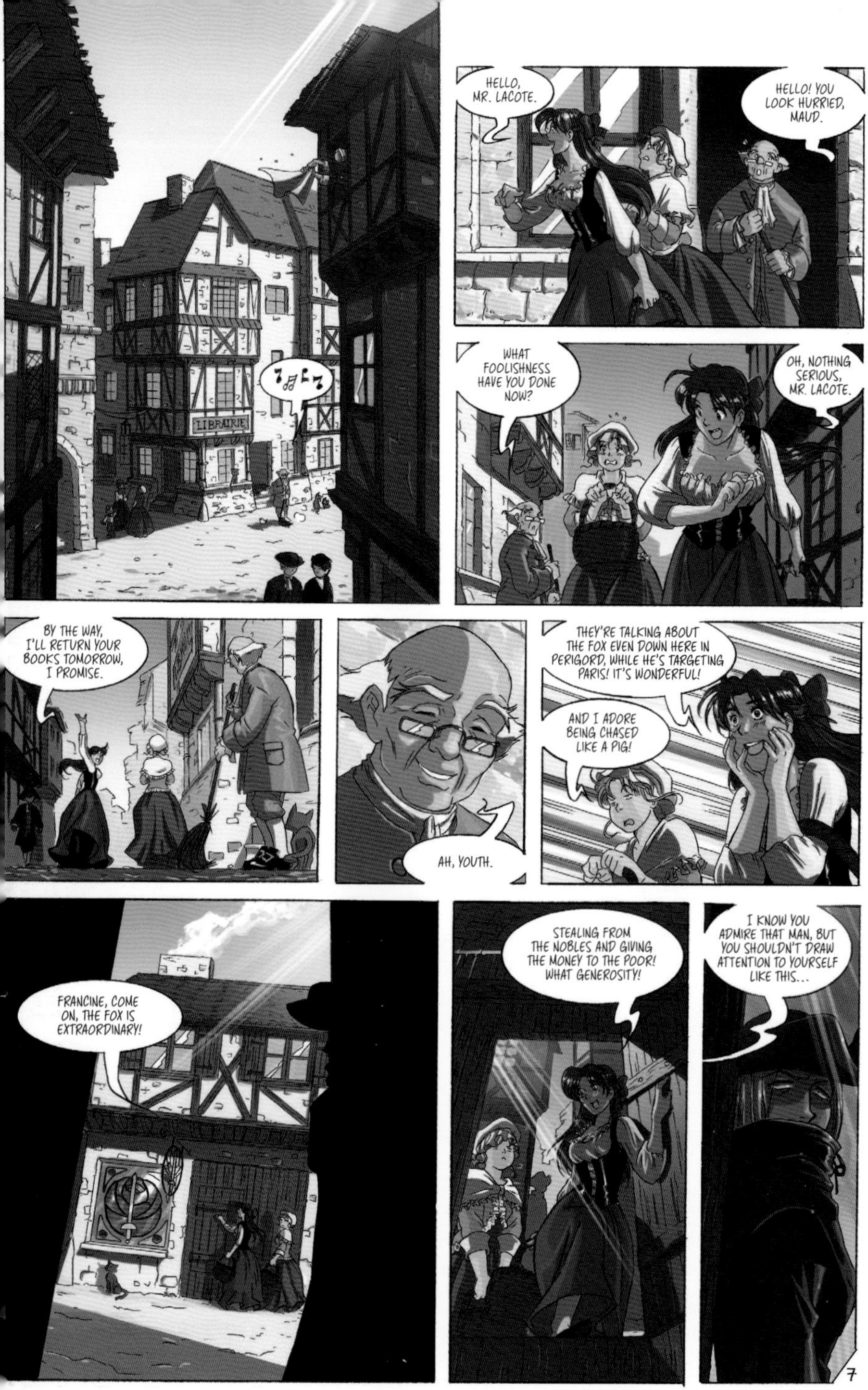
LIBRAIRIE
HELLO, MR. LACOTE.
HELLO! YOU LOOK HURRIED, MAUD.
WHAT FOOLISHNESS HAVE YOU DONE NOW?
OH, NOTHING SERIOUS, MR. LACOTE.
BY THE WAY, I'LL RETURN YOUR BOOKS TOMORROW, I PROMISE.
AH, YOUTH.
THEY'RE TALKING ABOUT THE FOX EVEN DOWN HERE IN PERIGORD, WHILE HE'S TARGETING PARIS! IT'S WONDERFUL!
AND I ADORE BEING CHASED LIKE A PIG!
FRANCINE, COME ON, THE FOX IS EXTRAORDINARY!
STEALING FROM THE NOBLES AND GIVING THE MONEY TO THE POOR! WHAT GENEROSITY!
I KNOW YOU ADMIRE THAT MAN, BUT YOU SHOULDN'T DRAW ATTENTION TO YOURSELF LIKE THIS...
7

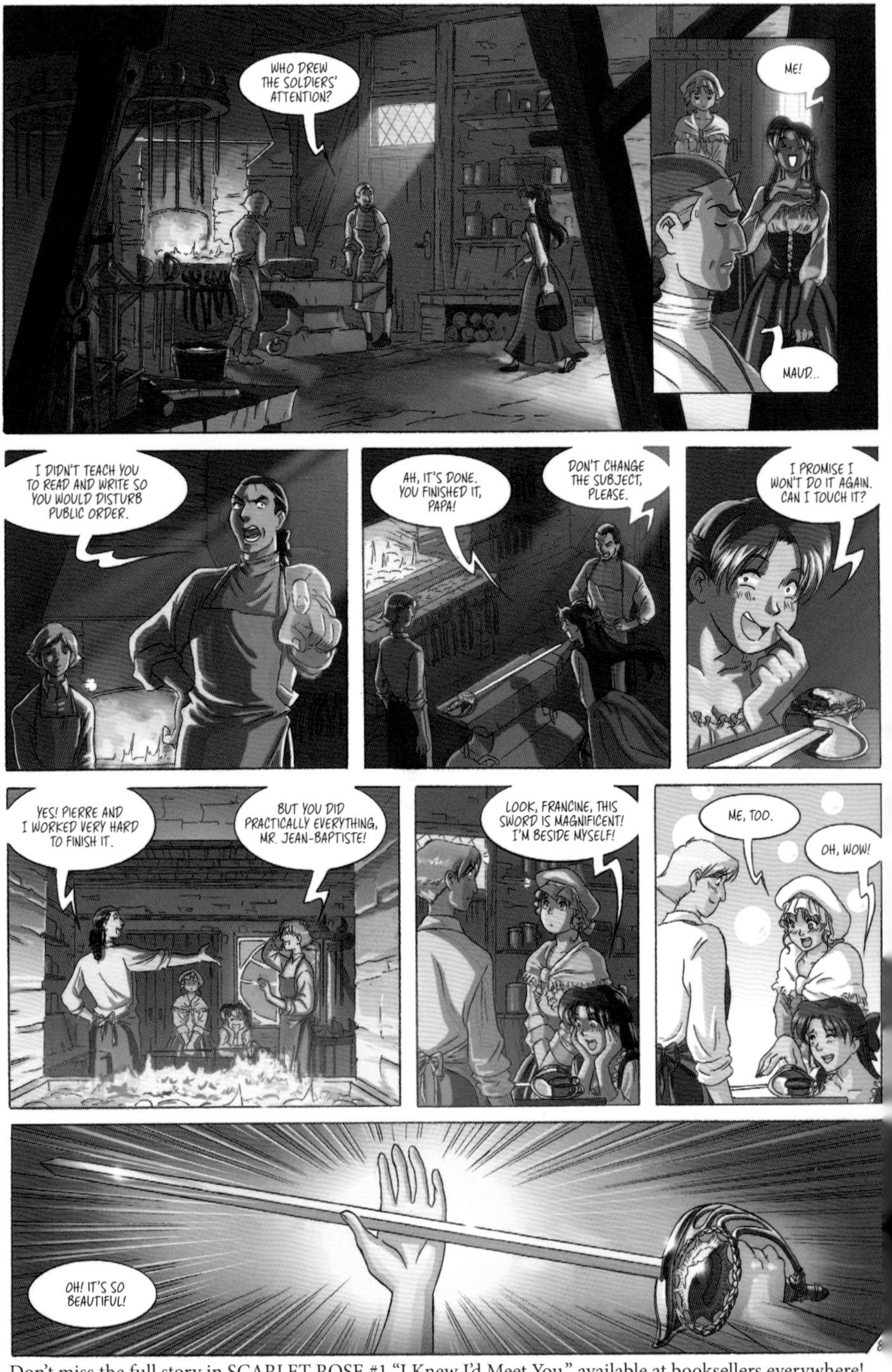
WHO DREW THE SOLDIERS' ATTENTION?
ME!
MAUD...
I DIDN'T TEACH YOU TO READ AND WRITE SO YOU WOULD DISTURB PUBLIC ORDER.
AH, IT'S DONE. YOU FINISHED IT, PAPA!
DON'T CHANGE THE SUBJECT, PLEASE.
I PROMISE I WON'T DO IT AGAIN. CAN I TOUCH IT?
YES! PIERRE AND I WORKED VERY HARD TO FINISH IT.
BUT YOU DID PRACTICALLY EVERYTHING, MR. JEAN-BAPTISTE!
LOOK, FRANCINE, THIS SWORD IS MAGNIFICENT! I'M BESIDE MYSELF!
ME, TOO.
OH, WOW!
OH! IT'S SO BEAUTIFUL!

Don't miss the full story in SCARLET ROSE #1 "I Knew I'd Meet You," available at booksellers everywhere!